"Will you come to my apartment this evening?"

He asked in a whisper, his breath feathering her ear.

"Chris, I . . . I—" She stammered and felt his fingers press into her shoulder more firmly.

"Please, love," he said huskily and brushed his lips over her sensitized ear. "I need to hold you close, lose myself in you, feel you lose yourself in me. I need that so much. Say that you want it, too."

Huddled so close to him, his arm around her, his warm body snugly aligned with hers, Ivy's private war raged with a new intensity. Tightening the grasp she had on his knee, Ivy sighed deeply. In a wisp of a voice, she said, "Yes, Chris, it is what I want...."

ABOUT THE AUTHOR

Bestselling Superromance author Kelly
Walsh's fifth book is an enthusiastic tribute to
the American postal inspection service.
"They're known as the silent service," Kelly
explains. "Most people have no idea what
they do. They really are the unsung heroes of
the law enforcement system." Kelly, who is
now hard at work on two more Supers, lives
in Florida with an aviary full of Princess of
Wales parakeets.

Books by Kelly Walsh

HARLEQUIN SUPERROMANCE
248—CHERISHED HARBOR
286—OF TIME AND TENDERNESS
336—A PLACE FOR US
360—A PRIVATE AFFAIR

Don't miss any of our special offers. Write to us at the
following address for information on our newest releases.

Harlequin Reader Service
901 Fuhrmann Blvd., P.O. Box 1397, Buffalo, NY 14240
Canadian address: P.O. Box 603,
Fort Erie, Ont. L2A 5X3

Starlight, Star Bright

KELLY WALSH

Harlequin Books

TORONTO • NEW YORK • LONDON
AMSTERDAM • PARIS • SYDNEY • HAMBURG
STOCKHOLM • ATHENS • TOKYO • MILAN

Published August 1990

ISBN 0-373-70415-1

Printed in U.S.A.

CHAPTER ONE

AN OMINOUS RUMBLING of thunder echoed throughout Ivy Austin's office, rattling the pictures on the wall and the slender bud vase on her desk. Going to the window, she frowned at the row of billowing dark clouds that was rushing in from over the Atlantic.

Below, on palm tree-lined Biscayne Boulevard, she saw that rush hour was in full swing. She hoped the rain would hold off for just a while longer; the traffic in Miami was nerve-racking enough without the added difficulty of driving during a storm.

"You'd better hurry if you want to beat the rain."

Ivy turned toward the doorway and smiled at Bob McDonough, the balding manager of Continental Marketing Research. "I'm almost finished with the report on the alumni survey. It will only take a few minutes to recheck the information on club memberships and corporate affiliations."

"A few minutes is about all the time we have before the clouds open up. I'm heading home now. You should do the same."

"I will, as soon as Scott gets here. I'm giving him a lift."

"See you in the morning, then."

As her boss turned to leave, Ivy stopped him. "Bob," she said warmly, "if Scott is accepted into the managerial training program, it will be because of the glowing recommendation you gave him. We're both very grateful."

"He earned it. That brother of yours is doing a great job." Draping his plastic raincoat over his shoulder, he gave her a chubby-faced smile and headed down the hall toward the elevator.

At her desk, Ivy turned her attention to the report she had been working on. As project supervisor, her job was to plan marketing research studies. She had worked at Continental's Miami office for nine years and had been project supervisor for three.

Merging information sent by branch managers in key cities across the nation, Continental was able to produce an elaborate psychographic portrait of virtually any neighborhood in America. Specialized mailing lists were then sent from the communications division to the home office in the Cayman Islands.

After reviewing the information on the alumni, Ivy initialed the project check sheet, placed the folder in a filing cabinet along the wall and glanced at her watch, wondering what was keeping Scott. She locked the files, gathered her things and headed for the communications division on the floor below.

The offices were empty except for the cleaning people, but as she neared the rear of the building, she heard the faint grinding of the machine that she knew was the shredder. Her steps quickened. Opening the door marked Authorized Personnel Only, her eyes widened in surprise. There was her brother, feeding documents into the shredder, the long strips of paper spewing into a brown paper bag he'd stuffed in a wastebasket. His head jerked up when he saw her.

"Scott, what are you doing? Lew is the only one who purges documents."

Biting down on his lower lip, he ran his fingers through his curly brown hair. "Close the door. I'm almost through." He fed the last of the papers into the shredder, eyeing his sister guiltily as he did.

She glanced at the printer on the opposite side of the room and saw that it was in operation. "Are you on overtime or what?"

"No," he said, switching off the shredder. "I'm trying to correct a mistake I made before anyone finds out about it." He hurried over to the printer and turned it off. Working quickly, he shoved the printed material into a file folder and inserted it between others in a cabinet. As he locked it, he said, "I need your help."

Alarmed by the nervousness she heard in her brother's voice, Ivy dropped her purse on his desk. "Listen, there's not an employee here who hasn't made a mistake, and there isn't anything that can't be corrected."

Scott faced her, fixing his anxious brown eyes on her blue ones. "I really screwed up good, though. One of the master disks I sent to the home office contains information that I merged incorrectly. If they sell that mailing list, the company that buys it will be targeting the wrong prospective customers. I've got to get it back."

He ejected a three-inch disk from the computer. "This is a new one I just made. I've shredded the erroneous printout and just filed away a corrected replacement copy. All that needs to be done now is to substitute this disk—" he held it up "—for the one in the home office. You could do that for me on Friday when you're at the department head meeting."

Wide-eyed, Ivy leaned down and flattened her palms on the desk, staring at her brother in disbelief. "Are you crazy? We could both be fired for trying to pull a stunt like that. Just tell Lew what happened. He'll straighten it out."

"Sure, and he'll make a big deal about it. That will be the end of any chance I have to be accepted into the managerial program at the home office." He slipped the disk in the inside pocket of his suit jacket.

Telling Lew Frazer about the mistake wouldn't help Scott any, Ivy realized. Her brother's boss, the head of the communications division, had fought Bob Mc-Donough all the way before Bob had submitted Scott's name for consideration. She knew Lew didn't want to lose Scott from his division, and she was also aware that he had wanted his sister-in-law to get the opportunity for advancement with the company. Still, what her brother was suggesting was out of the question.

"Scott, I can't—" Ivy spun around when she heard the office door open.

"Sorry," the maintenance man apologized, "I thought everyone had gone for the day."

"That's okay," Scott said. "We were just leaving." He picked up the brown paper bag, took hold of his sister's arm and hurried her out of the office.

As he hustled her down the aisle between rows of vacant desks, Ivy said emphatically, "We can't leave. You've got to put those files back the way they were."

"It's too late. The only way I could do that is if I had the disk I sent to Georgetown." He lifted the paper bag. "Lew wouldn't appreciate finding these strips in the file."

Ivy shrugged loose from his grasp. "Damn it, Scott. What have you gotten yourself into?"

At the elevator he punched the down button. "Look, I made one lousy mistake in two years. Should I broadcast it to everyone around here?"

When the doors parted, Ivy stepped in and leaned back against the side wall, glaring at her brother. Even as a child, his behavior had been unpredictable. There had never been a middle ground for Scott; he had either been as good as gold or a rambunctious brat. Scott's progress through high school had been similarly uneven. When he entered college, Ivy had hoped he had matured enough to apply himself and make something of his life, but he'd dropped out the following year.

From there he went downhill, making new friends Ivy hadn't approved of, behaving increasingly irresponsibly and finally leaving Miami altogether to live with a woman in Chicago. Emily Domsha had been in Miami on vacation, and Scott had followed her back home. Two years later Scott returned to Miami and surprised his sister by saying that the relationship was ended and he was ready to settle down in a steady job. Ivy had been leery when he had asked her to try to get him a job at Continental but, she had to admit, his work had been exemplary.

"Please, Sis," Scott pleaded, his features assuming a boyish expression, "help me out on this one. If I can make it into the training program, I'll work my butt off. You'll be proud of me, honest. Don't take this chance away from me. I'm begging you."

Ever since their mother died two years ago, Ivy had taken on her role in Scott's life. Walt Chandler, their father, hadn't been much help to his son; he and Scott had never gotten along. In many ways, Ivy thought, Scott was so like their mother. He was dark haired and dark eyed as she had been. And for better or for worse, he had inherited her ability to charm with a smile and just the right words. His charm worked on everyone except their father.

The elevator doors opened, and Ivy stalked into the plant-studded glass-and-steel lobby. Stopping abruptly, she fixed her eyes on her brother. "That was a stupid thing you did, destroying the file like that. Why didn't you talk to me first?"

Scott tossed the brown paper bag into a trash receptacle, then leaned back dejectedly against the wall of the adjacent parking garage. He shoved his hands into his trouser pockets, and his dark eyelashes flickered a few times. In a discouraged voice he said, "I've always been a disappointment to you, haven't I? I'm sorry. You deserve better. You know how much I've always looked up to you."

When he lowered his head, Ivy felt a sharp pain grip her heart. At twenty-four, nine years her junior, Scott still had a way of making her feel protective of him. She placed a hand on her brother's arm and softened her tone. "You're not a disappointment to me. It's just that . . . well, you have a knack for creating problems sometimes." She saw the night crew begin to mop the opposite end of the lobby. "Let's get to the car."

Minutes later, as Ivy drove onto Biscayne Boulevard, she switched on the windshield wipers against the pouring rain and turned on the headlights. "Did you call to see if your car's ready?" she asked.

"It is," he said quietly. "Thanks for the ride, and thanks for always being there when I need you."

Several blocks down, Ivy pulled into the left-turn lane and waited for the green arrow. Glancing over at Scott, she studied his crestfallen expression. The driver in the car behind her beeped his horn, and she made the turn, heading west onto the expressway.

After driving in troubled silence for a few minutes, she asked, "What makes you think I could switch the disks? You know how well they're secured."

His voice brightened measurably. "If anyone can do it, you can. I swear I'll never ask you to do another thing for me."

"I haven't said I will. I've got to think this through carefully."

"There's no other way, Sis. I've got a good chance to get into the program. You know how much weight Bob's recommendation carries with the home office. He recommended Leon for the training program, and look at the salary he's making now."

Briefly Ivy thought of Leon Torell, the Chicago branch manager. He had been working at Continental in Miami when she started with the firm. For a short time before she married, she and Leon had dated, but she'd soon decided he wasn't a man she could become seriously interested in. Not only had Ivy found something lacking in the chemistry between them, but she had discovered that Leon had a ruthless streak in him. She had seen several bright young people stomped on as Leon climbed the corporate ladder.

"Sorry, I'm making you so late in getting home," Scott said. "I know how Dad barks when he's hungry."

"Kim's fixing a seafood casserole for dinner tonight. I told them to start without me. They know I'm stopping at the house to pick up the last few things that are still there."

"You got a good deal on the house, but I think you could have done even better if you had held out a little longer."

"I was anxious to sell it."

"That's understandable." Scott nodded sympathetically. "Trying to run two households would drive anyone up the wall. How are you getting along living under the same roof with Dad again?"

"Fine. His being there when Kim gets home from school works out well for everyone."

"Ivy," Scott said hesitantly, "you won't tell him about our little problem, will you?"

She shot him a cutting sideways look. "*Our* little problem?"

His lips curved into a puppy-dog grin, and a light twinkled in his dark eyes. "All right, *my* little problem."

"Don't make it sound like a small deal. What you're asking me to do borders on stealing!"

"No way. You're actually helping the company without their knowing it. If they sell the mailing list on the disk they have now, it wouldn't be ethical."

"Ethical?" Ivy took a fortifying breath and sighed. "Scott, you could rationalize taking candy from a baby."

"Sis, I want to be a branch manager so bad that I can taste it, but you know that Lew's just waiting for me to screw up so he can ruin my chances. Please, help me out on this one."

Ivy cast him a dubious look, then concentrated on her driving.

Her thoughts went back to the time Scott was six years old and had bruised his knee while playing. She had wiped his tears. When he was thirteen, he had been caught trying to steal a model airplane from a five-and-ten while they were shopping. Ivy had paid for it to keep him from getting in trouble with the law and their parents. But, she was forced to acknowledge, there were good memories, too, and Scott was her brother. To Ivy, her family meant *everything*.

After leaving the expressway, she pulled into the gas station that was just around the corner from the apartment house Scott lived in. As he opened the car door to get out, she said, "I'm not making any promises, but I'll think about your 'little' problem."

He leaned over and kissed her cheek. "You're the best, Sis. Say hi to Kim for me." Before she could object, he dropped the disk into her purse and closed the car door.

"Scott!" Ivy looked down at the disk, groaned and watched her brother disappear into the station.

She drew her lips into a tight line and returned to the expressway, heading toward the house in the Miami Springs community. It wasn't a stop that she wanted to make. The home she and Bill had shared during their six years of marriage was filled with too many poignant memories.

The rain decreased to a fine drizzle, and she slowed the windshield wipers, thinking how unfair life had been to Bill. He'd made it through two tours of duty in Vietnam, only to be hurt in a stupid helicopter accident in Okinawa. Ivy hadn't even known William Austin then; she had been in her freshman year at the University of Miami.

Smiling softly, she remembered the history course she had taken as an elective in her senior year. Bill, ten years older than she, had been the professor. A year after graduation she had met him again at a party, and eight months later they had married. The future had never looked so bright. She was happy in her job at Continental, she was loved and she was in love. And Bill was having minimal difficulties with the back injury caused by the helicopter crash—until last year when he entered the

Veterans' hospital for what was to be a fairly simple operation to correct a ruptured disk. He died of postsurgical complications.

When Ivy turned onto Morningside Drive, she could feel her heartbeat accelerate as she approached the house. She had sold it furnished. There were only two cardboard boxes of personal things left to be removed before the new owners took over. Parking in the driveway, she glanced at the yellow allamandas and scarlet poinsettias that she and Bill had planted. Her eyes drifted to the mango tree, and she recalled how much Bill had enjoyed the sweet fruit. Forcing away the painful recollections, she hurried inside.

The cardboard boxes were in the living room, where she had left them two days ago. She placed her purse on the coffee table and looked around slowly, saying her final goodbye to the happy years that she and Bill had shared together. Her gaze drifted back to the front door, and she recalled their laughter when he had carried her over the threshold. He had nudged the door shut with his foot, still holding her in his arms: *I love you so much, Mrs. Austin, so very, very much.*

Ivy jerked her head away from the door and scanned the living room. Without the touches that their personal things had given it, there was a dismal formality about the room. Her fingertips trailed along the back of the green velour sofa as she moved slowly to the sliding glass doors that led to the patio and pool. Drawing back the yellow drapery panel, she stared out blankly, visualizing Bill and Kim laughing and splashing each other in the pool.

"Kim," Ivy whispered and closed her eyes, reliving the shock of Bill's hesitant words three years ago.

The letter's in the form of an inquiry, but I . . . I know that she's my daughter. A United Nations refugee camp in the Philippines is a rotten place for a twelve-year-old to spend Christmas.

Turning away from the glass doors, Ivy slumped back against the wall, recalling her initial confusion and the pain in her husband's voice when he admitted having fathered an Amerasian child while in Vietnam. Quickly, though, her confusion had turned to resentment, then to self-recrimination for blaming Bill for something that had happened years before she met him.

With a shake of her head, she forced away the troubling memories and made her way upstairs. She entered Kim's bedroom first. Gone were the pink-and-white-chintz spread and matching drapes; they were now in Ivy's father's house, in the room that had once been hers. Her gaze slid over the cherry-wood furniture as she recalled the nervousness she had felt while getting the room ready for Kim.

For two days before the girl's arrival, Ivy hadn't been able to eat anything substantial. To this day she could remember the look of astonishment in Kim's almond-shaped green eyes when she first saw the room that was to be hers. Only later did Ivy learn that Bill's daughter had often had to sleep on dirt floors in refugee camps in Thailand and Malaysia, and in the rain on wooden planks in overcrowded sampans.

Ivy's upbringing had been so different. Her parents, particularly her father, had doted on her, and their love had provided her with a happy and stable childhood, enabling her to reach out to others with a security that Kim had never experienced.

Slowly Ivy went through the other bedrooms, more because she wanted to see them one last time than because she believed she might have forgotten something. After returning downstairs, she carried the two boxes to her car and took off for her father's house in Coral Gables, the two-story Spanish-style house on Majorca Avenue that had been her home until she married Bill.

"WHERE IS EVERYBODY?" Ivy called, dropping her car keys and purse on the table in the foyer. "I could use some help unloading the car."

"In here, darlin'," her father hollered from his study.

She went to the doorway and smiled at Walter Chandler as he sat at his desk, typing in his hunt-and-peck method on an ancient, manual machine. "When are you going to get an electric typewriter?" she asked for the umpteenth time.

He looked up and peered at her over the steel rims of his glasses. "That's the trouble with this throwaway society of ours. Get the newest model, no matter if the old one's still working. This typewriter and I have gotten along just fine for more than a quarter of a century. It's got a home here until it gives out—" he pushed back the auburn hair now laced with gray that hung over his forehead "—or until an editor can't tell the a's from the o's."

At fifty-nine, Ivy's father was a gifted writer, a Florida State University English major who had become a police reporter for a Miami newspaper before he began writing full-time about his first love—sports. Before his wife's death, he had been a frequent contributor to national magazines, writing about everything from college football to all-night Ping-Pong parlors. He had crisscrossed the country to interview the likes of Muhammad Ali and Billie Jean King, and had even found time to add a dozen books on various sports to his writing credits.

Ever since Miriam's death, however, he had shown little zest for life and rarely left the house. He went through the motions of working, but his output during the past two years had been limited to an occasional article while he dallied with his current manuscript on competition and the human species. It hurt Ivy to see his gait becoming slower, and she missed his hearty laughter, now heard so rarely.

"How's the book coming along?" she asked, leaning down to kiss his cheek.

"So-so." Glancing up at her, he smiled. "Every time I look at you, I wonder how I fathered someone so lovely. But then I remind myself how beautiful your mother was."

"I have your eyes and the Chandler nose."

"And Miriam's sweet disposition." Her father sighed. "God, I miss her. But I guess if you live long enough, everything falls apart. My hair's thinning, I have to worry about my cholesterol level and I don't sleep so good."

"Where's Kim?" Ivy asked, hoping to get her father's mind off his brooding thoughts.

"Upstairs in her room. She didn't eat supper."

Ivy tensed. "Is something wrong?"

"Eddie Whitaker phoned and said he couldn't take her to the movies Friday evening."

"Oh? Did he tell her why?"

"He didn't want to talk to her. He asked me to let her know he had to make other plans." Walt took off his glasses and wiped them with a handkerchief. "The kid sounded apologetic. I'm guessing his mother made him do it."

A surge of heat flushed Ivy's face. "That's the second boy from school who's done that to her. I can think of a few choice words I'd like to say to Eddie and his mother.

What are the parents afraid of...that their darling sons are going to catch something?''

"Kim's a little different. Folks are wary of anyone who is. And Eddie's father was killed in Vietnam.''

"Does it make sense to hold a sweet fifteen-year-old girl responsible for the war?'' Ivy shook her head slowly. "I should have been here,'' she said as she left the room.

Climbing the stairs, she tried desperately to think of something to say that would ease the hurt she knew Kim was feeling. Ivy always tried to be truthful with her stepdaughter. She wished that the truth in this case was not so painful.

Knocking softly on the closed door, she asked, "Kim, may I come in?''

There was no response, so she opened the door and looked inside. Her stepdaughter was lying sideways across the bed, her face buried in the crook of her arm, her long, shiny black hair draped over her shoulder. When she looked up with tearful eyes, Ivy's heart wrenched.

Sitting on the bed beside her, she gently smoothed back the strands of silky hair from the girl's beautiful face. Her eyes, as Bill's had been, were emerald green, compelling and warm; her complexion was the color of burnished gold.

"I know you're disappointed, darling,'' Ivy said softly as she raised Kim and cuddled her, "but other boys will ask you out.''

In the gentle manner of speaking she had, Kim murmured, "I...I do not think so.''

"Yes, they will,'' Ivy insisted quietly.

What a delightful composite the girl was, she thought as she held Kim. She'd had an American father, and a

Vietnamese mother, and she spoke English with a French accent.

Drawing back, Kim looked at Ivy with soulful eyes. "What is so wrong with me, Mother? Why do the students make fun of me? It makes me feel terrifically bad." She placed a delicate hand over her heart. *"Tôi dâu dây,"* she said in Vietnamese: *It hurts here.*

It had taken Ivy almost a year to coax Kim into calling her Mother. Before that it had always been *Bà* Austin, Mrs. Austin. "Sometimes," Ivy explained, "people, especially young people, say and do things without realizing how much they can hurt someone."

Kim sniffled and lowered her eyes. "In Vietnam, I was called *côn lai*, a half-breed, and *bui doi*, the dust of life. My aunt told me that if I will have an education in America, I will be more respected, but I am not respected. Now I am not sure what I am."

Ivy took hold of the girl's shoulders gently and looked deeply into her tearstained eyes. "You're a beautiful, wonderful girl, and I love you very much."

"Am I truly lovable?" Kim asked dubiously.

"There's no daughter in the world who's loved more than you are." Ivy rose from the bed and pulled a tissue from the box on the night table to wipe the tears from Kim's cheeks.

When she turned, she saw the girl looking down at the pin she had clutched in her hand, a small butterfly of silver filigree. Kim had told Ivy that William Austin had given the pin to her mother long ago. Ivy knew that it was her stepdaughter's most treasured possession.

Sitting down next to Kim, she said, "It's such a lovely pin. You should wear it sometimes."

Silently Kim moved to the dresser. With great care she laid the pin in front of the small picture in the silver frame that Ivy had bought for her.

Ivy's eyes shifted to the picture Kim had brought with her from Asia. It was a photograph of Bill in his marine fatigues, his arms around a lovely, petite Vietnamese woman, Kim's mother. They were both smiling.

For long, quiet moments, Kim stared at the picture, and Ivy heard her sniffle again. To distract her from her sad thoughts, Ivy said, "As for Eddie changing his mind about taking you to the movies, let me tell you what happened to me when I was your age."

After Kim turned, Ivy said, "A boy, Roger Kaufman, asked me to a high school dance, my very first dance, mind you. My mother bought me a beautiful new dress, and I felt so very grown-up. My father even had a corsage ready in case Roger forgot to bring one." Ivy looked into Kim's wide, attentive eyes. "Seven-thirty came, and no Roger. I waited and waited. He never did come. He took somebody else to the dance. I had been stood up."

"Stood up?" Kim repeated, not familiar with the idiom.

"That's what we say when someone asks us out, but doesn't show up."

"I was stood up," Kim repeated, filing the expression in her memory. "What did you do?"

"I cried, just like you did, but I got over it and so will you, honey. One day the right young man will come along, and you'll forget the hurt you're feeling now. I promise you, you will."

"The right young man," Kim repeated softly. "That seems to be too beautiful a dream."

Ivy rose and went to her. Her voice was loving and gentle as she tilted the girl's chin up. "There's nothing wrong with having a beautiful dream, darling. It's not having one that's sad. Come on now, let's try that casserole you made. I'm starving."

As they descended the stairs, Ivy wondered if she should cancel her trip to the Cayman Islands. Kim needed her right now. But then, so did her brother, considering the mess he had gotten himself into.

Damn you, Bill, she thought, *I'll never forgive you for dying on me.*

CHAPTER TWO

AFTER GOING OVER the next day's exercises for Kim's TESOL class, the special class that taught English to speakers of other languages, Ivy returned to the living room, where her father was watching the Boston Celtics outmaneuver the Detroit Pistons.

"Move it, kid! Muscle him away from the ball!" Walt directed, leaning forward in his chair. "Hot damn, he's got it!"

Despite having lived with sports most of her life, Ivy had never learned to appreciate the spectacle of grown men battling it out with sticks and balls. Working at Continental provided enough of the thrill of competition for her. "Who's winning?" she asked to make conversation.

"The Celtics. I wish Miriam was here to see this. She was their biggest fan. One thing about her, she loved basketball."

Smiling, Ivy said, "Mother loved you. Sports just came with the package."

She slipped off her pumps, sat down on the sofa and curled her feet under her. Ivy missed her mother terribly. She had always been there whenever Ivy needed her, and she certainly needed her now.

The raucous sounds from the TV faded away as Ivy stared at the screen blankly, her thoughts centered on the disk her brother had shoved into her purse. *If only he hadn't destroyed the original files,* she thought. *But if that did come to light now, it would only compound his problem.*

Ivy glanced over at her father. She knew without asking what he would say if she told him about the situation. His advice would be to make Scott be forthright, stand up like a man and take whatever consequences came. Propping her elbow on the arm of the sofa, she ran her fingertips over her forehead, wishing her mother were alive. Ivy knew she could have talked to her about it. Scott would have listened to their mother; he always had.

The phone rang and she reached over for the receiver. It was Carol Wilson, their next-door neighbor, a psychiatric nurse at a Miami hospital. She wanted to know if Ivy could come over for a minute. Welcoming a reprieve from her troubled thoughts, she said she'd be right there.

Ivy found Carol in white silk pajamas, sitting on the carpet by the fireplace, her legs crossed yoga style, an almost empty box of chocolate-covered cherries beside her. Ivy smiled at her attractive neighbor, who was a year older than she was and some fifteen pounds heavier.

"I need your advice," Carol said. "Would you think my brain's running in slow motion if I dated Lamar?"

Ivy had heard enough about Carol's ex-husband, a foreign-exchange trader for a Miami bank, to make her think her friend would be making a mistake. The man was a philanderer of the first order. Rather than point this out, however, Ivy merely shrugged.

"Thanks for the sage advice," Carol quipped.

"Give me a reason why you'd want to date him," Ivy said and sank onto a beanbag chair near Carol, who held the box of chocolates toward her.

"I don't suppose my being masochistic would be a good one."

"Hardly." Ivy reached over and took a chocolate. "It's not as if he'd made just one mistake."

"One mistake?" Carol threw back her head and chuckled. "If Lamar puts his arms around a woman and his fingertips touch, he thinks he's in love."

"In that case, you might be better off listening to your head and not your heart."

"I guess you're right. I just had to hear someone else say it." Selecting a chocolate, she stared at it. "What I really want to do is to meet a sex-crazed Texan and marry into oil." After popping the candy into her mouth, she mumbled, "Oh well, instead of letting Lamar fawn over me, I'll pick up a quart of pistachio ice cream on the way home from work Friday. Why don't you come over? I'll get two quarts."

"I can't. I'm going out of town on business Thursday and won't be back until Friday afternoon. I want to spend the evening with Kim."

"Speaking of spending an evening with someone, are you ever going to see what's-his-name again, the blind date you had two weeks ago?"

"Ralph Owens." Ivy grunted and adjusted her position in the mobile chair. "I haven't had the greatest luck with blind dates. The ones my well-meaning friends have fixed me up with have turned out to be either divorced and bitter, widowed and maudlin or perennial boys."

"Well, there are still good men out there, but they aren't going to come knocking on your door if they don't know where you live."

"I don't have time for a man in my life right now."

"Hush your mouth, girl! God may take you seriously."

"I am serious. Between work, Kim, Scott and my dad, it's difficult enough keeping some control over my life."

"Control," Carol repeated dryly. "Lamar always had to be in control. There was another thing about him that bugged me. What is it with men? Why do they always have to be totally in charge, whether it's on the football field, the office or in their love life? And why is it so hard for them to give the same commitment to women that they give to their work?"

"You're the psychiatric nurse. You tell me."

Assuming the lotus position, Carol said, "It's easier to understand the crazies on the ward than it is the average man on the street." She studied Ivy's pensive expression. "Something's bothering you, isn't it?"

"A bunch of little things."

"Such as?"

"Kim, for one."

"Is she still having a hard time adjusting to school here?"

"That, and today a boy canceled a date he made with her. I suspect his mother had something to do with it."

Carol's expression was serious. "Not because of a sudden attack of the zits, I take it."

"No explanation was offered."

"Oh. Prejudice rears its ugly head. Being black, I know how that can hurt, whether it's done with an iron fist or a velvet glove."

"I just can't understand it. Kim's intelligent and lovely. She's more mature emotionally than most girls her age, but considering what she's been through, it's no wonder. And she's so sweet. How could anyone be mean to her?"

"You don't have to convince me. She's a living doll, but too many people can't deal with people of other races. Seems like they have to find someone to put down to make themselves feel superior. How's Kim taking it?"

"I found her crying when I got home." She looked over at Carol. "One letdown would be bad enough, but this is the second time it's happened."

"Poor kid." After a moment, Carol suggested, "While you're gone Thursday, why don't I take her to Wolfie's for dinner? She loves their cheesecake, not as much as I do, of course."

Ivy's face brightened. "I'd be indebted to you for the rest of my life. I was tempted to cancel my trip—" she thought of her conversation with Scott "—but it's important that I go."

Carol held out the candy box again. "Take the last piece."

"No, no. You have it."

"Can't. I'm on a diet."

Giving her friend a knowing smile, Ivy took the last chocolate-covered cherry.

"Before your fifty-minute hour is up," Carol asked, "is there anything else troubling you?"

After swallowing, Ivy said, "It's my father."

"Somebody break a date with him?"

"Just the opposite. I can't get him out of the house. His social interaction nowadays is limited to the mail carrier and the meter reader."

"You do carry a burden, don't you?" Carol said sympathetically.

"Sometimes I want to cry, but it would only make me feel worse." Pushing herself up from the beanbag chair, she said brusquely, "I'd better get on home so you can finish your yoga exercises."

"Discipline is the key to my having lost three ounces so far this year. Don't forget to tell Kim that we have a date for Thursday."

At the doorway, Ivy glanced back. "You're an angel."

THURSDAY AFTERNOON, as Ivy sat in the Cayman Airways jet waiting to take off from Miami International Airport, she opened her purse and peered at the disk her brother had given her. She told herself again, as Scott had insisted, that she was helping the company by correcting the mistake he had made. But even though she desperately wanted him to get into the managerial training program, she still felt like an archcriminal.

Once the plane was airborne, a flight attendant in a red blazer served her a complimentary drink called the Cayman Welcome, a blend of exotic fruit juices and the islands' own Tortuga rum. As she sipped her drink, she glanced across the aisle. Smiling at her was one of the handsomest men she had ever seen.

He was ruggedly attractive, a Marlboro-man type with sultry eyes. His wavy brown hair shone with golden highlights and suited his ruddy complexion. Impulsively, Ivy smiled back, then turned toward the plane window. Concentrating on the billowing fluffs of white clouds, she felt oddly affected by the man's more than friendly smile.

FROM ACROSS THE AISLE, Chris Laval studied Ivy, mentally reviewing the report about her he had submitted yesterday to Matt Shapiro, his boss at Postal Inspection Service Headquarters in Miami.

He had been following Ivy Austin for several days now and had little to show for it other than a record of her drives to and from work, an occasional stop at the supermarket and the two trips she had made to the house she had sold recently. Chris reflected that her driving her brother to a service station to pick up his car certainly didn't prove they were working together outside of routine office business. But Matt believed that someone at

Continental could be misusing their store of information.

Though he was not at all comfortable with the deception required for his assignment, Chris had agreed to it, knowing that time was running out. Each day more reports of people being swindled were coming in from across the country.

Prospective investors were contacted by phone and mailed a flashy prospectus, a financial statement and a newsletter to induce them to buy oil certificates and investment contracts. They were given counterfeit securities, then the swindlers would disappear with the investment money.

Chris glanced at Ivy again. He had recently transferred from Chicago headquarters, and when he had gone over the files the Miami office had on the executives of Continental Marketing Research, everything he'd read about her had been complimentary. Ivy Austin certainly didn't look like the type of woman who would be involved in a mail fraud scam, but it would be interesting to see if she had business in Georgetown other than at her company's home office.

Matt suspected that the money from the fraudulent investments scheme was being channeled to an offshore bank for laundering, and the secrecy laws in the Cayman Islands made them a likely location, since the banks there offered a confidentiality similar to those in Switzerland.

Sampling his fruit drink, Chris thought of Ivy Austin's raising her deceased husband's Amerasian daughter. That had impressed him. For a single parent to cope with a teenager and a career was difficult enough, he imagined, but he could only guess at the problems inherent in bringing up a stepdaughter born in such tragic circumstances.

His dark brown eyes glanced Ivy's way again. In her rust-colored business suit and white blouse, she looked both efficient and feminine. This impressed him as well. But impressed or not, Chris told himself sternly, he had a job to do.

As Ivy TRIED to concentrate on the magazine she had been reading, she found herself stealing glances at the man across the aisle. When she saw him get up, she gave the magazine her full attention, until she heard his voice beside her.

"Would you mind if I join you? I think my neighbor there could use a little more room."

Ivy looked over at the woman he had been sitting next to. She was holding a squirming toddler in her lap. "No, of course not." Moving her briefcase from the vacant seat next to her, Ivy placed it on the floor. "It's very considerate of you."

Still standing, the man put out his hand. "Chris Laval."

Extending her own, she smiled. "Ivy Austin."

She liked his smooth, baritone voice, and she liked his handshake, too. His firm yet gentle grip caused a warm sensation to ripple across her fingers.

Sitting down beside her, Chris commented, "Traveling with a child that age can be difficult. They want the whole world for their playground."

From the easy smile on his face, Ivy knew he wasn't complaining. "Do you have children, Mr. Laval?" she asked.

"No, but my three sisters and my brother have nine kids altogether. Do you have children?"

"A fifteen-year-old daughter."

"Fifteen? That's hard to believe."

"She's my stepdaughter."

"Ah, I see," he said with a nod, wondering if she had any idea of what that lethal smile of hers could do to a man. He glanced at her briefcase. "I take it you're on a business trip."

"My company's home office is in Georgetown. I'm attending a meeting in the morning. And you?"

"A long-postponed vacation. What kind of business are you in?"

"I'm project supervisor for a marketing research firm."

"Oh? What kind of research does your company do?"

"We collect information from various sources, merge it, then market the mailing lists we produce. The service caters to businesses that want to target specific consumers. What kind of work are you vacationing from?"

"Nothing quite so interesting. I'm an internal auditor for a Chicago firm, but I'm not even going to think about the job during my vacation."

"I don't blame you. I haven't had a real vacation in almost three years."

"Three years?" He smiled. "You're long overdue for one. Listen, I don't know a soul in Georgetown. Would you consider having dinner with me this evening? I'm a perfect gentleman, honest."

Ivy was not prepared to accept a dinner invitation from a stranger, even as attractive a stranger as Chris Laval. She lowered her eyes briefly. "I'm sure you are, but I have some work to finish for the morning meeting. Thank you for the invitation, though."

Chris didn't pursue the matter. Changing the subject, he said, "I envy your living in Miami. Winter's already hit the Windy City. Have you ever been to Chicago?"

"Once, five years ago. At the time, my husband's parents were living in Winnetka, just north of the city. They moved to New Mexico shortly after."

Chris noted how the sunlight streaming in through the plane window rayed over Ivy's lovely features and her silky auburn hair. More than a few times during the past several days, he had wished that their paths had crossed under different circumstances. He'd even fantasized about meeting her in a restaurant or in a supermarket, anywhere not related to his investigation.

Forcing away the useless wishes, he asked, "Does your job take you to the Cayman Islands very often?"

"Two or three times a year."

"I understand it's quite a financial center."

"Are you interested in banking, Mr. Laval?"

"Somewhat," he answered casually.

The seventy-five-minute flight passed more quickly for Ivy than any she had taken over the years. She enjoyed talking to Chris, and she loved his dazzling, easy smile. She began to regret having turned down his dinner invitation.

After landing at Owen Roberts Airport, Chris walked Ivy to the line of waiting taxis. She wished him a happy vacation and instructed the driver to take her to the Sunset House, where Cora Bennings from the home office had made reservations for Ivy's overnight stay.

During the short drive south of Georgetown, her thoughts returned to the disk in her purse. She knew it wouldn't be a simple matter to make the switch. Security in the file room was as tight as that in a bank vault, and Cora, who was in charge of communications divisions for all of Continental's branch offices, took her job as watchdog over the files seriously. Well, Ivy decided, all she could do was try.

It was late afternoon when she finished unpacking the few things she had brought with her. She went directly to the Royal Bank of Canada to exchange some American currency for Cayman Islands dollars, then headed for Cardinal Avenue to take advantage of the bargains in the duty-free shops and to do some early Christmas shopping.

She selected a single strand of pearls for Kim, a watch for Walt and a navy-blue blazer for Scott. Getting in the mood, she also bought two sundresses for Kim and a white swimsuit and some cologne for herself. Loaded with her packages, she returned to the hotel.

Although it was early November, the temperature was eighty-five degrees, so she showered before slipping into a blue print shirtdress and going to the dining room.

As she scanned the menu, a waiter brought a champagne cocktail to her table. "I didn't order this," she said politely.

"A card comes with it, Mrs. Austin." He handed it to her.

Happy vacation, Ivy read silently and looked up at the waiter.

"It's from the gentleman at that table." He nodded to his left.

Ivy turned her head to see Chris Laval smiling and raising his glass. Pleasantly surprised, she reached for the champagne glass and returned the gesture. She was about to sip, but paused when she saw him get up and head toward her table.

An unexpected excitement shot through her as she watched him move toward her. His walk was graceful, yet totally masculine, his shoulders even broader than she had thought on the plane.

"What a coincidence, Mrs. Austin. If you're dining alone, may I join you?"

Ivy couldn't understand why she felt so unnerved by his request, nor did she feel comfortable with the pleasurable sensation she experienced at seeing him again. With a nonchalance she didn't feel, she said, "Of course."

Her waiter asked, "Would you care to order later?"

"Yes, please," she said, moving her fingers nervously over the stem of the wineglass.

After Chris asked the young man to bring his drink to the table, Ivy picked up her champagne cocktail. "This was very thoughtful of you, Mr. Laval."

"Could we make it Chris and Ivy?"

"Chris," she said, beginning to relax. "For Christopher?"

"Christian, after a grandfather."

The waiter placed the glass of bourbon and water on the table, and Chris picked it up. "To an evening's vacation," he toasted.

Ivy sipped her champagne cocktail slowly, not able to take her eyes from the dark brown ones that held hers. Setting down her wineglass, she asked, "Are you staying here at Sunset House?"

"Yes...luckily."

Unsettled by the intensity of his gaze, Ivy averted her eyes. To cover her confusion, she quickly changed the subject. "Shopping is one of the reasons people come to the islands. There are some marvelous men's shops on Harbour Drive." Feeling her composure return as she spoke, she looked up again and smiled. "This afternoon I made my obligatory visit to some of the stores. It was a sensible spree compared to my last trip here. My daughter was on school holiday, so I was able to bring her with me. We really shopped that day.''

"Do you have a picture of her?''

Ivy beamed and reached into her purse for her wallet. "This was taken earlier this year.''

"She's lovely.''

"I think so.'' Ivy saw the question in his eyes. "Kim's mother was Vietnamese.''

"I've read about the Amerasian children. They're the true victims of the war,'' he said sincerely.

"My husband and I learned a lot about their situation. It's quite sad. In Vietnam they're shunned and treated miserably because of their racial mixture. We were told that only about two percent of the four thousand children who have come here have been reunited with their fathers. They say as many as fifteen thousand more may still be in Vietnam.'' She shook her head. "You wouldn't believe the red tape we had to go through to get Kim to the States.''

"I can imagine,'' Chris said, who came up against red tape regularly in his own work. "You and your husband are to be commended.''

Ivy lowered her eyes. "Bill died last year.''

The pain that Chris heard in Ivy's quiet statement made him feel like a lowlife. He hated this damn deception, but Matt had convinced him of the necessity for it. In his job, Chris often came up against criminals motivated by greed to steal and even murder, but the more he learned about Ivy Austin, the more certain he was that she could never be placed in the same company.

After they ordered and were served, Ivy tasted the coquilles St. Jacques she had requested, then glanced over at the lasagna on Chris's plate. "I take it you don't care for French cooking."

Chris dabbed his lips with a napkin. "Uh-uh. I was raised on it, had wine sauce coming out of my ears. My parents emigrated from Marseilles and opened a French restaurant in Bladensburg, Maryland. My father died when I was seven." Chris's voice took on an edge. "My mother remarried. Now her husband runs the restaurant."

"I'm surprised you didn't wind up being a restaurateur."

"If my stepfather had had his way I would have. My younger brother and one of my sisters will eventually take over the business. I put in my time, though. All during high school I waited on tables six nights a week."

Ivy smiled. "Somehow I can't picture you waiting on tables."

"Neither could I, but my stepfather wasn't a man to say no to." After a sip of red wine, he asked, "How is your stepdaughter adjusting to life in the States? I imagine it was quite a culture shock for her."

"It was a shock for Kim," Ivy agreed. "It still is in many ways. She was used to living with only the bare essentials, then suddenly she was faced with things like escalators, television and automatic doors at supermarkets, things that we take for granted. The independence of American teenagers still confuses her. Kim was raised never to question authority, to be obedient and downright subservient."

After reflecting briefly, Ivy continued. "I worry about her. She's extremely passive and finds it difficult to express her feelings when strangers are around. I've tried to interest her in joining Vietnamese clubs in Miami, but because of the harassment she experienced in her own

country, she won't. I'm certainly not going to force her
to do so."

"It can't have been easy for you, either," Chris said
sympathetically.

"To be honest, it hasn't been. After my husband died,
I felt a lot of pressure. I was expected to be a supermom,
superdaughter, supersister and super career woman. It
left little room for me to be just me." As though in confidence she lowered her voice and smiled. "Believe it or
not, there are times when I want to just goof off and relax... like I'm doing now."

Matching her smile, Chris said, "I'm happy you feel
relaxed."

"You make it very easy for me. You're easy to talk to,"
she admitted candidly.

During the remainder of dinner, Ivy discovered that
Chris had been divorced, and Chris learned about Ivy's
family. She spoke lovingly of her parents and told Chris
of the void that her mother's death had left, particularly
in her father's life.

Afterward, Chris wanted them to take in the floor
show at the Cayman Islander nightclub, but Ivy said she
had to be bright eyed in the morning and suggested a
short walk on the beach behind the hotel.

As they walked, they passed palm trees and thick clus-
ters of sea grape trees. On the other side of a mound of
coral rocks, they came upon a cove—a narrow, sloping
beach that met the placid sea. A full moon rayed over
sand and surf, casting the idyllic scene in muted tones of
blue and silver.

Chris was struck by how comfortable he felt, the ease
of the silence that lingered between him and Ivy. It gave
him a feeling of contentment that he rarely experienced.

Ivy glanced over at him, smiled softly, then looked out to the horizon where the immense star-studded sky met the shimmering water. "This is about as close to heaven as a person can get, I guess."

His eyes followed her gaze. "It is peaceful here. It makes you forget all the craziness that goes on in the world."

She stopped walking and faced him, wondering at his comment and craving to know more about this man she had just met. Crossing her arms, she grasped her shoulders. "Life does get pretty crazy at times. I think that's what families are for. They help you get through the bad times. Mine certainly did." After a momentary pause, she smiled and said, "I've talked you to death about my family. Do you get home often?"

Chris stared out over the water. "I haven't been home in almost four years."

"Four years?" Ivy repeated with obvious surprise.

"My stepfather isn't one of my favorite people, and my brother and sisters are busy with their own lives."

"What about your mother? Don't you miss her?"

"At times, but she's convinced that I've never even tried to be friends with her husband. All in all, I get along better with my family on the phone than I do when I'm in the same house with them."

That kind of thinking was totally foreign to Ivy. Through the good and the bad times, she had always found happiness and security being close to and concerned for her family. They had lauded her achievements and comforted her when tragedy struck. She didn't see how a person could survive without a family's loving support. She wondered how Chris did.

Moving to the nearby coral rocks, she leaned back against them and listened to the sound of the surf rolling up on the shore. The scent of saltwater and island night blooms filled the air. For quiet moments she mulled over what Chris had said, then thought of Kim before remarking, "Being part of a family can be crucial."

"To people like you," he suggested, resting back next to her.

"Yes, but I was thinking of Kim just now. If it hadn't been for her family, she wouldn't have survived."

"I imagine she's had a hard time."

"That's putting it mildly. Her life's been a nightmare until recently."

Curious, Chris asked, "How long have you known about her?"

Not having anticipated his interest, Ivy hesitated, then told him, "Not until three years ago when Bill was notified that she was in a refugee camp in the Philippines. He thought she and her mother had died years before. Bill met Kim's mother when he was a marine assigned to the American embassy in Saigon. She taught French at a Catholic high school there. Bill was transferred to Okinawa, then he was in a helicopter accident, hospitalized and sent home with a medical discharge."

Ivy cast a sideways glance at Chris. Seeing the interest in his expression, she continued. "He never got Kim's mother's first letter telling him that she was pregnant. A year later he did receive one and learned he had a daughter. He tried desperately to get them out, but then Saigon fell to the Communists. Kim's mother was sent to a reeducation camp, as were most of the South Vietnamese teachers. She died there of cholera."

Gently Chris said, "If you'd rather not talk about this, please don't."

Ivy smiled weakly. "I'd like to. It might help to get it out instead of keeping it bottled up inside."

Chris nodded encouragingly, and Ivy resumed her story.

"Kim was taken care of by her mother's family despite the taunts of the rest of the village because of her racial mixture. When matters became intolerable, an aunt and Kim joined the boat people and left Vietnam. They spent years in refugee camps in Thailand and Malaysia, then they were herded into a sampan and shipped back to Vietnam.

"When Kim was in school, she was constantly tormented by teachers and students because her father had been an American, so her aunt requested that she be sent to the States, hoping her father could be located. All the aunt knew was that his name was William Austin and that he had been an American soldier. Two years later Kim ended up in a refugee camp in the Philippines."

Ivy shook her head slowly. "She was so young, I don't see how she ever lived through all that." Easing a finger across her cheek, she apologized. "I'm sorry, Chris. This is hardly the way for you to begin your vacation."

"I wouldn't have it any other way," he said softly and walked beside her as she headed toward the water's edge.

Placing a hand against her chest, Ivy realized that for all the pain of reliving Kim's ordeal, she actually did feel better. It was as though talking to Chris had put the troublesome thoughts to rest, and for that she was grateful. Accepting the handkerchief he offered, she wiped her eyes, then chuckled at herself. "So much for my being the pillar of strength I pretend to be."

"Don't let it bother you. I've shed a few tears in my life." Glancing at the water, he said, "It's too bad we don't have bathing suits with us. A swim would do us both good right now. How about when we get back to the hotel?"

"My meeting starts early in the morning. I wish I could ask you for a rain check, but I'll be returning to Miami tomorrow afternoon."

"So soon," he remarked quietly.

Ivy couldn't define the emotion she saw in his eyes, nor could she understand the reason for the keen set of his jaw, but she had to believe that his seeing her again really mattered to him. The realization of that took hold of her with a force that was overwhelming.

"Maybe," he suggested softly as he moved closer and took hold of her shoulders, "we could get together before you . . ."

His voice trailed off, and a tense silence enveloped them as their eyes met and held. Wishes flurried in Ivy's unsettled thoughts. She wished she were staying longer. She wished that Chicago wasn't so far from Miami. And yes, she wished Chris would take her in his arms and kiss her.

Ivy closed her eyes, but then she felt his fingers tighten on her arms.

"I'm sorry," he whispered and released her.

Opening her eyes, she saw that he appeared confused and embarrassed.

Chris was bewildered. College athletics and fairly regular workouts had strengthened his leg muscles, but at the moment they could barely support him. What the hell had happened? he wondered. How had he almost lost all the control he prided himself on? Why was he having to fight the frantic urges he'd experienced as a teenager?

"Ivy," he stammered, "I—"

Summoning a tenuous smile, she forced her eyes from his and conquered the turmoil that swirled within. Looking over the moonlit cove, she said quietly, "No need to explain, Chris. It's the magic of the islands. Nothing more.''

Quickly she turned and started down the beach toward the hotel.

CHAPTER THREE

THE RECEPTIONIST at the home office greeted Ivy cheerfully and advised her that Cora wanted to speak with her before the meeting began. Ivy went directly to the woman's office. Janice, Cora's secretary, told her that her boss was in the adjacent file room where the information disks were stored.

Cora Bennings, Ivy decided long ago, had never smiled in her life. In her late forties, the vice president was a workaholic who had a penchant for wearing ties. Today was no different. Looped under the collar of her white shirt was a blue-and-gray paisley tie.

"Nice tie, Cora," Ivy commented, placing her briefcase on the table next to the long row of four-inch-high file drawers.

"How nice of you to notice." Cora's gray eyes took in Ivy's rust-colored linen suit. "You've lost weight."

"How nice of *you* to notice," Ivy said with a lilt in her voice as Cora replaced two disks in a wide drawer and closed it.

Turning, the woman smoothed back the sides of her red hair, which she wore in a French twist. "I need to talk to you about Scott. Let's go to my office."

Ivy watched the woman close the vaultlike door behind them, and her heart sank when she heard the click that came from a newly installed electronic panel.

Cora motioned Ivy to a chair and sat down behind her neatly arranged desk. "Bob McDonough's recommendation isn't taken lightly, and Scott's work has been impressive, but I'm concerned about his background."

Knowing that the woman was on the selection committee and would have a lot to say as to which candidate would be brought to the home office for grooming for a managerial assignment, Ivy asked, "What is it that bothers you, Cora?"

She opened a folder on her desk. "After a year in college he dropped out, and there are two years where he traveled."

"Yes."

"Ivy, you know how conservative our company is."

"After nine years I'm aware of that."

"Traveling is rather vague. I could understand if he had taken the grand tour of the Continent. Did he?"

"Really, Cora, that wasn't an issue when Scott was hired."

"He wasn't being considered for a managerial slot then. I'll have to give my input soon, and considering how well you've progressed, I'm leaning toward Scott. But this two-year period has me concerned, and why did he drop out of college?"

Ivy tried to explain her brother's behavior in the most favorable light. "Scott met a young woman who was in Miami on vacation. He fell in love and followed her back to Chicago. He had several odd jobs there that wouldn't enhance a resumé. The relationship didn't work out, and he returned home. But certainly during his time at Continental he's more than proved his abilities. Remember, it was his suggestion that we convert to the three-inch disks for information storage."

"True." Cora's eyes narrowed. "His fingerprint check cleared, so we know he wasn't in prison."

"Of course he wasn't! Do you think I'd have recommended him to the company if he had been?"

"Don't get upset. It's just that the information we handle is quite sensitive. I'm going to be asked the same questions I'm asking you if I back up Bob's recommendation. For those two years I can't come up with one reference."

"Yes, you can...Leon Torell, our Chicago branch manager. I asked him to keep in contact with Scott while he was there. He was more or less his big brother away from home."

Cora lifted her pencil-thin eyebrows. "As I remember, Leon was almost his big brother-in-law."

"That was a long time ago, before I married Bill. I haven't seen Leon for some time."

"Well, if he'll give Scott a recommendation, there shouldn't be any problem in getting your brother approved for the managerial program."

Ivy's heart skipped a beat. "You're definitely going to recommend him?"

"Scott's bright, and as long as he's settled down, he can have a good future with the company. Don't tell him, though. Wait until it's definite. I'll give you a call."

"Cora, I could kiss you."

"Let's not get mushy. I'm simply making a decision that should be good for the company." She glanced at the wall clock. "We'd better get to the conference room."

Gathering her things, Ivy realized that now more than ever she had to find a way to switch the disks for her brother.

Halfway through the meeting, Ernie Williams, the vice president in charge of project supervisors, declared a coffee and pastry break. Ivy bided her time, and when she saw Cora and Ernie with their heads together, she slipped out of the conference room.

As she walked briskly down the hallway, she removed one of her gold earrings and put it in her purse. When she reached Janice's office, the secretary was on the phone. *Please hurry,* Ivy thought impatiently. The minute the woman put down the receiver, she said, "Janice, I've lost one of my earrings. Could I check Cora's office and the file room?"

"You can look in Cora's office, but I can't let you in the file room. Sorry, but you know the rules."

Frowning, Ivy pleaded, "Please, it will only take a second. Cora is tied up in the meeting and I didn't want to bother her. The earrings belonged to my mother."

"Oh…well, in that case, but Cora would kill me if she knew I let you in there."

Ivy watched intently as Janice flipped over her desk calendar to check the new lock's numerical combination. After she opened the door to the file room, Ivy said, "You're a doll. I won't be but a minute."

The instant she was alone in the room, Ivy pulled the disk from her purse and checked the code number on it: D173. As quickly as she could, she scanned the drawers, locating the one marked C and the one marked E. Between the two was an empty space where drawer D should have been. Ivy wanted to cry.

"It's not in Cora's office," Janice said, standing at the door to the file room.

After shoving the disk into her purse, Ivy turned. "It's not in here either. Well, so much for that. Thanks a million, Janice. I've got to get back to the conference room."

Feeling like a failed Mata Hari, Ivy sat through the remainder of the meeting, wondering what to do next. Of the hundreds of drawers in the file room, why did someone have to be working on the D's? Dear God, she thought, what if that someone was using information on the disk that Scott had sent?

Try as she did, she couldn't think of another way to get back into the inner sanctum later on. Ivy's plane was due to leave for Miami at two o'clock, and she knew that tomorrow, Saturday, the building would be closed. No one would even be around, except the guard in the lobby.

No one!

A rush of adrenaline shot through her, and she knew what she had to do.

AFTER RETURNING to Sunset House, Ivy told the desk clerk she would be staying over for another day. In her room, she phoned her father to let him know.

"Dad, I hate to ask you, but would you take Kim to a movie tonight? It might help to get her mind off the date she was supposed to have with Eddie."

"No problem there. Randy's taking her out."

Ivy tensed. "Randy? Randy who?"

"You know him . . . Carol's brother. He went to dinner with Carol and Kim last night."

"But he must be eighteen."

"And Kim's fifteen. What's a three-year difference?"

"At their ages, a lot." Her questions tumbled out. "Where's he taking her? What are they going to do?"

"Calm down. Randy's a regular gentleman. He asked me if it would be all right to take her to a country music festival in Coconut Grove, and I said sure. I thought you'd be pleased that she had a date with a nice boy."

Ivy knew she should be pleased for Kim, but instead all she felt was anxiety. "I want Kim home by eleven o'clock at the latest. Make sure Randy understands that. And, Dad, you will be there when he picks her up and brings her home, won't you?"

"I will, darlin', I promise."

After hanging up, Ivy paced, thinking about Randy Wilson. She'd met him just after Carol moved in three years ago, but Ivy had only seen him a few times since. He had always been polite, but because of his height and athletic build, Randy had always seemed older to her than he was.

Carol had only good things to say about him, Ivy recalled. His grades were excellent, he was captain of his high school basketball team and active in the ROTC program. She remembered Carol saying that Randy was planning on a career in the air force after graduation and that he was going to apply for officer candidate school.

Still, Ivy was bothered by the idea of Kim's first date being with a boy who was almost a man. But he's Carol's brother, she countered to reassure herself, and he's a nice young man. "Young man" sounded better to her than just "man."

Going to the window, she gazed out past the palm trees to the colorful sailboats skimming over the emerald-green water of the Caribbean. Despite the cheerful sight she felt more depressed by the moment, realizing that she would be missing one of the most important events in Kim's life: her first real date. Ivy wanted to be there with her to help her decide what to wear and to brush her hair—and to tell her how far a good-night kiss should go.

She thought of the frightened thirteen-year-old girl Bill had brought home. Frightened? Kim had been terrified, and Ivy's heart had gone out to her immediately. She had come to love Kim as though she were her very own, but she was growing up so quickly, Ivy realized.

Shaking her head, she felt the need to get out of her room for a while and remembered the new swimsuit she had bought yesterday. Minutes later, with sunglasses on and towel and tote bag in hand, she made her way toward the rear of the hotel lobby, heading for the beach. She was passing the entrance to My Bar, a thatch-roofed seafront lounge that was popular with the local people, when a familiar voice called her name.

Inside the lounge, she saw Chris getting off a bar stool. He was wearing a burgundy-and-white-striped chambray shirt and khaki slacks, looking very much like a tourist.

"Hello again," he said, moving toward her, his easy smile reminiscent of the way he had looked at her last night on the beach. "I thought you were leaving this afternoon."

"A change in plans...a business matter," she explained. "I'll be leaving tomorrow."

"Wonderful. That gives us time for a piña colada." Before she could object, he took her arm gently and headed back into the lounge.

At the bar, Ivy placed her towel and tote bag on a vacant stool and sat down, resigned. She would have preferred to be alone with her thoughts, but she didn't want to appear rude.

"Danny," Chris called to the bartender, "another piña colada for me and one for the lady."

"Gotcha."

Chris straddled the bar stool, and when his knee brushed Ivy's, he felt her pull her leg away. He tried to ignore the tingling sensation aroused by the contact by concentrating on his job.

He wondered what kind of business matter was keeping Ivy in the islands, and if it had anything to do with the visit she had made to the Royal Bank of Canada yesterday. When he saw her leave Continental earlier, he'd thought she seemed preoccupied. He was further intrigued when he learned from the desk clerk that she was staying over.

"Nice little place they have here," he remarked, noting her faraway expression.

"Uh...yes. I always stay here. I prefer its casual atmosphere to the luxury hotels on Seven Mile Beach."

"Casual it is," he agreed, glancing around at what he guessed was the local fishing fraternity comparing stories.

Seeing a small group of divers with their snorkeling equipment come in through the beachside entrance, Ivy asked, "Do you like water sports, Chris? The islands are one of the top scuba-diving places in the world."

"Uh-uh, but recently I've become interested in walking on the beach in the moonlight." He grinned, then placed some money on the bar when Danny brought their drinks.

Ivy blushed slightly at the reference to last evening. She had had a wonderful time—until the last few awkward moments. Looking at Chris now, she still couldn't decide whether she should be thankful or hurt that he hadn't kissed her.

"I enjoyed last night," Chris said and sipped through the straw in his glass.

After taking a bite out of the pineapple wedge stuck in the frothy white drink, Ivy said with forced calm, "About last night...things look different in the daylight here in the islands."

His eyes raked over her slender figure clad only in the white swimsuit. "Yes, they certainly do." When Ivy faced him, he inquired, "Do you have a black eye?"

"Of course not. Why would you think that?"

"The dark glasses."

She slipped them off, laid them on the bar and looked at him, inexplicably annoyed. "So, Chris," she asked somewhat curtly, "is this how you plan to spend your vacation, downing piña coladas?"

"Would you believe this is only the second I've had in my life? Danny recommended it as the perfect vacation drink." He took another long sip and smacked his lips. "I agree. It tastes like an ice cream soda with fruit juice in it."

"A few more of these ice cream sodas and you'll wish you had stuck to bourbon and water."

Grinning, he said, "The voice of experience, I take it."

Ivy lifted her glass that was the size of a large brandy snifter. "Think of it as a word to the wise."

Silently, she chastised herself for sounding as if she had got up on the wrong side of the bed this morning. It wasn't like her at all to snipe at people, and Chris had done nothing to deserve it. It wasn't his fault that he unnerved her as no other man ever had.

She had always felt secure with Bill. He had been a gentle man from the beginning, and they had grown more comfortable with each other as time passed. There had been no surprises and no being put off balance suddenly. Chris was different; he made her feel different.

When he held her last night in the moonlight, she had felt as though she were an eighteen-year-old cheerleader again—hoping that the captain of the football team would kiss her. It was as if she had been possessed by some free spirit who didn't know the meaning of words like *tomorrow*, *regret* or *control*.

That worried her, for Ivy considered herself a sensible person. She wore sensible shoes, balanced her checkbook each month and trekked religiously to the dentist twice a year. But every time Chris smiled, she found herself feeling dangerously out of control.

"If you keep palming that glass the way you're doing, the cracked ice will melt."

"What? Oh." She pulled her hands away, realizing her fingers were almost numb.

"Didn't you sleep well?" he asked. "You seem different somehow today."

"I have a lot on my mind," she said with little emotion in her voice.

A steel band began playing calypso music, much to the enjoyment of the locals. Over the din, Chris suggested, "Let's move to the cabana on the beach. I'll take the drinks, and you gather up your things."

Ivy followed him, and they snaked their way through the dancing crowd. When they reached the thatch-roofed hut, Chris set the glasses down on the picnic table and told Ivy he'd be right back.

As he headed toward the lounge, she wondered what had happened to the fairly routine life she had been leading. It had all started with Scott and his trouble. That had led to her skulking around at the home office today, and only God knew if her plan for tomorrow would work. She was also bothered about Kim's going out with Randy. But thoughts of Chris pushed their way through her other concerns.

She sipped her piña colada, deciding that if he asked her to dinner, she would say she had other plans. Or would she? she pondered, chewing her bottom lip. Ivy had to admit that Chris interested her. He was a man who would stand out in a crowd. She liked the way he laughed, low and intimate, and he had a heart-hammering smile that made her feel all mushy inside. Turning toward the hotel, she wondered what was taking him so long.

Several more minutes passed before she checked again and saw him come sauntering toward her, wearing a yellow bikini swimsuit that left little to the imagination. His physique was quite impressive, Ivy decided immediately, and she could tell from the tan line on his thighs that he usually wore a boxer-style bathing suit. Yes, he was definitely an attractive man.

Chris slipped down on the bench next to her quickly and grinned. He hadn't expected to go swimming during his stay on the island, so the best he could do at short notice was to borrow a suit from his new friend, Danny, the bartender. So much for planning, he thought and started in on his drink.

Again his knee brushed against Ivy's leg, but this time he pulled his away. That overwhelming physical urge he'd thought he outgrew years ago shook him again. After several self-conscious moments, he cleared his throat and managed to ask, "So, what made you get involved in marketing research?"

Ivy's straw made a slurping noise at the bottom of her glass, then she tilted her head toward his. "I've always had a passion for research when it involves people and places. I guess I take after my father. He has to do a lot of research in his job. He's a sportswriter. Do you like sports?"

Chris sat up a little straighter. "You're looking at a former college track star, and I wasn't too bad at basketball, either."

Thanks to the heat of the day and the piña colada, Ivy began to relax a little, and she smiled. "You're in great condition. That says a lot about a man." Suddenly realizing she was staring at Chris, she ran the back of her hand across her forehead. "It's hot. I'm ready for a swim. How about you?"

Right now, the last thing Chris wanted to do was get up from the table in the skimpy swimsuit. He had always been obsessed with the need to be in complete control of his life, including his relationships with women. But dealing with Ivy Austin was a totally new experience for him. Just her smile triggered lustful thoughts in him. At the moment, she had affected more than his smile.

Standing, she asked, "Ready?"

"You go ahead. I'll be right behind you."

He watched her lithe form jog down the beach and waited until she had entered the water. Then he glanced around, tore over the sand and dived in. Surfacing behind her in the chest-high water, he grabbed her waist. Ivy let loose a cry of surprise and whirled around to face him.

"I thought you weren't into water sports," she challenged lightly.

"Since meeting you, I'm changing my mind about a lot of things." Suddenly his smile faded and his expression became serious. He eased his fingers slowly up over her arms.

The cool water had dispelled the effects of the piña colada Ivy had drunk, but the sultry look in Chris's eyes had an even more sobering effect on her. When he lowered his head to kiss her, she moved her face to the side and said quietly, "Chris, I'm not used to playing games like this."

Gently he tilted her face back toward his and said just as softly, "I haven't played games since I was a kid." He drew her closer, feeling his heart thudding against his ribs. Again he wished to hell that she was just a woman he had met while on a real vacation.

Placing the palms of her hands against his broad chest, Ivy tried to move backward in the water, but the hold he had on her was firm. "Chris," she said, meeting his eyes, "there are many tourist attractions here in the islands, but I'm not one of them."

With a seriousness that surprised even him, he countered, "You'd be an attraction anywhere in the world."

Disconcerted by his remark, she stammered, "Chris, I . . . I do think you're nice, but—"

"Nice?" He smiled halfheartedly. "You might not say that if you knew what I'm thinking."

Ivy raised both her hands and smoothed back the wet hair from her forehead. "Do you always rush things the way you're doing now?"

"Am I rushing?"

"As far as I'm concerned you are."

"Time is of the essence. You're leaving tomorrow."

"Exactly. We haven't had time to . . . to really get to know each other."

"You mean we should talk more before rushing into anything."

"Yes."

"Okay." He drew her closer until he felt her breasts rub against his chest. "What should we talk about?"

To clear her thinking, Ivy took a deep breath, but when she did, it only made matters worse. Her sensitized nipples were pressed into Chris's solid chest, and she could feel the pressure of his firm thighs along hers. Needing space and time to collect herself, she flattened her hands against his chest once more and tried to back away again. "For one thing, we should talk about the dangers of taking too much for granted."

Her admonition shook him and brought him back to reality. Instantly he released her, then lowered himself into the water and began moving his arms back and forth. "I'm sorry," he apologized sincerely. "I didn't mean to give you the impression I was taking anything for granted. It's just that you make me feel so... so alive." With that said, he swam away with quick, powerful strokes of his arms and legs.

For a while Ivy stood in the water, trying to make sense out of what had just happened. No one in memory had looked at her with such passion, and the pleasure of it forced her to acknowledge how much she missed feeling loved and wanted by a man and loving him in return. The need was suddenly so great that it became an ache, a desperate longing for a companion to laugh with and with whom to make plans for the future. But it couldn't be just any man. It would have to be someone special.

Yet, she admitted, Chris *was* special. He had taken the time to listen to her at dinner and on the beach last night, and there was no way of pretending she wasn't attracted to him. But giving in to those feelings now, she realized, would be ludicrous. Tomorrow they would have to say goodbye. She would leave for Miami, and he would eventually return to Chicago. What would be the point? A few intimate hours, and then what? Self-condemnation? Regret?

No, that wouldn't make any sense.

Having decided that, she trod through the water back to the beach. After drying herself, she spread the towel on the sand, sat down and tried to concentrate on the sail-boarders and jet skiers skimming over the sunlit aquamarine water. But her eyes kept returning to Chris as he swam back and forth furiously, as though he were in competition.

When he finally left the water and started up the beach, Ivy became acutely aware of his manly form: his broad chest, flat stomach and well-shaped arms, thighs and calves. When her attention slid to the way the wet bikini molded onto his masculinity, she quickly slipped on her sunglasses.

Chris lowered himself onto his stomach next to her and rested on his forearms, oblivious to the sand that coated his wet skin. "The water's nice," he said matter-of-factly, then looked up at her as she sat there silently, staring straight ahead.

After brooding moments, he said, "Look, I'm sorry if I spoke out of turn awhile back, but I meant it when I said you make me feel alive." He chuckled softly. "Call it chemistry or whatever you want, but there's something about you that gets to me. I don't know if it's the way you smile or the way you laugh so openly. Hell, I even like the way you walk."

When she remained silent, he asked, "Haven't you ever met someone and known instantly that that person was special? Well, I think you're special. You may not want to hear that, but I hope you appreciate my honesty."

To still the nervous movements of her fingers, she interlaced them around her knees. "Chris, we barely know each other."

Rolling onto his side and resting his jaw in his curved palm, he rattled off lightly, "I'll be thirty-eight next week. I did a tour of duty in the army. I have a degree in accounting from the University of Maryland. One marriage, one divorce. I work hard. I'm kind to children and animals. And I happen to think you're one of the most beautiful women I've ever seen in my life.''

"Chris, please, you're making me nervous."

"I don't mean to."

Averting his eyes, Ivy realized he was doing it again. He was knocking her off balance, and the feeling was scary. She wasn't so naive that she didn't recognize a come-on when she heard one, but she couldn't dismiss Chris's words that easily.

Ivy had never thought of herself as being beautiful. Averagely attractive, yes. For some reason, though, Chris made her feel beautiful. More disturbing, he made her painfully aware of her feminine need for a man's caress—and love.

Her eyes sought his again, and she said firmly, "I try to take care of myself, but I'm hardly one of the most beautiful women in the world. For one thing, my nose isn't quite straight. And I have a slight overbite."

The look he gave her was sensual and sincere. "Don't change a thing about yourself, not one damn thing." Slowly his eyes drifted up from her slender feet to her auburn hair, which looked darker now that it was wet. "You know, there have only been a few times in my life when I've really been astounded. As a kid, I remember being amazed when I realized the whole world was in Technicolor. My second shock came when I was around fourteen and had a date with JoAnn Dawson. I went through a long, dry spell until the first time I saw you. Wham, another zinger."

When Ivy didn't respond, he cupped his hands behind his head and lay back on the sand. "I'm tempted to ask you to dinner, but if you accept it's pretty certain that I'll make a pass at you. I know you wouldn't want me to."

He shaded his eyes against the strong sun and peered up at her. "You wouldn't . . . would you?"

Chris's question echoed in her ears, and she had to bite back the "yes" that was on the tip of her tongue. As much as she wanted to accept his invitation, there were too many other things on her mind right now, her precarious plan for the morning not being the least of them.

Gathering her things, she said softly, "I can't, Chris."

"More work to do?"

She was standing now, looking down at him with eyes shielded by sunglasses. Nodding, she said quietly, "I hope you enjoy your vacation."

Chris followed her movements with his eyes as she walked toward the hotel. "Ivy Austin," he mumbled, "you haven't seen the last of me . . . not by a long shot."

CHAPTER FOUR

EARLY IN THE MORNING, Ivy greeted the daytime guard at the home office and wrote her name in the sign-in book. She experienced a momentary panic when she saw that Ernie Williams had signed in a few minutes before. She hadn't expected that, but she knew his office was in the opposite wing of the building, so she went directly to Janice's office.

Quickly she flipped over the pages of the secretary's desk calendar, noted the combination of the lock to the file room door and fingered the numerals on the electronic panel. Hearing the click, she breathed a sigh of relief and entered the long room.

The drawer marked D was in place now. She put her purse on the table and saw that her hands were shaking as she retrieved the disk Scott had given her. The little three-inch plastic disk felt as though it weighed a ton as she stared at it.

I shouldn't be doing this! an inner voice warned, and she pulled her hand back from the drawer. But then she thought of her brother's future and how he had redirected his life during the past two years. No, she decided firmly, she had to help him now. Quickly she exchanged disks and dropped the one from the drawer into her purse.

She left the file room and quietly shut the heavy door, but when it clicked, Ivy had a disturbing thought. What if someone wondered why she had signed in this morning? She went to Cora's desk and started to write a note.

"Hello again."

Ivy gasped and her head shot up. "Oh . . . Ernie," she said, her voice shaking. "You startled me."

The gray-haired man said, "My wife tells me I have the same effect on her sometimes. How's my favorite project supervisor, and what are you doing here on Saturday?"

While she finished writing the last few words, Ivy explained, "I'm leaving a note for Cora." She looked up at Ernie again. "I lost an earring yesterday, and I want her to be on the lookout for it."

After discussing business for a few minutes, Ivy left the building. Once outside, she inhaled deeply several times to steady her nerves, then started to cut through the alleyway to get to the taxi stand around the corner.

Halfway down the long, narrow alley she saw a hulk of a dark-haired man enter and start toward her. His strides were slow, his face solemn, and he was staring directly at her. Sheer panic tore through her when she saw him raise his hands and come right at her.

The man lunged, and she groaned with pain when she felt her back hit the stone wall of the building behind her. In the next instant, she realized he had grabbed her purse.

"Stop!" she cried out as he tore back down the alley—right into Chris.

The events of the next few moments were almost a blur as the two men struggled. Picking up a stray brick from the ground, Ivy ran toward them, raised the brick and swung at the mugger's head with all her strength. Seconds later, the man tore out of the alleyway, and Ivy looked down at Chris, horrified.

"Oww," he moaned, holding the back of his head, his eyes squinched tightly.

Crouching beside him, Ivy placed a hand on the side of his face. "Chris, I'm so sorry. Did I hurt you?"

Through slits in his eyelids, he looked up at her. With a twisted smile, he said, "I guessed you were a heart-breaker, but I didn't think my head was in danger." He raised her purse by the straps. "At least I got this back."

Ivy draped the straps over her wrist and took hold of his arm. "Let me help you."

Both of his hands flew up, palms toward her. "I'm not budging until you put down that brick." When she did, he pushed himself up from the ground and rubbed the back of his head.

"Are you bleeding?"

He checked his fingers. "No, but I'm going to have one hell of a bump."

"Maybe you should see a doctor."

"No, some ice will help...after we report this incident to the police."

Feeling guilty enough for hitting Chris by mistake and also for having switched disks, Ivy didn't want further complications by bringing the police into what was an unsuccessful mugging attempt. "No, no police!" she said, her words pouring out. "I've got to get ready to leave, and who knows how long they'd keep me here. I can't miss my plane today. Let's get back to the hotel so I can put some ice on your head."

"Okay," Chris said, distressed that she had been so quick to rule out going to the police.

As Ivy wrapped some ice cubes in a towel, she said, "It was lucky for me that you came along when you did."

She glanced at him, her expression curious. "How did you happen to be at Continental?"

Laying his suit jacket across her bed, Chris said, "Morning exercise. I'm an avid walker."

"Oh. Well, thanks again." She went to him after he sat down at the bottom of the bed. Gently she parted his thick brown hair and studied the bruise. "Ooh, you do have a bump."

"Let me," he suggested, then took the ice pack from her and pressed it against the back of his head. "You know, I understand that mugging is almost nonexistent in the islands." He looked up at her and grinned. "The bartender and I have become great friends. Danny told me they have an exceptionally low crime rate here."

"That's true," she remarked as she packed her overnight bag. "The economy is in good shape."

"Thanks to their banks being an offshore haven for stateside people who have large sums of money they would just as soon the IRS didn't know about."

Turning, Ivy looked at him quizzically. "What brought that on?"

"Just my interest in banking." He thought about the visit she had made to the bank the day she arrived in Georgetown. "I understand that wire transfers of money between banks here and those in the States don't have to be reported to the IRS."

Ivy smiled lightly. "And you think the man who tried to mug me was collecting for his upcoming bank deposit?"

Chris studied her expression before saying quietly, "If he was a mugger."

"If? He tried to steal my purse, didn't he?"

Nodding, Chris rose, went to the wet bar near the sliding glass doors and dumped the ice into the sink. Despite Ivy's reluctance to report the incident to the police, he still couldn't believe she'd be involved in a mail fraud or money-laundering scheme. Most of last night he had lain awake debating his dilemma.

Ivy Austin had gotten under his skin; he didn't want to let her walk out of his life. They would both be returning to Miami, and he wanted to see her again. But he'd already given her his cover story about living and working in Chicago. If they did see each other in the near future, she would soon learn he was a postal inspector who was checking on the people in the company she worked for. What to do? The answer hadn't come during the night, but now he knew he had to make a decision.

He glanced back at her and watched her snap the locks on her suitcase, then he squeezed out the towel and draped it on the faucet of the wet bar. "Ivy," he said, without looking her way, "I'm flying to Miami today, also."

Her features expressed the sudden excitement she felt at hearing that. She liked Chris, but she refused to consider a one-night stand with him. It would be another matter if he were to spend the remainder of his vacation in Miami and they could learn more about each other. Her smile dissipated, though, when she realized he might have other reasons for going to Miami than to be with her. Jokingly she asked, "Tired of paradise already, Chris?"

He turned, stood straight and shoved his hands into his pants pockets. "There are things about me you don't know."

"There are things about me you don't know," she said softly. "Isn't that what time takes care of?"

"I don't live in Chicago anymore. I've just transferred to Miami, and I'm not an internal auditor. I work for the Postal Inspection Service. I'm an inspector."

Ivy felt her facial muscles tense. Slowly she sat down on the side of the bed. Ever since they met on the plane, she'd had a vague feeling that something was awry. Chris had had an uncommon interest in her work, and he had surprisingly shown up at the same hotel. Then there was his sudden appearance in the alleyway earlier. But what would a postal inspector want with her? she wondered.

Tilting her head up, she searched his measuring gaze, then asked, "Why the deceit, Chris?"

"You really don't know, do you?"

"I don't know what? Please stop being so cryptic. Just tell me why you thought it was necessary to lie to me. Did you think you'd make more points with a woman if you were an internal auditor and not a postal inspector?"

"I wish it were as simple as that." He took slow steps away from the wet bar, then leaned back against the wall and crossed his arms. "I'm part of a team that's investigating a nationwide swindling operation. Sharp promoters are using the mails to defraud people. Often they target the elderly, people who are trying to stretch their retirement dollars. The con men prey on their loneliness, their lack of mobility or fear of running out of money. After defrauding their victims, they pack up and move on to new territory, leaving no trace of their operation."

As Ivy listened, she became more confused. "What does any of that have to do with me?"

"We've narrowed down our investigation to several large marketing research firms, companies that accumulate in-depth information on people. It's possible that someone at one of the firms is supplying the swindlers with selective mailing lists.''

Slowly Ivy rose from the bed, her self-restraint dwindling as she realized he was just about accusing her. ''And you think I could be involved?'' Raising a hand, she ran her fingers through the side of her hair. ''You've actually been following me ... spying on me?''

''We call it surveillance.''

Becoming more furious by the second, she spit out, ''I call it an invasion of my rights!''

''My job at the Postal Inspection Service is to protect people's rights, not invade them.''

''Is it part of your job to send women champagne cocktails and invite them to dinner?''

''No,'' he answered quietly, his eyes directly on hers. ''I did that because I wanted to.''

''Why should I believe anything you say to me now?''

''Because it's the truth.''

''Ah, I see,'' she said with an icy edge to her tone. ''Now you're being honest and open with me. Why didn't you try *that* approach a little sooner? Why did you let me pour out my heart to you about my family, as if you cared?'' Her hand shot up. ''No, don't tell me. You were convinced I was swindling the elderly out of their life savings.''

Slowly and calmly he said, ''Ivy, my job is to get all the information I can. I don't believe you are involved, but someone in your company could be.''

''That's ridiculous! Continental is a legitimate, respected firm.''

''Will you help me prove that?''

''How? By spying on my co-workers?''

''No, I wouldn't ask you to do that, but you could keep your eyes open for anything out of the ordinary.''

"Believe me," she informed him curtly as she took rapid strides to the door, "my eyes are open. I'd like you to leave now. I've got a plane to catch."

Chris picked up his jacket from the bed. "I'm asking you not to mention this conversation with people at work, not for the time being, anyway." He looked at her flushed face and waited for a response.

"And have them laugh at me?" Ivy asked.

When she reached for the knob to open the door, Chris placed his hand over hers and lowered his voice. "I'd like to see you after we get back to Miami."

"I don't think that would be wise, Mr. Laval," she said, her voice tense, clipped.

"You can still call me Chris."

"Mr. Laval, there's little chance of my calling you anything."

DURING THE RETURN FLIGHT to Miami, Ivy sat as far behind Chris as she could. She felt brutally betrayed and used by the man, and thought herself foolish for thinking that he had cared for her at all. Her head was aching from the tension that had built up during the day. Her entire trip to Georgetown had been one big disaster, but at least she had retrieved the disk Scott had wanted so desperately.

The disk.

Just the thought of it grated on her. Why should it now? she questioned. Her brother had made a mistake and had turned to her for help. She had done what he had asked, and it was over with. But, she told herself, this was the last time she would pick up the pieces for Scott.

Scott. He had always been pampered by her and their mother, and he usually conned them into helping him get out of trouble before their father found out. In fairness to her brother, though, Ivy wondered if it had been his fault that he had always been easily influenced by the older boys he had run around with.

Certainly their father hadn't been of much help while Scott was growing up. His work had taken him away from home so often after Scott was born that he'd had to fulfill his role as disciplinarian in short spurts. Her brother had been the one to receive the brunt of their father's ire then, not that Scott hadn't deserved it, she reflected.

Ivy forced away her mind's wanderings and glanced down the aisle of the plane to where Chris was sitting. She still couldn't believe that nonsense about someone at Continental being in cahoots with swindlers. She knew just about everyone who worked there, and they were all ordinary people like her, people who had families, paid their taxes and griped about it. *Well, Mr. Laval,* she thought, *you're barking up the wrong tree at Continental.*

Yet, she admitted, trying to temper her anger at him, he had said Continental was only one of the companies being investigated. She allowed that the man had to do his job, but did he have to make her like him in the bargain? That was what really hurt. Chris had gained her trust and confidence, and then he had thrown that trust back in her face by telling her what he had done.

Of course, he didn't have to tell you, she argued silently, and wondered why he had. *To get you to spy for him, that's why!* Well, his plan hadn't worked, she concluded, and set her attention on the clear sky outside the plane window.

Soon, though, her thoughts returned to the disk in her purse, and she decided to make a stop at the office in Miami before handing it over to her brother.

WHEN THE JET LANDED in Miami, Chris left the plane ahead of Ivy, and she waited as long as she could before following the last of the passengers from the plane. Heading toward an exit door in the terminal, she saw Chris at one of the phone stalls, making a call. He saw her, too, and waved a hand in a friendly gesture. Ignoring it, she hurried to where she had parked her car and headed for downtown Miami.

Once inside her office, she closed the door, inserted the disk in her computer and made a printout of its contents. As the information was printed, she checked the first few pages. Just as Scott had told her, it was an alphabetical mailing list. She noted that the addresses were in Denver, Colorado. Ivy wasn't sure why, but she decided to keep the printout and took it with her when she left the building and headed for her brother's apartment.

"I KNEW YOU COULD DO IT!" Scott exclaimed, his eyes riveted to the disk he clutched. Quickly he went to the kitchen and tossed it in the garbage. Returning to the living room, he asked, "How about a drink to celebrate?"

Ivy dropped her purse onto the sofa and sat down. "I hardly think celebrate is the word. I'm ashamed of what I did, and you should be for asking me to do it."

"God, you're square. People in business do things like this every day. Why make such a big deal about it?"

"Because it *is* a big deal, that's why. And who are these people you know who do this kind of thing every day? No one at the company, I hope."

Scott slumped down on an easy chair and slung a leg over the cushioned arm. "Jeez, you're uptight. Have lousy weather in the islands? Listen, after I get back from vacation, let's do a weekend in Nassau. I've got some money saved, and we can—''

"Since when have you started saving money?"

"Since the horses at the racetrack have dropped their personal grudge against me. Any more questions, big sister?"

"Yes. What information did you merge incorrectly on that disk?"

Standing quickly, Scott went to the curved counter that separated the living room from the kitchen. As he poured himself a Scotch on the rocks, he said offhandedly, "I mistakenly included the names and addresses of some middle-income people on that particular disk." He turned, his smile innocent. "Sure I can't fix you a drink?"

Ivy shook her head, realizing how useless the list would be if the company had sold it to a buyer who wanted to contact only upper-income people. In a way she felt relieved that the correct information was now on file.

"Well," she said, thinking the case closed, "as long as you learn from this experience and are more careful in the future, I guess no real harm has been done."

"Trust me. You're looking at a reformed man. From now on, even Dad will be proud of me. How is the ol' grouch?"

"He's not a grouch. He just misses Mom."

Scott's smile withered. "Yeah, I miss her, too." Leaning back against the counter, he took a long swallow of his drink.

"You know, Scott, it wouldn't hurt you to stop by and say hello to Dad once in a while."

"Why? To let him ruin my day? He's never forgiven me for not turning out to be the jock he thinks he is. I near got killed on that damn football field in high school, trying to pretend I was. No thank you. I'll use my brains to get ahead, not my bones.''

Ivy reached for her purse and stood, knowing it was no use trying to patch things up between father and son, not now, anyway. To end the conversation on a lighter note, she said, ''Don't forget to toss anything in the refrigerator that will spoil while you're gone.''

Scott chuckled. ''There's never much in there.''

Ivy couldn't help but smile at him. For all the grief he sometimes caused, her brother could still look like an angel when he wanted to. In his handsome, dark features, she again noted his resemblance to their mother. Smoothing back the curly black hair that fell over his forehead, she said, ''Be sure and take warm clothes with you. You know how cold it can be in Chicago this time of year.''

He took her hand between his and shook it gently. ''I will, and stop worrying about me. I'm a big boy now.''

''Are you, Scott?'' she asked softly, then tried to ward off her doubts. Starting toward the door of the apartment, she asked, ''Are you going to see Emily while you're in Chicago?''

''Emily...oh, sure. I talked to her on the phone last night.''

''I thought that's why you decided to go there.''

Scott opened the door. ''I'll walk you to the elevator.''

''Is there any chance you two will get together again?''

''That's exactly why I'm going, to find out.''

Sincere, Ivy said, ''I liked Emily, and Dad would be so pleased if you did settle down.''

''If I got married and came up with grandchildren for him, you mean.''

''Dad will be happy if he knows you're happy.''

"And the sun rises in the west." The elevator door opened. "Now get out of here so I can pack," he said, grinning broadly. "Say, why don't *you* come up with some grandchildren for him?"

"Go pack," she said and lost sight of him when the door closed.

In his apartment, Scott fixed his eyes on the phone. He smoked one cigarette, then another before making a long-distance call.

"This is Scott," he said, a thickness in his voice. "Ivy's made the switch." He blinked several times as he listened. "No, you're not getting the disk. I got rid of it. It's the only thing that proves my involvement in your operation." Again he listened while lighting another cigarette.

"Bull! I don't trust anyone, particularly you, and I've made up my mind. One more trip and I'm through, out of the organization for good! I'm sorry I ever let you talk me into getting mixed up with it." He listened for tense moments, then calmed his voice. "I'll be in Chicago Wednesday night, but remember, this is the last trip I make for you."

As Ivy's CAR NEARED the house, she saw a motorcycle zip from the driveway. When it passed her, she caught a fleeting glimpse of the rider, a woman. Silver-gray hair bushed out from under her helmet, just touching the collar of the plaid jacket she wore.

After parking, Ivy grabbed her suitcase and hurried into the house to hear about Kim's date with Randy. She had mixed feelings when she learned the two teenagers had gone to the beach for the day.

"What time did Randy bring Kim home last night?" Ivy asked her father.

"One minute before curfew."

"What time did he pick her up today?"

"Nine o'clock sharp."

"Did she take sunscreen with her?"

Walt stopped leafing through the pages of his manuscript and looked up at his daughter. "You know, you're a worrywart, just like your mother was. You worry about me, you worry about Scott and you worry about Kim. You're spreading yourself kind of thin, don't you think?"

"Someone has to be concerned about the family, and I don't see any other takers," she informed him matter-of-factly.

Slipping off her linen suit jacket, Ivy laid it over the back of the chair next to her father's desk. Then she leaned down and kissed his cheek. "Who was that on the motorcycle I saw hot-rodding out of the driveway?"

"My new employee." Smiling that he had piqued Ivy's curiosity, he added, "She's the Kelly Girl, the temporary office worker who's gonna type my manuscript."

"A rather mature girl, isn't she?"

"Would you be happier if I hired some teenybopper in tight shorts to parade around here? Trudy's a widow, and she's experienced—" he peered over the rims of his glasses "—as a typist. In England she was a copy editor for one of those women's magazines."

"She's British?"

"Most people who were born in England are." He chuckled. "Wait until you hear her accent. It's kind of cute."

"What time did you tell Kim to be home?"

"I didn't tell her. For God's sake, she's a young lady, not a baby."

"She's barely fifteen," Ivy reminded him as she picked up her jacket and suitcase.

"When you were fifteen you sometimes stayed out all night."

At the doorway, she looked back at her father and grinned. "At slumber parties, three houses down the block."

She headed for the stairway but looked around when Walt said, "You had a delivery a little while ago. It's on the dining room table."

Ivy searched her memory for something she had ordered, but nothing came to mind. Putting down her suitcase and jacket, she went to the dining room. In the center of the table were a dozen scarlet roses and sprigs of white baby's breath.

"There's a card," Walt said, resting a shoulder against the doorframe.

Slipping it out of the little envelope, Ivy read silently: As was the champagne cocktail, these roses are my idea. A phone number served as the signature. Ivy guessed it was Chris's home phone number and read the card once more. Then she smiled softly and tapped it against her chin.

Walt said, "The last time I saw roses that pretty they were the ones I took to your mother in the hospital."

"What? Oh, yes, they are nice." She touched one lightly, then sniffed the half-opened bloom. "They're from a man I met on the plane to Georgetown."

"Does this man have a name?"

"Chris Laval. He's a postal inspector."

"Works for the government, huh? What'd you do...use a stamp twice?"

Ivy bristled slightly. "I didn't *do* anything. We just happened to meet." Moving by her father, she started toward the stairway.

"Well, it's about time you were courted again."

Halfway up the stairs, Ivy stopped and looked down at him. "I am not being courted."

Resting an arm on the railing, Walt grinned. "You got twelve roses in there that say you are. When do I get to meet this Chris Laval?"

"Are you that anxious to get me out of this house again?"

"I'm anxious for you to get on with your life, Daughter. I don't want you spending the rest of it alone as I'm doing."

"With two women in the house, how do you figure you're spending your life alone?"

"You know what I mean. Someday Kim will get married and what are you and I supposed to do...play Scrabble until our eyes give out?"

"If that happens, we'll hire a Kelly Girl to read the letters to us." With that said, Ivy climbed the rest of the stairs and went down the hall to her room.

She strode over to the window that faced the garden in the rear of the house. A gentle breeze rustled the fronds on the palm trees that edged the swimming pool. She thought of the palms along the beach near the hotel where she and Chris had walked, and she remembered how intently he had listened when she talked to him about Kim. The card was still in her hand, and she glanced at it. Then she shook her head, placed the card on her dresser and began to unpack.

Moments later her eyes drifted over to the card again. Well, Ivy decided, the polite thing to do would be to at least call and thank him for the roses.

CHAPTER FIVE

"HELLO."

Hearing Chris's deep voice, Ivy smiled and twirled the extension cord of the phone around her finger. "This is Ivy," she said softly.

"I was hoping you'd call."

"The roses are absolutely beautiful."

"I'm glad you like them."

"It really wasn't necessary, though."

"I didn't send them because I thought it was. I just wanted to apologize for behaving like a klutz. You were right. I should have been more honest with you from the beginning."

Ivy didn't know why, but she found herself defending him. "You were only doing your job. I was a little unnerved by what you said about suspecting that someone at Continental was involved with criminals. It was a little hard to—"

"Let's not talk about that now. How's Kim? I imagine she missed you."

Ivy chuckled. "I have a sneaking suspicion she was glad I wasn't here. Her dating has picked up considerably since I left. She's at the beach with a friend now."

A lengthy silence followed, and Ivy eased herself down onto her bed, wondering what to say next, wondering how to prolong the conversation. But nothing came to mind.

"Are you still there?" Chris asked.

"Yes, I'm here."

"Ivy," he said hesitantly, "Wednesday is my birthday. I don't know many people in Miami yet. Would you have dinner with me?" Before she could answer, he added, "If you won't, I'll probably celebrate it alone."

"That would be awful," she said, feeling her heart begin to race.

"Then you will?"

"Would you like to have dinner here? You could meet Kim and my father. He'll probably talk you to death about sports, but I think you'll like him."

"You're sure I wouldn't be imposing."

"Not at all. Is seven o'clock all right?"

"Armageddon wouldn't keep me away."

Ivy could hear his smile in the words. "Seven o'clock then."

"Seven," he repeated. "Bye for now."

"Chris!" she said quickly.

"Yes?"

"Thanks again for the lovely roses. It was sweet of you."

"Thank you for phoning. That was sweet of you."

"Bye, Chris."

"Bye."

Ivy heard the click, leaned back against the cushioned headboard of her bed and slowly cradled the receiver. The past few days had been a constant series of ups and downs, but right now, she had to admit, was one of the high points. She knew her pulse was beating rapidly, and a touch of her cheek told her that her face was flushed.

It was a long time since a man had sent her flowers, she realized. Not since Bill, who used to send flowers on her birthday and on anniversaries.

It had been sweet of Chris to send the roses to apologize, Ivy thought. Now that she knew he was living in Miami, there was no reason they couldn't see each other occasionally. She no longer had to be concerned about Scott and his problem. That was over and done with.

Stretching out her arms languidly, she felt certain that her father and Kim would like Chris. How could they not? Chris could be charming when he wanted to be. More than charming, she corrected, remembering the way he had looked at her in the moonlight in the cove, the way he had swaggered down the beach in the yellow bikini and the way he had held her and gazed at her in the water. Yes, she confirmed, Chris was more than charming. He was a man that any woman would like to—

Good Lord, she chided, jumping up from the bed, *you're behaving like a schoolgirl!*

While she finished unpacking, she tried to decide what to have for dinner Wednesday night. Then she heard a car door slam in the driveway and went to the side window.

She saw Randy opening the car door for Kim. His automobile was an old-model Camaro that he obviously kept in beautiful condition. It troubled Ivy to see Randy and Kim head for the front door hand in hand, but the smile on her daughter's face alleviated her concern.

Kim's call greeted Ivy as she started down the stairs.

"Hi, honey." Ivy shifted her eyes to Randy, and she could certainly see why Kim could be attracted to him. Athletically trim, with a crew cut and handsome features, he reminded her of a youthful Harry Belafonte. "It's good to see you again, Randy. Did you two have a good time at the beach?"

"Sure did, Mrs. Austin."

Draping her yellow windbreaker over the banister, Kim asked, "Can I have dinner at Carol's?"

"Did she invite you?"

"I did," Randy said quickly. "Carol wants me to stay for dinner, and she always cooks enough for an army."

"That's fine with me, but I think you should check with your sister first."

Randy nodded, tugged at his white sweatshirt, then told Kim, "I'll take care of that now. You get your books together and come on over."

"I have to shower and change," she said, smiling up at the young man, who was a good foot taller than she was.

"Yeah, well, don't be long, okay?"

"I won't."

Ivy could see the obvious adoration in Kim's eyes, and in Randy's she saw the same thing. Quickly she searched through her memories, trying to recall if she had ever looked at anyone quite that way after two dates. When she remembered the short-lived crush she'd had on the captain of her school's football team, some of her concern returned.

As soon as Randy left, Kim started to dart up the stairs, but Ivy stopped her. "Just a minute, young lady. Take your jacket with you."

Kim smiled. "Yes, Mother." She sailed down the stairway and grabbed her windbreaker.

"Aren't you forgetting something else?"

"Something else?"

"Well, I've been out of the country. Don't I at least get a welcome-home kiss?"

From her position on the third step, Kim threw her arms around Ivy and kissed her cheek. The warmth of the young girl spread over her, filling her with an immense feeling of happiness and contentment.

"That's better," Ivy said, smiling, and she started up the stairs beside Kim. "Now what's his about getting your books together?"

"Randy is going to help me with English, and I am going to help him with French. He says that in school he learns to read and write French, but that little time is spent to talk it."

As they rounded the top railing, Ivy said, "That sounds great for both of you. You like Randy, don't you?"

"He is *très gentil*, very nice." Inside her room, Kim laid her windbreaker on the bed. "He is kind to me and—" she faced Ivy, then lowered her eyes "—I like to be with him. He makes me feel safe." Looking up, she smiled. "And I like the way he laughs."

Going to her, Ivy ran her fingers over Kim's dark, silky hair. "Being with someone you like is a nice feeling, isn't it? It was that way with your father and me."

Having said that, Ivy experienced the same feeling of hesitation she always did when she mentioned Bill to Kim. She wanted Kim to know about her father, but she was also aware of the trauma it had been for Kim to lose him so soon after he had begun to play such an important role in her young life. To change the subject, she asked, "What are you going to wear to Carol's?"

"Jeans and the white top you gave me for my birthday."

"I'll get them while you shower." After Kim went into the bathroom, Ivy asked, "Has Randy told you he's joining the air force after he graduates?"

From the bathroom she answered, "Yes. He is going to be an officer." She stuck her head out the doorway. "That's a very large responsibility, especially for someone as young as Randy."

"As young," Ivy repeated and seized at the opening Kim had given her. "He's eighteen, isn't he?"

"He will be in two months."

"Do you think you'll be seeing a lot of him?"

Dressed in her robe, Kim came out of the bathroom and neatly placed the clothes she had been wearing on the bed. "Randy says that he likes me a lot." Again she lowered her eyes. "He says that I am beautiful." Slowly her long, dark lashes lifted, and she looked into Ivy's eyes. "Do you think I am truly beautiful, Mother?"

Ivy took hold of Kim's shoulders and gently turned her so she could see herself in the mirror over the dresser. "You are one of the most beautiful young ladies that I have ever seen. I'm not surprised that Randy thinks so, too. One thing, though, honey, and I want you to think about this. Randy is a fine young man, but he's only the first young man who will be important to you. It's good that you two have become friends, but he has definite plans for his life."

Sitting on the bed, Ivy added, "When he leaves in June, I don't want you to—" she wanted to say "be hurt," but she modified her warning "—to miss him too much. For now, enjoy his company, but keep in mind that you're only fifteen years old. That's a little young to become serious about a boyfriend. Okay?"

For long seconds, Kim thought about Ivy's words, then she said, "Okay."

Ivy stood. "Take your shower now, and we'll talk about this again another time."

Downstairs in the living room, she phoned Carol to check on dinner arrangements.

"Sure, she's invited," her neighbor said. "And don't think I'm being a sweetheart. I haven't seen my brother three days in a row since I don't know when. He's used the excuse that my parents' home is clear across town, but I've this strange feeling the ride here has suddenly become much shorter, thanks to Kim.''

Ivy thought the same thing. ''Well, just send her home whenever you're ready for her to leave.''

''I may never let her leave. You should see Randy right now. He's poring over one of my old college English textbooks like it was an ROTC manual.''

''It's nice that they're going to help each other out with schoolwork.''

''Nice? In this day and age, two teenagers getting together to actually study is spooky. I just hope I've got film in my camera. Ivy, the timer just went off. I've got to get busy. If this dinner doesn't come up to snuff, Randy will disown me. I'll talk to you later.''

Ivy started toward the kitchen, but she caught a whiff of the roses and went into the living room to look at the flowers Chris had sent. As she admired them again, she remembered that she hadn't decided what to have for dinner Wednesday evening.

Chris had said he wasn't much on French cooking. That figures, she thought ruefully, for she had become fairly proficient at preparing French cuisine because Bill had enjoyed it. She half decided on lasagna, but Chris had ordered that in the restaurant the night they had dined together. Baked chicken, she decided, would be a safe bet…or maybe a rib roast. She wondered if, like her father, Chris was a meat, potatoes and gravy man. A birthday cake! She'd have to have a birthday cake, but she'd buy it at the Danish bakery. There just wasn't enough time to—

''Do I look okay?'' Kim asked as she came into the dining room, carrying her books.

Ivy turned and examined her. Had she never noticed before, she wondered, or was Kim suddenly filling out? The white top with the rounded eyelet collar emphasized the girl's petite figure, as did the soft blue jeans she wore. Ivy also detected a glow on the girl's face that she hadn't noticed before. "You look great," Ivy assured her and saw Kim's eyes focus on the roses.

"How beautiful they are," Kim exclaimed. "Did you buy them?"

"No, a friend sent them to me, a man I met when I was away on business."

Kim's green eyes shifted from the roses to Ivy. "You just met him, and he sent you roses?"

"Yes, wasn't that a thoughtful thing for him to do? You'll meet him Wednesday. I've invited him for dinner."

"Why?"

"For one thing, it's his birthday, and he doesn't know many people in Miami. His name is Chris, Chris Laval. He's very, as you say, *gentil*, and he's anxious to meet you. Would you like to take Carol a rose?"

Kim backed away from the table, rather too quickly, Ivy thought, and she became more concerned when she saw the girl's fingers move nervously.

In a quiet voice, Kim asked, "Did my father ever send you roses?"

Ivy hadn't been prepared for that question, but the import of its coming at just this moment was all too clear, as was Kim's sudden negative reaction to the flowers.

"He did many times," Ivy said and managed a smile. "Your father knew how much I loved roses."

Softly Kim asked, "You still think of him, no?"

"Of course, just as you do." Ivy glanced at her watch. "You'd better not keep Randy and Carol waiting. I don't know what time she's planning on eating. Are you sure you don't want to take her a rose?''

Kim shook her head. "They are for you, Mother."

MONDAY MORNING, after Randy picked up Kim to drive her to school, Ivy was just finishing her second cup of coffee in the kitchen when she heard the deafening roar of a motorcycle tearing up the driveway.

"That's Trudy," Walt said and went to the door.

"The Kelly Girl," Ivy muttered, lifting her eyebrows. After a last swallow of coffee, she went into the living room to greet her father's new employee.

"You're Ivy, aren't you, dear!" Trudy bubbled as she held out her hand and sailed across the room. "I'm Trudy Kerr."

Bemused by the sudden onslaught, Ivy extended her hand. She guessed the woman to be in her mid-fifties. Her features were rather sharp, but she was attractive, and her makeup had been applied tastefully and judiciously. She was large boned, rather than stocky; her hair billowed around her face like a silver halo. Her ample, gleaming white teeth, Ivy decided, would do justice to any toothpaste commercial.

"It's good to meet you, Trudy," Ivy said as the woman pumped her hand. "You've got your work cut out for you."

"A Kelly Girl is a trained, tested, skilled worker, my dear."

"I'm happy to hear that. My father isn't the most organized person in the world."

"Show me a writer who is. They all have their heads in the clouds—" she glanced down at Walt's slippers "—and their feet in comfortable shoes. Bertie, my dear departed husband, was a writer. He was fascinated by the

Etruscans and their love of phallic symbols, or was it the Pompeians? Whoever. I'm sure your father and I will get along smashingly." She trained her turquoise eyes on Ivy's father. "Won't we, Walter?"

Ivy glanced over at him, noting the shocked expression on his face, then she said to Trudy, "How nice that you've worked with writers before. Well, I've got to run." As she passed her father, she touched his arm and grinned. "Have a nice day, *Walter*."

THAT EVENING, Ivy's father ranted on about the mistake he had made in hiring Trudy, claiming she was dictatorial and had a mouth that wouldn't stop. But when Ivy checked her father's office, she was amazed at the order the woman had brought to it already. The following evening, his comments about Trudy were somewhat softer, and when Ivy returned home on Wednesday, she found her father trying to make friends with the new word processor that had been delivered that day.

A little after seven, just as Ivy and Kim finished setting the dining room table, the chimes at the front door sounded.

"It's Chris," Ivy said and nervously glanced at the now fully opened roses on the sideboard. "Kim would you turn on the heat under the broccoli?" After adjusting the belt of her blue silk dress, she went to the door.

Ivy had thought of Chris often during the past few days—and nights—and when she saw him standing on the threshold, smiling and looking handsome in his sport jacket and tie, her heart started pounding again.

Their eyes lingered on each other for long silent moments, then Chris said softly, "Hello again."

"Hello and happy birthday."

"You look lovely."

"So do—" Ivy cut herself off in mid phrase and stepped back. "Come in."

In the foyer, he handed her the brown bag he held. "I brought some white wine. I hope it's appropriate."

"It's perfect. We're having baked chicken. Is that all right?"

"I love chicken," he said quietly, but his thoughts were on the soft blueness of her eyes and the sheen of her lovely hair.

"I love chicken, too," she said, her voice almost a whisper, not aware that they both had their hands on the wrapped bottle of wine.

From the archway to the living room, Walt advised, "The bird is going to be cooked to a crisp if you two don't finish saying hello."

Ivy's head spun toward him, then she flushed and introduced the two men. As Walt led Chris into the living room, she took the wine to the kitchen, where Kim was spooning fruit cocktail into stemmed appetizer dishes.

"Come meet Chris," Ivy said excitedly as she put the wine in the refrigerator.

Kim's response was glum. "I'll watch things in here."

"Everything's fine, honey. Chris is looking forward to meeting you."

Putting the appetizers in the fridge, Kim asked, "Why should he want to meet me?"

Ivy knew the girl was anxious about Chris's coming for dinner, but she hadn't expected her to act like this. Tilting up Kim's chin with gentle fingers, Ivy answered, "Because you're my daughter, that's why. I'm proud of you, and I want to show you off. Come on now, please?"

"Okay," she said quietly, her eyes downcast.

As she and Kim entered the living room, Chris stood and smiled. "Hello, Kim. You're even prettier than the picture your mother showed me."

An awkward silence followed, then Kim slowly lifted her almond-shaped green eyes and looked over at him. "You are very tall," she remarked coolly.

From the bar cart at the far corner of the room, Walt asked, "Would you like a ginger ale, Kim?"

"No, thank you. I have things to do in the kitchen." She turned and left the room quickly.

"What's wrong with her?" Walt asked Ivy as he handed Chris a bourbon on the rocks.

"Nothing. You know she's shy in front of strangers."

"Chris won't be a stranger around here, I hope. Did you know that in college he did the eight hundred meters in a little under two minutes?"

"One of my better days," Chris said, wondering why Ivy was pensive.

"Here you go, Daughter." Walt handed her a napkin and a bourbon and water, then returned his attention to Chris. "Ivy tells me you're a postal inspector."

"Yes. I just transferred from Chicago."

"Hate to admit it, but I don't know much about what postal inspectors do."

Chris grinned. "That's why we're known as the silent service. We investigate mail and wire fraud, extortion, burglaries and counterfeiting as well as assaults and murders. We also work closely with all federal law enforcement agencies."

"Well," Walt said, "I imagine Miami will keep you busy enough. This place has changed from the sleepy town it once was. I can remember back when they rolled the sidewalks up at dusk and the tourist season lasted only a few months in the winter. Now it's a regular international city, not like it was when I was a police reporter. Do you have to testify in court, too, Chris?"

"Oh, yes. The Service has a ninety-eight-percent conviction rate of the cases we take to court."

Ivy was pleased that Chris and her father were hitting it off, but she was worried about Kim. Putting down her glass, she said, "I'd better see how my helper is doing in the kitchen."

WHILE THEY ATE, Chris learned about the book Walt was working on, and he tried to counter Kim's coolness to him by engaging her in conversation about Vietnam, telling her how he had spent a year there while in the army. He talked about the Vietnamese people he had met, and explained that in his job as a translator, he had been able to use the French he had learned at home as a child. Ivy's heart sank when his attempts to make friends with Kim failed miserably.

After they all had birthday cake, Walt and Kim offered to do the dishes, and Ivy and Chris went out onto the deck at the rear of the house.

Glancing out over the garden and the pool, Chris said with palpable disappointment in his voice, "Kim doesn't seem to like me."

"She will," Ivy assured him, hoping it would be true. "I'm not sure she's ready to see any man come into our lives. Kim is just beginning to feel secure. Any change could seem threatening to her."

Chris thought about that as he followed Ivy down the two steps leading to the antique brick pathway that wound through the beautifully kept garden area surrounding the pool. After commenting on the azaleas blooming under the palm trees, the clumps of scarlet salvia and orange-flowered heliconia, he asked, "Are you the gardener, or did your father do all this?"

"My mother and Scott did most of the work originally, but now I've taken over. I enjoy it, it's relaxing. Are you interested in gardening?"

"I don't know much about it. I grew up in an apartment over the restaurant. Then, Kendal, my ex-wife, and I had our careers to keep us busy. The nearest we got to gardening was watering the few plants we had in our apartment in Chicago."

Ivy didn't mean to pry, but she was curious about Chris's ex-wife. "Is that where Kendal is now?"

"Uh-huh. She's a biochemist for a drug firm, and good at her work." After a caustic chuckle, he said, "Kendal believed that my job was the only thing I was really good at. I guess I can't really blame her for thinking so. I did a lot of traveling, and I am ambitious. Someday I hope to be chief postal inspector in Washington, the big honcho, the man at the top. Tell me, how did you and your husband manage the two-career business?"

Sitting down on the white wrought-iron bench that circled the trunk of a golden shower tree, Ivy said, "It never really was an issue. Maybe it wasn't one because I had a nine-to-five job, and Bill pitched in when necessary."

"A fifty-fifty arrangement with home chores, huh?"

Ivy smiled. "Not exactly, but Bill was easy to get along with. He liked things to go smoothly."

Chris sat down next to her, crossed his legs and rested an arm on the curved back of the bench. "Can't say as much for Kendal. She had a knack of reminding me how boring I was to live with."

"Boring?" Ivy repeated, looking over at him. The light coming from the deck cast a golden glow over his handsome face. From what she knew of Chris so far, she wondered how any woman could find him boring. "How long were you married?"

"Two years, but we had lived together for almost a year before that." He shook his head. "She became a different woman after the ceremony. I guess she thought she would be able to change my mind about transferring with the Service again. I had worked out of San Francisco before moving on to Houston, where I met Kendal. We were married there, then I was transferred to Chicago."

Chris looked over at Ivy and smiled. "Let me know if I'm boring you now."

"You're not," she said honestly.

"After two years in Chicago, I requested a transfer to Miami. Kendal knew that was my plan, and then it would be on to New York before going to Washington, but she wasn't about to move again. So it was back to the single life for both of us. Last year she married one of the chemists she works with."

"That's too bad—the divorce, I mean," Ivy added quickly.

"Oh, I don't know. I like the idea of having complete control over my life again."

Ivy remembered telling Carol something similar about herself.

"Now," Chris said, "there's no one to hassle me to be someone I'm not." He faced Ivy. "They say that a man is what he does, and a woman is what she is. I don't know why it has to be that way, but it seems to be true. What did Bill do?"

"He was a history professor at the University of Miami."

"How long were you married?"

"Six years."

"It must have been difficult for you when he died."

"It wasn't easy," Ivy admitted, her expression somber. "One of the worst things, strangely enough, was boxing his clothes and personal items like his razor." Her lips parted in almost a smile. "Bill never liked electric razors." Her smile evaporated. "It was hard for Kim, too. She had never known what it was like to have a father, then just when she started getting used to having one, she lost him. A father is important to a young girl, Chris. Mine was to me, and he still is, of course. Bill tried so hard to make up for the lost years he and Kim never had together. He was a loving father and husband."

"Sounds like he would be a tough act to follow."

Ivy didn't respond to that. Instead she rose from the bench and took slow steps to one of the lampposts by the edge of the pool.

Chris followed and braced a hand on the post. "You still miss him, don't you?"

"I do, and I've been quite lonely at times, but I have Kim and my family...and I work hard."

"When I hear you talk about your family, you make me feel as though I'm missing something in life."

Facing him squarely, she looked deeply into his eyes. "My family is everything to me, Chris. I wish you had known my mother. My parents were beautiful together."

"Mine never were. My mother tends to nag, and my stepfather lives for the restaurant. I always thought he saw us kids as cheap labor."

"Do your brother and sisters feel that way, too?"

"I honestly don't know how they feel. We've never been really close. Maybe I'm just the black sheep in the group, but sending a Christmas card is enough family life for me."

"That's sad," Ivy whispered and looked away, realizing how different she and Chris were as far as family loyalty and settling down were concerned.

Brightening suddenly, he said, "Birthdays aren't a time for being sad. Thanks again for taking the trouble to make mine special for me this year."

As she gazed back at Chris's compelling eyes, Ivy felt a renewed longing for a companion in her life, someone she could love with all her heart, someone who would love her equally. Yet, she felt certain that Chris could never be that man. Tearing her eyes away from his, she said, "It wasn't any trouble. We just added a cake for dessert."

"You did forget one thing, though."

She faced him again, and this time she saw a mischievous glimmer in his eyes. "What?"

"A birthday kiss."

Her heart started to race, something it often did when she was with Chris. Steadying her voice when he placed a hand on the side of her face, she asked, "Isn't it supposed to be a healthy whack for each year?"

"I'm partial to the kiss."

When he lowered his face toward hers, Ivy moved her head slightly and kissed his cheek, but in the next instant he held her face between his hands, and she felt his lips brush across hers before settling on them, gently, lovingly.

CHAPTER SIX

IVY SANK WILLINGLY into Chris's embrace. His kiss was soft, almost unbearable in its tenderness, and his body heat spread over her like a comforting, warm cover. Then a more potent heat ignited deep within her and spiraled upward until a languid dizziness overtook her. Without thought she moved her hands over his shoulders and guided her fingers to his nape and through the thick waves at the back of his head.

She felt a strong hand move downward over her spine and ease her against his firm body, molding hers to his. Urgent desire shot through her without warning, creating a desperate need for more of him, for all that he wanted to give. It was her lips that parted and her tongue that sought his, bringing forth a moan from him that drove her to a higher pitch of excitement. She deepened the kiss; she clung to him, firmly pressing herself against him.

Chris finally tilted his head up and inhaled a deep breath. "Happy birthday to me," he gasped, then gazed down at her with sultry eyes. "Stop me if I'm taking too much for granted again, but did you enjoy that as much as I did?"

Slowly Ivy withdrew her hands from around his neck, then moved backward, struggling to get her bearings. Embarrassment swept through her, and she averted her eyes. "It was nice," she whispered inanely.

"There we go with 'nice' again. I thought it was fabulous."

"That, too," she agreed, now tempted to give him a kiss for each of his thirty-eight years.

"What are we going to do about it?"

"Do?" she asked evasively. "Why do we have to do anything?"

"We don't have to. I was hoping you'd want to."

Turning aside, Ivy crossed her arms and began moving her fingers over them nervously. "Chris," she began tentatively, "I—I'm not ready to jump into something serious right now."

"Neither am I, but that doesn't mean we have to turn off our natural feelings."

"It's just too soon," she countered. "This is happening too fast."

He moved behind her and cupped her shoulders with his hands. Softly he said, "Ivy, you loved Bill and you lost him. I'm sorry for that, but you're alive. You're an intelligent, vibrant woman. You have every right to make a life for yourself. If I mean anything to you at all—"

Ivy turned abruptly. "You do, but I wasn't thinking of Bill. Right now I'm just not in any position to plan my life for myself. I have Kim and my father to think about."

"The family again," Chris said, perplexed. "I'm not saying that we should start looking at silver patterns. All I am saying is that there's something going on between us. At least for me it feels like something special. Couldn't we let it take its course and see what happens?" When she remained silent, he asked, "Is it my imagination or are you less than thrilled with my suggestion?"

"Chris, you just moved here."

"One city is a lot like the next."

"It's understandable that you're lonely."

"I could remedy that in five minutes at any lounge on Miami Beach. You're the one I want to be with."

"How can you be so sure of that so quickly?"

"I know myself, Ivy, and I want you to take the time to get to know me, too. What would be wrong with our seeing each other on a regular basis?"

Smiling wistfully, she said, "Nothing, I suppose." To herself she added, *For you.* In an attempt to sound light-hearted, she asked, "Am I to believe you're one of the endangered species known as the one-woman bachelor?"

"When the woman is as special as you are, I am." She shuddered when Chris placed gentle fingers at the side of her neck and ran his thumb over her chin. "And you are special, you know, so very, very special," he added quietly.

Tingling all over, Ivy wasn't certain if she was having a moment of weakness or insanity, but she heard herself say, "If we do go on seeing each other, there has to be the understanding that there's no commitment between us."

Taking her in his arms again, he said, "We go by whatever rules you set."

"I'm serous about this, Chris."

"Oh, lady, I am, too."

Before she could say another word, his mouth covered hers again, but this time his kiss was anything but gentle.

"Mother!"

Kim's voice drew Ivy's attention toward the house, where she saw the girl standing on the deck, staring at her and Chris. "Yes, honey?"

"I . . . I just wanted to say good-night before I went upstairs."

Ivy and Chris joined Kim, and the three of them went inside. Chris said it was time he left, and after thanking Walt and Kim again, he walked with Ivy to his car.

"Is it all right if I call you at work?" he asked.

"My extension is 324."

"I'll phone tomorrow."

"Afternoons are best," she said, trying to memorize the planes and angles of his strong, handsome face.

Leaning down, he kissed her lips softly, then got into his car.

What are you letting yourself in for? Ivy wondered as she watched Chris's car pull out of the driveway.

She started back to the house, but stopped at the pot of white geraniums that rested on a stone pillar at the bottom of the steps. It was quiet, so very quiet that she could almost hear the rapid beating of her heart. Vibrant, excited and happy, she gazed upward at the night sky. One star shone brighter than the others. Fixing her glistening eyes on it, her words came in little more·than a whisper. "Starlight, star bright, first star I've seen tonight, wish I may, wish I might have this wish I wish tonight."

Her eyes closed for a moment, then she smiled as she thought of what Chris's reaction would be to the wish she had made.

NOT LONG AFTER she had fallen asleep, Ivy was awakened by a scream coming from the next room, and she realized Kim was having one of her nightmares. Ivy hurried to her and saw Kim crouched in bed, sobbing and shaking.

Sitting beside the terrified girl, Ivy took her in her arms and began rocking her. "Hush, darling. You were dreaming. Everything's all right. I'm right here with you."

With her slender arms braced around Ivy's neck, Kim pleaded through her tears, "Promise that you won't send me back, Mother. Promise me."

"I'd never do that," Ivy assured her.

"Promise me."

"I promise. You're my little girl, and I love you. And Granddad loves you. We couldn't let you go."

Kim drew her head back and murmured, "Even if Mr. Laval wanted you to?"

Ivy fought a rising anguish, but she smiled as she gently smoothed away the tears from Kim's cheeks. "Why on earth would he want that? Chris and I are only friends, just as you and Randy are. You come first in my life, before any friend that I have, and you always will."

"What if you fall in love with Mr. Laval? He may not want me here, no?"

"Well, that would be just too bad for him."

"You will never send me away?"

"Never. In fact, you're the one who will leave me someday."

Hugging Ivy tightly, Kim murmured, "I would never leave you."

"When you're older and the right man comes along, you'll fall in love and marry him, but that doesn't mean you and I will stop loving each other. One day you may have a daughter of your own, and you'll understand how much I love you. Now, lie down and go back to sleep. I'll stay with you for a while."

As soon as Kim drifted off, Ivy rose from the bed and moved quietly to the window. Pulling aside the sheer panel under the chintz drapes, she looked up at the stars again, wondering if it was possible to take back a wish.

Troubled, she glanced back to where Kim was sleeping peacefully. She realized that the girl was still so insecure that seeing her and Chris kiss had probably brought on her nightmare. Just the possibility of that caused a pang of guilt in Ivy's heart.

When Bill died, she remembered now how Kim's nightmares had increased because she feared being sent back to Vietnam. It had taken time and constant reassurance to convince her that wouldn't happen, that Ivy loved her as if she had been her own flesh and blood. Now, apparently, Chris was rekindling the child's darkest fears.

Should she continue to see him? Ivy wondered. At what cost to Kim's peace of mind? Would Chris understand? Not likely. A man so detached from his own family would hardly understand her devotion to hers. Yet, as he had told her, there was something special between them.

She had thought as much in the Cayman Islands and when she had received his roses; their time alone this evening had confirmed it. She had never felt so alive and so giving, so desired and so excited as she had in Chris's arms. No, she didn't want to give up those feelings! But she had to protect Kim.

Gazing through the windowpane to the stars above, Ivy whispered, "Mother, what should I do?"

CHRIS EYED the wall clock in the empty conference room and took another swallow of black coffee, thinking it wouldn't be too long before he could phone Ivy. He shook his head and grinned, remembering the difficult time he'd had sleeping last night. This morning the covers on his bed looked as though they'd been purposefully wadded up and piled in a heap.

For a good part of the night he had tossed and turned, thinking of Ivy, either smiling in the dark or groaning with pent-up frustration. He wondered if she had thought of him, or if she had merely drifted off peacefully.

There was so much he liked about her, he reflected. The woman looked like a dream, but she was just as beautiful inside. He admired the way she loved Kim and how protective she was of her father. Chris could hardly fault her for her loyalty to the company she worked for, either.

The door of the conference room opened and he looked up to see his boss enter, carrying another armload of papers.

Pushing aside a pile of documents that lay on the table, Matt plunked down the new additions. "These just came in from the Denver office."

Chris eyed the stocky, redheaded man. "I haven't even finished the complaints from Evanston yet."

Matt propped his hands on the conference table and scanned the reports from postal authorities across the nation. "I had Ellen spot-check these new complaints. They follow a pattern similar to the ones from Evanston."

"Then I'll bet my retirement that the same operators are running the swindle. So far, every one of these victims received a prospectus in the mail and bought counterfeit securities in a nonexistent oil company. It's the old pyramid-type operation. A few victims made some quick dollars and induced friends to buy into the deal." Chris shook his head. "How the hell can people be so gullible?"

"Well, I'll leave you with Denver here. Ellen's still sorting through the complaints that came in from Dallas."

"Dallas?" Chris got up and went to a wall map of the United States. Taking two pins with blue flags on them, he stuck one in Colorado and one in Texas. "If we're right in thinking that the swindlers are getting their mailing lists from a marketing research firm, it rules out all the companies except Continental." His eyes drifted over the numerous blue flags on the map. "Theirs is the only firm that has branch offices in all these states."

"I told you Continental was a good prospect. They've got an excellent reputation, but it would take just one rotten egg to foul up a legitimate operation. It could be anyone who has access to their mailing lists." Matt paused, then said, "I read your reports on the people at Continental. You make Ivy Austin sound like a saint."

"She comes near to it," Chris said as he returned to the table.

"Any ideas on the other employees?"

"They're all living within their means, no ostentatious expenditures. Of course, the one we're looking for could be smart, socking away whatever he's being paid in a dummy account somewhere."

"Or whatever *she's* being paid."

Chris looked over at him. "Right."

"What about the saint's brother, Scott Chandler? I didn't see a report on him."

"I haven't finished that one yet. He flew to Chicago yesterday."

"So?"

"He bought a one-way ticket. Could be he's planning on driving back with someone. I'd like to spend a few days at Chicago headquarters, do some further checking on the Evanston complaints."

"Sounds reasonable, but what about this mess here?" He swept a hand over the table.

"I'll finish going through these complaints this evening, and I thought I'd catch a flight tomorrow after work."

"Okay," Matt said as he opened the door to leave, "but watch the expenses. Accounting is moaning about the budget cuts."

As soon as the door shut, Chris picked up the phone and punched the number for Continental.

"Extension 324, please."

He got Ivy's secretary, then smiled when he heard Ivy's voice.

"Hi, it's Chris," he said in a low, melodious tone. "How's your day going?"

"As usual, everything has to be done yesterday."

Chris glanced at the documents strewn over the conference table. "I know what you mean. Listen, I was hoping we could have dinner alone tonight, but I've got to work, and tomorrow evening I'm leaving town for a few days. Any chance we could get together when you get off work tomorrow?"

Because of Kim, Ivy had decided to take things slowly where Chris was concerned, and she had rehearsed several reasons for having to put him off for the time being. But now that he said he was going away, caution flew out the window.

"Yes," she replied, trying not to sound too excited. "I'll try to leave a little early, around four-thirty."

"Great. I'll wait for you in the park across from your office building."

AFTER CONCLUDING the brief conversation with Chris, Ivy returned her attention to the two-page questionnaire she had been designing. It was a new project for a nationwide grocery manufacturer who offered free coupons to consumers who returned the filled-out questionnaire.

Most questions asked about the brands and types of foods usually purchased; others inquired about family health, insurance coverage and income levels. As Ivy checked the questions on life-style habits and retirement plans, she had a difficult time concentrating on the project.

Her thoughts kept going back to Chris and his suspicion that someone at Continental was misusing the personal information the company gathered. But who at the company would violate the confidentiality rules? No one she knew would do that. If some marketing research firm was involved, she told herself once and for all, it certainly wasn't Continental.

Casting the troublesome thoughts aside, she forced herself to concentrate on the job at hand.

CROSSING BISCAYNE BOULEVARD Friday afternoon, Ivy despaired when she didn't see Chris, but then she spotted him leaning against one of the palm trees in the park. She slowed her pace and tried for a casualness she didn't feel.

The moment Chris saw her, he started toward her, his strides long and rapid. Before she could even say hello, his lips were on hers in a quick but loving greeting.

"You look great," he said, holding her at arm's length and letting his eyes roam over her.

"After a day at the office, I'm sure I do," she said lightly. "What's this about your having to go out of town?"

Placing an arm around her shoulder, he followed a pathway into the park. "I've got to go to Chicago for a few days."

"The investigation you told me about?"

"Right. A lot of people are getting ripped off in the Evanston area. One retired couple mortgaged their home to make an investment and lost everything. Now the con men are operating in Denver. They don't stay in any one place very long, just time enough to get their money and run."

Chris felt a sudden pang of conscience. "You know, I shouldn't be talking about any of this to you. If Matt knew I was, he'd have a coronary."

"Matt?"

"Matt Shapiro, my boss."

"Oh." Ivy thought about that for a few seconds. "Then why *are* you telling me?"

He stopped and drew her aside to let a couple pass them. Once they were out of earshot, he said, "Because I don't want to run the risk of you thinking that I'm working behind your back again."

"You still believe someone at Continental could be involved in this business, don't you?"

Chris sucked in a deep breath of air and let it out slowly as he glanced out over the park. Looking back at her, he said, "We're fairly certain the swindlers are using information such as Continental gathers in order to target select victims. In this case, it's middle-income people who are retired."

"But why does it have to be Continental? There are a dozen companies that do the same kind of research."

"None does it as extensively as your company. We've been tracking the areas that have been hit, and Continental is the only firm that operates in every one of them."

"That doesn't prove anything."

"Ivy, if we could prove it, we'd be able to shut down the entire swindling operation. That's what we're trying to do, but we've got to stay within the law to do it, and that means following the trail of mountains of paperwork. The only shortcut to putting the operation out of business would be through information that could get us on the right track now."

"I understand that you've got to do your job, and believe me, if anyone at Continental is doing anything illegal, we'd want to know about it. But I told you that I'm not going to spy on my co-workers."

"I'm not asking you to. I'd feel just as lousy if I were put in that position." He took her arm, and they started down the pathway again. "There is something I could find out in a roundabout way, but I want things to be honest between us, so I'm going to ask outright."

"Ask."

"What's your brother doing in Chicago?"

Ivy stopped in her tracks. "Scott's on vacation." Then the reason for his question dawned on her. Glaring at him, she asked accusingly, "You've been following him, haven't you, just as you followed me?"

Chris nodded. "I have to file a report on all the executives at Continental."

"Scott is *not* an executive."

"But he's your brother, so he was included."

Heat surged up Ivy's neck and onto her face. Turning, she started back toward Biscayne Boulevard.

Chris caught up and met her rapid pace. "A minute ago you said you understood that I had to do my job. That's all I'm doing."

"Are you also following my father because he's related to me? And what about Kim? Is she on your list of suspects?"

"Now you're being ridiculous."

"And you're sounding more like an investigator in a police state. This is still a free country, Chris."

Stopping, he spun her toward him. "We hope to keep it that way. But with companies like yours building up personal dossiers on individuals, our job becomes more difficult, and the criminals' work becomes a little easier."

Ivy stared at him in disbelief. Through clenched teeth she asked, "Are you through?"

"Yes," he said quietly.

"Then let go of my arm."

"No, not until you calm down."

"Chris, I *am* calm."

"Sure you are, and I'm J. Edgar Hoover."

"You're acting as he did with this business of spying on American citizens. My brother is in Chicago on vacation. Is that so sinister?"

"Why did he buy a one-way ticket?"

"You checked the kind of ticket he bought?" She raised a hand. "No, don't say it. It's part of your job, right?"

"He works in the communications division and has access to mailing lists."

Ivy felt as though a lightning bolt had just struck her, and she wondered why she was still standing. But what Chris was implying was too fantastic to even think about. Surely her own brother wouldn't be involved in robbing the elderly of their life savings. No, it was too ridiculous to even think about.

Wresting her arm from Chris's hold, she threw back her shoulders and locked her angry eyes on his. "I have access to our mailing lists and so do others at Continental. Don't you think you're pushing a little hard to come up with someone to blame?''

"I have to follow up on every possibility."

"By being attentive to a suspect's sister?"

Chris felt a heaviness in his chest, and his voice was deeper than usual when he asked, "Is that what you really believe?"

Ivy couldn't dismiss the hurt she heard in his voice, nor could she excuse herself for having caused it. Chagrined at her sudden outburst, she sat down on a nearby bench and ran her fingertips over her forehead. When he sat next to her, she asked sadly, "What should I believe, Chris?"

"That I care for you a great deal, and I thought you cared for me." He leaned forward and clasped his hands. "Ivy, why are we arguing like this? I get a feeling that there's more going on here than my job and your brother. It's as though you're deliberately building a barrier between us. I hate it. I just hate it."

A barrier, Ivy repeated mentally, and judged the word to be quite accurate. True, she was upset that Chris could think her brother capable of working with criminals. True, she didn't want anyone in her family spied on. But she also had the sense to appreciate the work that all federal investigation agencies did. His accusation, however, struck a nerve. Was she unconsciously building a barrier between them? she wondered. If so, why? Because of Kim's fears? Or her own, maybe?

But why was she so afraid? She had agreed to see where their budding relationship would lead them, and she was the one who had said there would be no commitment between them. She knew that his career goals necessitated his moving on. Hadn't she advised Kim that she and Randy could be friends until he left? Now Ivy wondered why she couldn't accept the same advice herself. So, Chris would leave in a year or two. Couldn't they be good friends until then?

Yes, she decided, knowing that was what she wanted— so very much, in spite of Kim's attitude toward him.

Looking over at Chris's dejected profile, she asked softly, "Will you phone me while you're away?"

He looked at her sideways, doubt shading his expression. "Are you sure you want me to?"

Ivy nodded.

Reaching over, he covered her hand with his and squeezed it gently. "Then I will." After checking his watch, he stood. "I've got to get back to headquarters to pick up some files before I leave. I'll walk you back to the parking garage."

"I'm going to stay here just a while longer," she said quietly, needing time to think.

"Okay. Take care of yourself while I'm gone, and say hi to Kim and your father for me." He leaned down and kissed her, then headed for Biscayne Boulevard.

Ivy watched him go down the pathway, mulling over the conversation they had just had. She recalled his remark about the swindlers now operating in Denver. "Denver," she whispered, wondering why the name of that city seemed significant. Suddenly she knew.

The printout she had made from the disk she had taken from the home office and given to Scott was a mailing list for the Denver area. She had almost forgotten that she had put it in the bottom drawer of her dresser.

A coincidence, she told herself uneasily, then rose and retraced her steps out of the park.

As she waited for the traffic light to change, she wondered if she should get rid of the printout when she got home. Why keep it? What difference would it make? It wasn't as though she thought her brother could in any way be involved with crimes that were being committed in Denver, Colorado.

Yes, when she got home she'd throw the papers out.

CHAPTER SEVEN

TRUDY REMOVED her glasses and let them dangle on the silver chain that circled her neck. After shutting down the word processor for the day, she looked across the room at Walt, who sat in an easy chair, checking one of his research books.

"My Bertie used to say that people who write are dreamers."

"Your Bertie had a lot to say, didn't he?"

"He spoke his mind."

Walt raised his head and peered at her. "Good for him."

"I was just wondering if you were a dreamer."

"Sure, sometimes I even dream in color—usually when I'm dreaming about food."

"I'm not talking about nighttime plays of the mind."

"Then why don't you say what you mean?"

"I merely wanted to now if you live your life as analytically as this book you've written."

"I always check to make sure I've got gas in the car before I drive off somewhere."

"That's exactly what I thought. Don't you ever take chances, do something spontaneous just for the sake of doing it?"

"What the hell are we talking about?"

"I've watched you for a week now, Walt. Do you realize that you do the same thing every day at almost the exact same time? At eight-thirty you start going over the pages I typed the day before. Precisely at ten you fix tea for us. At noon you collect the mail, then you prepare lunch. When you begin reading, I know it's exactly two in the afternoon.''

"So what's your point?"

"Don't you ever get a craving to live dangerously, to kick up your heels a little? Studies show that boredom is a great killer.''

"A glass of tap water has a lot of stuff in it that could probably kill me, but I don't dwell on it.''

"There's not much you can do about tap water, but Ivy told me you haven't been out on a date since your wife died.''

"How did we get from tap water to my Miriam?"

"There you go again, being analytical.''

"One of us has to figure out what you're talking about, other than you think I'm boring.''

"I didn't say that. I think you're attractive and intelligent, and I'd like to take you to dinner tonight.''

Walt focused his eyes on her. "Your treat?"

"My treat.''

"Including the tip?"

"And the parking fee, if there is one.''

"You got a deal. Do we go as is, or do you want to get gussied up?''

"Do you own a tie?"

"And a jacket.'' Grinning, he added, "Just don't think I'm easy.'' When he heard the front door close, he put aside the book he was holding and got up from the chair. "Guess I'll have to tell Ivy about the phone call. She's not going to like it.''

Ivy had one thought on her mind as she came in: to get rid of the printout she had upstairs. But when her father came into the foyer, she saw his dour expression. "How are things going with the book?" she asked, wondering if he and Trudy were having difficulties.

"No problem there, but—" He nodded toward his office, and his eyes rolled heavenward. Taking hold of Ivy's arm, he walked her into the living room. "I've got to talk to you."

As she dropped her purse on one of the two matching sofas, she asked, "Is something wrong?"

"You had a phone call from a Mrs. Miller, one of the guidance counselors at Kim's school."

"A guidance counselor?"

"Yeah, sit down." Ivy did. "It seems like Kim's been skipping some classes."

"What?" She jumped up from the sofa.

"Oh, she's been going to school, but she's got some unexcused absences from her English literature and social studies classes. Apparently this has been going on for two weeks now."

"Is she upstairs?"

"No, she hasn't come home yet. Mrs. Miller wants you to come in Monday morning at nine o'clock, or else Kim will be suspended."

Forgetting about the printout, Ivy slumped back down on the sofa. "This has not been my best day. Why would Kim behave like that? She knows how important school is, particularly her English classes."

"Don't come down on her too hard."

Ivy looked up at him. "I take it you're not going to have any part of being a disciplinarian."

"I'm only her grandfather. I'm afraid you're it."

"Thanks for the vote of confidence. Will you at least stand by while I find out what's going on?"

"Can't. I've got a date with Trudy"

"Oh? How'd you get up the nerve to ask her?"

"She asked me."

"Wonderful. Are you sitting in front of her or in back of her on the motorcycle?"

"Don't make light of this. I haven't had a tie on for almost two years. I'm not sure my neck can take it."

"It's not your neck I'm worried about."

Hearing a car door slam in the driveway, Ivy rose, and Walt bounded for the stairway. At the window, she saw Kim and Randy heading for the front door. Ivy began to pace, waiting for them to come inside the house. The door opened and closed, and she heard the two of them laughing. Ivy took deliberate steps to the archway that led to the foyer.

Excitedly, Kim asked, "Can I go to the basketball game to see Randy play?"

"Not tonight."

Randy's face dropped. "Mrs. Austin, it's our homecoming game."

"I'm sorry, Randy. Kim and I have a family matter to discuss."

"But, Mother, I've never seen Randy play."

"I said not tonight, Kim."

Randy hooked his thumbs into the front pockets of his jeans and rubbed the toe of his sneaker on the tiled floor. In a disgruntled tone, he said to Kim, "I'll call you tomorrow." Then he gave Ivy a pained look. "G'bye, Mrs. Austin."

"Goodbye, Randy."

As soon as he closed the door behind him, Kim glanced at Ivy uneasily.

"We have to talk, Kim. Let's go into the living room."

After the girl followed her, Ivy said, "Sit down please," trying to sound firm, but hating the role she now had to assume. "Mrs. Miller, the guidance counselor at school, phoned today. She said you've been cutting some of your classes. Is that true?"

Kim shifted her eyes to her tightly clasped hands, but said nothing.

Sitting next to her on the sofa, Ivy asked calmly, "Why? I know there must be a reason." Still the girl remained silent. "Kim?"

Slowly she lifted her head, and Ivy could see that she was on the verge of tears. Placing an arm around Kim, she said, "Honey, we've got to talk about this. If something is wrong, we'll work it out."

"I hate school," Kim murmured.

Ivy managed a hint of a smile. "Well, I wasn't exactly thrilled with it myself, but just as I go to the office, your job is to go to school. It's the work that you do there now that will pay off in the future."

"Why can't I quit school and go to work? Other kids do."

"For one thing, the law says that you must attend school until you're at least sixteen. But that aside, what of the plans we've discussed about your going to the University of Miami after high school?"

"I don't want to go to the university."

"What's changed your mind about that?"

"At school some girls my age are mothers already."

Ivy drew back her arm and sat up erect, feeling as though a big fist was squeezing her stomach. "We're talking about school, not teenage mothers. And, Kim, you're much too young to even be thinking about something like that."

"Mother, how old were you when you married my father?"

"I was twenty-six. I finished high school and college before I even contemplated marriage." Thinking of Randy, she added pointedly, "And your father was thirty-six."

After giving Kim some time to let that sink in, Ivy said, "Let's forget about babies and marriage right now. I want to know why you've been cutting classes. I'm sure there has to be a reason. Now what's the problem?"

"Some students laugh at the mistakes I make in English."

"You speak perfectly well."

"Not when I am nervous, and when I have to read in class, they say I sound funny."

"I'd like to know how many of them speak three languages. I know it's difficult if a few of the kids tease you, but that's no reason to give up going to class."

Kim looked up at Ivy with soulful green eyes. "Sometimes the boys call me a gook and slant-eyes."

Ivy felt as though her blood was beginning to boil. She realized that the name-calling was the real reason for the problem at school, and she knew that Kim had had enough of that while in Vietnam. "Well," she said with determination, "that will stop after I speak with Mrs. Miller, I promise you."

Seeing the downcast expression on Kim's face, Ivy asked, "Do you think you could reach Randy at home and tell him I've changed my mind about your going to the homecoming game?"

Immediately Kim's face lit up, and she dashed to the phone. "He won't be there yet, but I'll leave a message."

After the talk with Kim, Ivy felt drained. Deciding to get a cola from the fridge, she headed for the kitchen. On the way, she bumped into Walt and Trudy as they were about to leave.

"Congratulations, Trudy," she said, taking note of her father in his suit and tie. "You've done the near impossible. You look positively handsome, Dad."

Trudy flashed her white teeth. "He does, doesn't he? Would you like to come with us, Ivy?"

"No, she wouldn't," Walt interjected, then lowered his voice. "How did it go with Kim?"

"I think everything will be all right after I talk to her guidance counselor."

"Good." He crooked his arm, and Trudy slipped hers around it. "I'm driving," he said to his daughter, "in my Chevy."

As Ivy was about to close the front door after them, she noticed Carol's car pull into the driveway next door. She turned when Kim came charging out of the living room and dashed up the stairs.

Ivy hollered up after her, "Don't lock the door if you leave before I get back from Carol's, and come home right after the game."

Silence answered her, and Ivy groaned. "One word from me and everyone falls into line." Then she headed next door.

"Anybody home?" Ivy asked as she knocked on the screen door of Carol's backyard patio. She could see her friend slouched on a chaise longue, still wearing her white uniform. Shoeless, her white-stockinged legs were stretched out languidly. In her hand she held a tall glass.

"Come on in and make yourself a vodka and tonic. I'd do it, but I'm paralyzed from the neck down."

"I could use one," Ivy said.

When she returned from the kitchen, she slumped on the lounge chair next to Carol and took a long sip of the cool drink. After resting back on the cushion, she tilted her head toward Carol. "Apparently your day was as good as mine."

With closed eyes Carol said, "It's Friday the thirteenth, and there was a full moon last night. What do you suppose my day was like at the funny farm? I thought we were going to run out of Librium for the guys on the ward. God, they were uptight."

She looked over at Ivy. "I had a flat on the way to work and was late. We lost two patients during a fire drill. They were found in the bar across the street, talking to a two-headed monster they said lived in the stone wall. Then the chief nurse made a surprise visit to the ward to check things out. Naturally I hadn't had time to finish my charting, *which* she gleefully pointed out to me. By the time I left work, I was ready to scream." After a swallow of her drink, she asked, "So what was your day like?"

"Nothing quite so colorful. I have to meet with a guidance counselor at Kim's school Monday morning."

"Oh?"

"Some of the kids in her classes are giving her a hard time, so she's been skipping them."

"Maybe you should put her in a private school."

"I'm not sure that would solve anything."

"Probably not. I remember my high school days and the way I teased poor Althea Burns. 'Fat, fat, that's where you're at.' God, I was a rotten kid."

"I guess your average teenager can cope with some taunts, but poor Kim already carries a lot of hurt with her."

"Well, maybe running around with Randy will bolster her morale. It sure has done wonders for his."

Ivy sat up on the side of the lounge chair and placed her glass on the small table between her and Carol. After folding her hands in front of her, she said, "I need to talk to you about them."

"Friend, tell me this is going to be good news. I'm not sure I'm in any shape to handle anything else right now."

"It's serious, Carol. I spoke to Kim about cutting classes, and out of the blue she tells me she wants to quit school and go to work. Then comes this stuff about some girls being mothers at her age. From there we somehow got into marriage."

"Marriage? She's still a baby."

"She's not quite a baby, but I don't think it's good for her to see so much of Randy."

Carol's hazel eyes darkened. "Ivy, I doubt if Randy is the one suggesting she quit school. He knows the value and the necessity of an education."

"I'm not saying it's his idea."

"Just what are you saying?"

"He's . . . too old for Kim."

"What do you want him to do, disappear from the face of the earth?"

"Of course not. It's just that Kim is so vulnerable, and Randy's been very attentive."

"From what I've seen, Kim has been just as attentive."

"That's the problem. She likes him too much," Ivy explained.

Sitting up, Carol said, "Well, it seems to me you should be talking to Kim about this, not to me. She's your responsibility. I have enough of my own to cope with."

Ivy realized Carol was becoming upset, but she chalked it up to her having had a bad day at work. To ease the tension that was building between them, she said, "I'm probably not making myself very clear, Carol. What I'm trying to say is that I just don't think Randy is the right young man for Kim to be dating."

Misunderstanding Ivy's intent, Carol plunked her glass down on the table and rested her palms on her thighs. "You may not have noticed, but Kim's skin is the same color as my brother's. If you don't think he's good enough for your darling stepdaughter, just come out and say so."

Stunned by the implication, Ivy's eyes widened. "Carol! This is Ivy you're talking to. The color of Randy's skin has nothing to do with what I'm trying to say. Kim's had a rough time of it, and she still doesn't have many good things going on in her life. I'm just afraid that she's going to read more into Randy's friendship than he thinks she will. If they get into a heavy dating situation, I don't know how she'll handle it when he leaves after graduation."

"Oh." Carol took in a deep breath and let it out in one rush of air, then she picked up her glass and held it out. "Let's toast to my controlling my big mouth. The only excuse I can offer is that I wish today had never happened."

"Ditto," Ivy said, and they clinked glasses before they drank.

"I hadn't thought that far ahead," Carol admitted. "I'll have a talk with Randy, but I'm not sure he thinks his older sister is capable of giving him advice on anything now that he's almost eighteen."

"That worries me, too," Ivy confessed. "Think back to high school. Remember how the boys walked around glazed-eyed and drooling with their tongues hanging out?"

"I remember too well. They were in a constant state of sexual frenzy. I'm surprised some of them had enough energy left to climb the stairs to get their diplomas. But Randy's not like that."

"No one's kid brother is. I certainly never thought of Scott as being that way when he was in high school. But look at it from Kim's point of view. Randy is handsome, popular and he's got a head on his shoulders. He's going to have a bright future. I wouldn't blame any young girl for falling in love with him, and I wouldn't be surprised if Kim does if they go on dating so seriously. I mean, he's with her more than I am now. Then I come home today, and she's talking about babies and marriage."

Carol got up. "I'm going to fix us another drink."

"Not for me. I've got to get back. Randy's coming by to take her to the basketball game."

"What does your father think about all this?"

"My father is starting to drool himself. I expect his tongue will be down to his kneecaps by the time Trudy is finished with him."

"The Kelly Girl?"

"The same. I could never get him to turn in his old Remington typewriter or even go to a movie with Kim and me. Suddenly he's the proud owner of a word processor and a laser printer, and he's wearing a suit and tie. Trudy, mind you, asked him out to dinner tonight."

Carol smirked. "Your experience as a stepmother might come in handy, as far as getting along with Trudy...if she becomes your stepmother."

"Ha! I don't give her very long. My father's too used to being pampered, and Trudy strikes me as being a lady with a mind of her own."

"So, what are you going to do about Randy and Kim?"

"I sure don't know. They say that if you push kids too hard one way, they're certain to do the opposite. It worked that way with Scott when he was growing up. I wish Bill were here. My shoulders aren't big enough to handle everything."

"Well, I don't know how much good it'll do, but I will talk to Randy, try to alert him to problems that could arise." Smiling, Carol added, "Although I could get used to the idea of your being my sister-in-law."

"Get used to the idea of that not happening for quite some time. You are a good friend, Carol," Ivy said sincerely and kissed her on the cheek.

"And you are one hell of a mother."

Kim had already left when Ivy returned to the house. She wasn't used to being alone, and she didn't like the feeling. Either Bill or Kim had always been with her in the old house, and since she moved back home, her father had usually been around. Ivy chuckled at herself. For two years she'd been trying to get him to socialize more, and she had been concerned that Kim never went out with friends from school. Now that they were both in demand, Ivy felt isolated and depressed.

Going to the stereo, she switched it on, then tuned it to a station offering soothing background music. After kicking off her shoes, she settled in the corner of a sofa and stared into the unlit fireplace, remembering how much Bill had enjoyed a cozy fire on a cool night. She wondered if Chris did.

She recalled how Bill used to make hot buttered rum during the few cold snaps that would pass through Miami in the winter. Did Chris like hot buttered rum? Although he had told her some things about himself, Ivy realized there was a great deal she didn't know about Christian Laval. What she was aware of, she decided, should frighten her off.

He was definitely not a family man. At least, he indicated he had little interest in his own family. She imagined he was probably closer to friends than family. He certainly was an ambitious man. His eyes were focused on the top position in the Postal Inspection Service, and he'd most likely work his way up to that spot.

She had a feeling that anything Chris set out to do, he would accomplish. Nothing would stop him—not family and not a wife. Apparently he was more than ready to give his job the extra time and effort that success would require.

That really wouldn't leave much time for anyone else, she cautioned herself as she sat alone in the living room. *Then why get involved with him?* The answer was all too clear.

It was just that there was so much about Chris that she liked! He was strong but not macho; sensitive but not wimpy; handsome but seemingly not aware of it.

His compassion had made an indelible impression on her the evening she had talked about Kim on the beach in the Cayman Islands. Ivy appreciated the subtle way he had tried to break through the girl's cool attitude toward him during his birthday dinner. He had also shown genuine respect for her father and a sincere admiration for his work.

But most important, Chris made her feel alive again.

Ivy wasn't sure when she had begun accepting less in life than she wanted. It had to have been shortly after Bill died, she decided as she tried to put her thoughts in perspective. At some point she must have determined that being a loving mother to Bill's daughter, a loving daughter herself and a loving sister would be satisfying enough. Now, though, after meeting Chris, she knew it wasn't.

Facing that fact, however, was like staring into a dark abyss alone, without a light to guide her. The truth brought with it an urgent yearning that frightened her more than the darkness of the imagined abyss.

Chris, though, was not a man who could permanently satisfy that yearning, and Ivy wasn't sure she wanted to settle for a temporary relationship. But did she really have a choice?

Of course you do! she insisted. *You just don't let things go any farther than they have. You tell Chris you've reconsidered letting things take their course. You already know what will happen. The two of you will wind up being lovers, and then he'll move on, forgetting you. That's what will happen.*

So? she responded to her own argument. *Who are you saving yourself for? The men you've dated haven't exactly been Prince Charmings, wanting to sweep you away to live-happily-ever-after land.*

More frustrated and confused than ever, Ivy began rhythmically patting the arm of the sofa, wondering how Chris would look on a white stallion.

THE RINGING OF THE TELEPHONE startled her, and she realized she had fallen asleep on the sofa. She reached for the receiver, her voice groggy when she answered.

"Hello."

"Ivy?"

"Chris?" Her senses sharpened immediately.

"Yes. It didn't sound like you at first."

"I was . . . preoccupied." She glanced at the clock on the mantel over the fireplace. It was a little after ten. "Where are you?"

"In the airport terminal at O'Hare."

"Is anything wrong?"

"I hope not. That's why I'm calling, to make sure. I hated to leave so quickly after our talk in the park, but I had to catch the flight out. Ivy, I...I need to hear you say that everything is all right between us. It is, isn't it?"

Her heart began thumping wildly, and she cradled the receiver with her two hands as she rested her head against the back of the sofa. "Yes," she whispered, "everything is all right."

"I miss you already," he said softly.

"I miss you, more than I realized I would."

"I'll try to get back by Tuesday, but I can't be sure of that. I've got to fly to Denver on Sunday. Can we have dinner when I return to Miami?"

"Yes, just let me know what night as soon as you can."

"I will. I have to go now. Think about me, okay?"

"Yes, Chris."

"Bye, love."

"Goodbye."

For silent moments after Chris hung up, Ivy held the receiver to her ear, smiling, her eyes closed. Suddenly they snapped open.

"Denver!" she said and quickly replaced the receiver.

Rushing upstairs to her bedroom, she retrieved the printout from the bottom drawer of her dresser. Nervously she flipped through the sheets of paper, checking the names and addresses on the list. They were all in Denver.

A nagging suspicion gripped her that her brother, knowingly or innocently, might be involved in something shady, but immediately she refused to accept even the possibility. Yet the Denver addresses kept taunting her.

She tried telling herself they were only names and addresses, just one selective list of the millions of names in the files at Continental.

Selective. The word struck a chord, and she wondered how different the printout would be on the disk that her brother had substituted the day she had caught him shredding documents. Being one of the few people authorized to have access to the files at any time, Ivy knew it would be a simple matter for her to find out. Still, Lew would wonder about her sudden interest in Denver, Colorado. Since tomorrow was Saturday, though, she decided that she could examine the files with no interruption.

Ivy didn't at all like the feeling she had about checking up on her brother, but she knew it was something she had to do for her own peace of mind—and to maintain her relationship with Chris.

CHAPTER EIGHT

"SO WHY ARE YOU GOING to the office today?" Walt asked at the breakfast table in the kitchen.

Spreading butter on an English muffin, Ivy said, "Just some work I want to finish. It won't take long. Would you like some more coffee?"

"No, no. Trudy says too much coffee is bad for you."

"Since when have you started taking anyone's advice on health matters?"

"Trudy can be quite persuasive. She expects me to lose at least ten pounds by the time she finishes typing the book."

Ivy made an imaginary check mark in the air with her index finger. "Chalk up another one for Trudy. She seems to have a direct line to your conscience. What time did you get in last night?"

"Actually it was this morning. You won't believe what we did after dinner."

"I'm not sure I want to know," Ivy teased.

"Not that. She talked me into taking a helicopter ride over Miami."

"I didn't think the tours made night flights."

"They don't, but she's buddies with one of the pilots. After that we took in the show at the Flamenco."

"So now you're into Cuban nightclubs, too. My, my, what a difference a Kelly Girl makes."

"She does make a difference. Seen my office lately? It's never been so organized."

"True, and I love the Degas prints she hung on the wall across from the photos of the Miami Dolphins in action." Ivy chuckled. "The prints and photos make quite an intellectual statement... graceful ballerinas on one side, on the other, grown men trying to maim one another."

Walt peered at his daughter over his coffee cup. "Trudy says a writer should broaden his interests."

"When did you get interested in ballet?"

"Trudy says the dancers are just as much athletes as high jumpers."

"Trudy says, Trudy says," Ivy repeated, mimicking her father. "Pretty soon you'll be talking with a British accent."

"Do I detect a note of displeasure in your tone, young lady?"

"Of course not. I've just got to get used to the new you."

"Something's eating at you. What is it? The phone call from Kim's school?"

After a sip of coffee, Ivy said, "That and a few other things in my family that have taken me by surprise lately."

"I've got pretty big shoulders. If you want to talk them out, you know where to find me. But not today. I'm taking Trudy to the jai alai games, and this evening she's dragging me to the symphony."

"Good," Ivy said in earnest. "I'm happy to see you getting out of the house. I've got to get, too." She rose and kissed her father on the cheek. "Kim didn't come home until almost midnight last night, so I let her sleep in, but I don't want her going anywhere until I get back from the office."

"Even with Randy?"

"Especially with Randy."

MIDMORNING, IVY RETURNED from Continental and saw Randy's car parked in the driveway. After taking her briefcase up to her bedroom, she returned downstairs and found Kim and Randy on the deck at the rear of the house.

Kim was sitting on one of the steps leading down to the pool area. Seeing Ivy, she jumped up. "Granddad said I couldn't leave until you came back."

"That's right." She looked over at Carol's brother, who was sitting cross-legged on the deck. "Hello, Randy."

"Hi, Mrs. Austin. I thought Kim would enjoy going to the Seaquarium today. She's never been there."

"I'm sure she will enjoy it," Ivy said with a semblance of a smile, "but before you two take off, we need to talk."

She and Kim sat down on the step, and Ivy waited for Randy to move to the step below theirs. "I hope I don't sound like the Wicked Witch of the West," Ivy began, "but it seems to me you two have been spending an awful lot of time together." Turning to Randy, she said, "I want Kim to have friends, but I'd also like her to meet and date boys her own age."

"But, Mother, I—"

"Let me tell you how I feel first, Kim." Again she turned her attention to Randy. "You're a fine young man, Randy, but you're almost eighteen. I know you and Kim have become friends, and that's good, but I'm worried about you two spending so much time together." Ivy saw the crushed expression on both teenagers' faces, and said, "Okay, I've had my say. What do you two think?"

Uneasy, Randy squirmed in his sitting position as he looked at Ivy and then at Kim. "I like being with her, Mrs. Austin. We get along great."

"Haven't you been dating seniors at school?"

"Well, yeah, but I don't anymore. Kim is different."

"How, Randy?" Ivy asked.

"She listens to me, like what I have to say is important. And she's calm and kind of delicate. She just makes me feel good."

Ivy couldn't argue with that, but she was concerned about what "making Randy feel good" might include in the future.

"Mother," Kim said nervously, "not many students at school has been...have been—" she corrected herself "—as kind to me as Randy. When I told him I want to leave school, he was very angry with me. Just as you did, he said it was important that I have an education. So you see, Randy is a good friend."

Ivy realized she was losing the battle, but she felt obligated to set some sort of limit. "All right, it's agreed that you can continue to see each other on a regular basis, but not every day of the week as you have been."

Randy asked, "You mean I can't drive her to and from school?"

"I don't think that's a good—"

"I'll attend every one of my classes," Kim said quickly.

"She has to get there somehow," Randy chimed in.

"Well," Ivy said grudgingly to Kim, "if you promise that you won't cut any more classes."

"I promise!"

"All right, but no dating during the week. You can make plans for the weekend, but that's all." She looked directly into Kim's green eyes. "And only if your schoolwork is good."

"Can Randy come here to help me with English on Wednesdays?"

Ready to wave a white flag of surrender, Ivy hesitated, then said, "Only for an hour...or two, maybe." She saw their faces brighten considerably. "Randy, I want you to remember that you're the first boy Kim is dating, and that she's only fifteen years old. When she's in your car, it's to be used for transportation *only*. Do I make myself clear?"

Randy's hazel eyes darted to Kim, then back to Ivy. Sheepishly he said, "Yeah, sure, Mrs. Austin," then he jumped up from the step. "Come on, Kim. Let's get going."

As they started around the house to the driveway, Ivy called to Kim. "I expect you home in time for dinner."

The minute they were out of sight, Ivy knew she'd have to have a mother-to-daughter talk with Kim, the kind of talk her own mother had never had with her. And, Ivy emphasized for her own benefit, she would have to make it crystal clear that she was not condoning sexual involvement for a girl Kim's age. The more she thought about it, the more concerned she became, since she realized how vulnerable Kim was to anyone who was kind and decent to her.

Ivy was well aware how starved the youngster was for true love and affection and for what most girls her age desired—acceptance by their peer group. But even the slimmest possibility of a sexual relationship between Kim and Randy made her realize how essential it was that the girl be well informed.

"YOUR MOTHER'S A COOL LADY," Randy said, glancing over at Kim as he drove toward the Rickenbacker Causeway. "I like the way she was up front with us, don't you?"

"She is a very wise woman."

He turned down the country music coming from the car radio. "You know, I meant what I told her. I sure like being with you."

"Many people do not know how to act around me," Kim admitted, lowering her eyes. "That is one of the things I like about you, Randy."

He eyed her sideways and grinned, "Hey, you're blushing!"

Kim kept her eyes trained on her slender fingers. "I blush too easily."

"No, you don't. Everything about you is just right."

She looked up at him, a faint smile of wonder brightening her delicate features. "You like everything about me?"

"Cross my heart and hope to die."

"Why would you hope to die?" she asked seriously.

"That's just an expression. It means if I'm not telling you the truth, I'd hope to die."

"Because you were lying to me?"

"Yeah ... well, it's a dumb saying." After a moment he asked, "Did you know what your mother was talking about when she said this car was to be used for transportation only?"

"We shouldn't kiss in the car anymore."

"Oh. I figured you'd pick that up. But she was probably worried we'd have an accident. She didn't say anything about not doing it outside the car."

Kim smiled and studied his handsome profile for several moments before asking softly, "Randy, do you want to make love with me?"

His foot jerked on the gas pedal, and the car jounced them both. "What?"

"Do you?"

"Well . . . uh, yes, but—"

"You're not going to." After a worrisome silence, she asked, "Do you still like me?"

He swerved off the road and bumped the curb when he parked on a side street. Looking at her, he draped an arm over the back of the seat and smiled. "I like you even more." He swallowed hard, then said, "In fact, I think I love you, Kim."

Blushing again, she remarked quietly, "In America, love is everything. People even marry for love."

"It's not that way in Vietnam?"

"Usually the family arranges a marriage for a girl."

"But wouldn't you want to choose the man you'll spend the rest of your life with?"

"My mother would have to like him, too."

"You mean Mrs. Austin."

"She is my mother now."

"Oh, yeah." After a moment's pause, Randy said, "You know, I feel for you. I mean, having lost both your parents. That must be a bummer. No one real close to me has ever died. It must be awful."

"I never knew my mother," Kim said softly, "and I only knew my father for a short time, but I will always remember him. He was very kind to me, like you are."

"Heck, you're easy to be kind to. But getting back to Mrs. Austin . . . to your mother, I mean. I think she likes me."

"I think so also, but she knows you will be going away soon."

"Not until June, and while I'm in the air force, we can write, and we'll see each other when I'm on leave. By the time you finish high school, I'll be an officer."

"Perhaps you will forget me, no?"

Randy took hold of one of Kim's small hands. "I couldn't forget you if I wanted to. I've known other girls, and not one of them even came close to being as special as you are to me."

Kim looked down at Randy's hand that held hers. "After high school, my mother thinks I should go to the university."

"I do, too. A person won't get very far in life nowadays without a good education." He looked away briefly, then said, "I think we should go steady now, don't you? Now that we've talked it over with your mother, I'm sure she won't mind."

She tilted her face up toward his, a seriousness tensing her expression. "You wouldn't be embarrassed to go steady with me?" she asked quietly.

"Embarrassed? Are you crazy? I'd be the proudest and the happiest man alive. Why would you even think that?"

Kim slipped her hand from Randy's, then folded hers in her lap. "In Vietnam," she said shyly, "everyone is Vietnamese. I was considered most shameful because my father was an American. I would not want you to be insulted because of me."

"I'd like to see someone try it!" Randy blurted out. Taking hold of her hand again, he softened his voice. "Kim, it's different here. Everyone's family originally came from somewhere else. Mine came from Africa. And look at Trudy—she came from England. Half of Miami is from Cuba.''

"That's what I don't understand. Why do some of the students at school make fun of me?''

"The boys that do are nerds, and the girls are probably just jealous. You're a knockout with those gorgeous green eyes of yours, and your hair is so...well, it's so soft and shiny.''

"My eyes have always embarrassed me," she admitted honestly.

"That's got to stop right now," he ordered, tilting her chin up. "Take my word for it, you are totally awesome.''

"Totally awesome," Kim repeated, not knowing what that meant, but from the look on Randy's face, she knew it had to be good.

"So," he asked, "do you think we could go steady?"

Kim lowered her head, thought seriously, then looked up at him through long, dark eyelashes. "I think I would like that.''

"You would!" After gulping down his Adam's apple, Randy unclasped the gold chain from around his neck and placed it around hers. "There," he said, "that makes it official. The chain binds you and me together." When he saw Kim's expression of surprise give way to one of pure delight, he swallowed hard again and asked, "Do you think we could step outside the car for just a minute, so I can kiss you?''

IN HER BEDROOM, Ivy compared the two printouts. Using a red pen, she checked off the names that Scott had deleted from the disk he had originally sent to the home office. She guessed they were the names and addresses of the middle-income people that her brother had told her shouldn't have been included.

Ivy knew it would take time to go through the files at work to see why those fifty names didn't belong in this particular mailing list. Or, she could just call Scott at the Palmer House in Chicago and ask him.

Going to the nightstand next to her bed, she picked up the phone. After a moment's thought, she put it down again, deciding she'd rather speak with her brother face-to-face.

And say what? she wondered. *By the way, Scott, do you happen to be part of a gang that's swindling people out of their life savings?*

But that was too ludicrous to believe. Her brother had behaved irresponsibly at times, but he wasn't a criminal. It just couldn't be true. *Then why keep thinking about it?* she asked herself.

It was all Chris's fault, she decided. He was the one who kept bringing it up, but he was sure to be apologetic if and when his organization did track down the people who were involved.

She glanced down at the printouts again, and the red check marks stood out like ominous warning flags. What if it was true, though? What if Scott had somehow become involved in a criminal scheme? Was she supposed to help Chris send her own brother to prison?

Quickly she grabbed the two printouts and started toward the bedroom door, planning to throw them in the trash downstairs. But something stopped her, and she placed them both in the bottom drawer of her dresser.

THAT EVENING, Ivy had her mother-to-daughter talk with Kim. She was surprised that the girl was exceptionally knowledgeable about the "facts of life." What had

floored Ivy was learning that Kim and her aunt had often
assisted women in refugee camps who had gone into labor. Their conversation left Ivy feeling emotionally
drained. Still, she felt better that she had met her responsibility as a parent for having discussed the subject
with Kim.

Until late in the evening, Ivy waited, but Chris didn't
phone.

Early Sunday morning, Kim and Randy, their textbooks in hand, took off in his car for the beach. Walt left
shortly after to pick up Trudy. They were heading to the
racetrack and then to dinner with some friends of Trudy's. The only thing that Ivy worried about, regarding
her father's new interests in life, was that he was going to
have a heart attack keeping up with the spirited lady from
the British Isles.

Alone again, Ivy busied herself mulching the garden
around the pool, remembering how Chris had liked the
colorful display of blooms. Although she had the air
conditioning turned on inside the house, she left one of
the back windows ajar so as not to miss hearing the
phone ring.

It didn't.

MONDAY MORNING, when Ivy met with the guidance
counselor at Kim's school, Mrs. Miller told her things
that she already knew: Kim was highly intelligent, extremely shy and she refused to interact with her peer
group.

"Can you blame her," Ivy asked the Nordic-looking
woman seated behind the desk, "when they call her gook
and slant-eyes?"

Mrs. Miller's eyes narrowed. "I didn't know they were
doing that."

"I'm not surprised that Kim didn't tell you, but now that you know, I hope you'll put a stop to it. She's had a rough life, and she doesn't need any more abuse, especially from the people in the country where she thought she was finally going to be safe."

"Really, Mrs. Austin, no one here is going to abuse your stepdaughter."

"There are all kinds of abuse, Mrs. Miller. I'm extremely proud of Kim and the progress she's made adapting to a life that was totally foreign to her two years ago. A great deal of that has to be credited to her intelligence, but she's also quite sensitive. Kim cut those classes because she was being humiliated. She was not brought up to be a fighter. She internalizes her hurts."

"I can appreciate what you've told me," the woman said sympathetically. "Be assured that I'll let her teachers know what's been going on."

"Thank you for that, but one more thing. If her teachers just come down hard on Kim's classmates, I don't know how much good it will do outside of class. It might only cause Kim more embarrassment. Couldn't all teachers be advised to be more sensitive to signs of racial prejudice? With the influx of immigrants we have here in the Miami area, I'm sure other parents are having the same problem I am. Perhaps it would be helpful if the teachers could get the students to discuss the situation in class."

Leaning forward in her chair, Mrs. Miller said, "I wish all parents were as concerned about their children as you are. We'll get things straightened out for Kim. Don't you worry about it."

As Ivy left the school and headed for Continental, she felt more hopeful than when she had arrived, but she realized that not all of Kim's problems would be settled overnight.

ON THE WAY HOME after work, Ivy pulled into the shopping center near the house and went into the supermarket. She had just taken hold of a cart when she heard Carol call her name. Turning, Ivy saw her coming from one of the checkout counters, carrying a grocery bag.

"Got time for a cup of coffee?" Carol asked.

"I'd love one. It's hardly on our menu at the house since Trudy arrived. She's a firm believer that coffee is bad for you. Of course she puts away tea like she has stock in the company."

Nearing the archway that connected the supermarket to the coffee shop, Carol asked, "How can you look so fresh after a day's work? I always feel like lettuce leaves that've been left in the sun."

"I had some great news today. Scott's been accepted into the managerial training program."

Carol propped her bag of groceries on the seat and slid into the booth across from Ivy. "I hate your brother. He gets to work in the Caribbean, and I get to start the night shift tomorrow."

"Come over and use the pool during the day whenever you want. You can keep an eye on my father for me."

"What's Walt up to that he needs watching?"

After a short interruption while they both ordered coffee, Ivy said, "Actually it's Trudy who needs watching."

"Why? Are you missing some of the family jewels?"

"I'm liable to be missing a father pretty soon. He's acting a lot like Randy."

"Lots of drooling with his tongue hanging out?"

"No, with my father it's a drastic change in life-style. He's letting his hair grow longer because Trudy just loves the waves, and he's thinking about trading in his Chevy for a convertible."

"That's bad?"

Tilting her head, Ivy said, "I guess not, but he's different from the father I'm used to. Trudy actually has him going to the symphony now."

"What's wrong with that?"

"My father's idea of classical music is listening to 'The Star-Spangled Banner' being played before a baseball game."

Carol sipped her coffee and put her cup down. "What I'm hearing is that you're afraid he'll marry this broad, and that the wicked stepmother will do mean things to you . . . like throw you out, maybe."

"She wouldn't have to. There's no way Kim and I could stay there if he did remarry. God, I sound awful. Tell me, psychiatric nurse, why is that?"

"How does it sound to you if Ivy Chandler Austin was to remarry?"

Ivy laughed. "I think you're the one who needs counseling, not me."

"Is the idea so farfetched? What about this Chris character, the postman?"

At the mention of Chris's name, Ivy's eyelashes flickered, and she felt a hot surge of excitement shoot through her. Trying to ignore her reaction, she said matter-of-factly, "He's a postal inspector, but he's not the marrying kind. He just parted with one woman who wasn't ready to follow him around the country because he wants to wind up numero uno in the United States Post Office."

"So? Aren't you interested in a guy with a future?"

"Right now it's all I can do to work out my own future. In a year or so Chris is going to transfer to New York, then he wants to go on to Washington."

Carol chuckled. "A lot of men think they need space."

"There's certainly a lot of space between Miami and New York."

"So, you're footloose and fancy-free. What have you got against traveling?"

"Fancy-free? Think again, friend. I'm not about to uproot Kim from Miami for anyone. She's just starting to feel secure in her environment here, and things may begin to improve with the kids at school. I had a meeting with her guidance counselor this morning. If Kim and I were to go traipsing from state to state and school to school, I'd probably be spending more time in guidance counselors' offices than at work, wherever that might wind up being. Uh-uh, no way. Kim's never had a really safe home before this, and no one is going to take that away from her as long as I can help it."

"I get your point. Maybe Chris would consider setting down roots here. He'd have a ready-made family."

"That would only scare him off. Apparently he and his family get along like water and oil."

"The guy has got to have some good points, or you wouldn't have almost fainted when I mentioned his name."

Ivy blushed. "Well, he does have a few."

"Such as?"

Her lips spread into a wide smile. "I think he's the most gorgeous man I ever laid eyes on. And he's so—"

"Wait, wait. If you're going to make me cringe with envy, I need appropriate sustenance." Signaling the waitress, Carol ordered two chocolate fudge sundaes.

"Carol," Ivy asked after the waitress left, "what about your diet?"

"I'm so hungry I could eat my hand. Now, tell me *all* about your postal inspector."

"As I said, he's nice-looking."

"You *said* he was gorgeous."

"Well, not like your Hollywood types. He's more rugged than that, more like the men you see in Marlboro ads."

Carol placed a hand over her chest and fanned her face with a paper napkin. "Be still my heart."

"And he's also shown concern for Kim. Deep down I really think he's caring, gentle and understanding. He's opened up to me in ways that Bill never did."

"I thought you and Bill had a storybook marriage."

"We did, but he never got excited about much, other than when Kim arrived on the scene. That almost blew his mind."

"I imagine it did a number on yours, also."

Ivy leaned back as the waitress set down their sundaes. After swallowing a spoonful of vanilla ice cream, syrup and nuts, she said, "I was shocked but—and this may sound crazy—it was the first time I thought of Bill as having had a romantic past. That gave him a new dimension in my eyes, even made him more interesting."

"As interesting as this Chris guy?"

"Bill never made me feel the way I do when I'm with Chris."

"Your legs turn to jelly, your heart does the samba and you have a hard time not gaping. Right?"

"Exactly."

"You're falling in love, friend, if you haven't already. Are you sleeping with him?"

"No, but I think I'd have a difficult time saying no if he asked."

"Don't worry, he'll ask. Men do when a woman's as attractive as you are."

Ivy wiped her lips with a paper napkin, then rested back in the booth. "I don't know. I'm afraid that I could fall in love with Chris very easily. It's the falling out of love when he leaves that scares me."

"You know what I tell my patients just before they're being discharged? I tell them to take it one day at a time, and to try like hell to enjoy each day. You, my friend, might want to consider doing just that." After spooning up the last of her sundae, Carol went on, "I've got to meet this Chris. Bring him along for Thanksgiving dinner at my place."

"Are you sure you want to go to all that trouble? My father said you invited Trudy, too."

"You're looking at one shrewd cookie, Ivy. I figure that if I have to face tons of food while cooking it, I'll eat less."

RESTLESS, IVY TRIED to concentrate on the old Bette Davis movie on television, but she was barely listening, hoping that the phone would ring. After her talk about Chris with Carol in the coffee shop, Ivy realized she had more than a mild interest in the postal inspector. With Carol's urging, she had decided to listen to her heart and not her head where Chris was concerned. Once Kim got to know him better, Ivy was certain the girl's attitude would change.

When the telephone did ring, she hurled herself to the opposite end of the sofa and grabbed the receiver. It was Chris.

"Are you in Chicago?" she asked, hearing the warmth in his voice even across the miles.

"No, I'm still in Denver. I can't wait to get back to Miami, but things are worse here than I thought. Another scam has surfaced. Senior citizens are being sold a bogus catastrophic health care plan. We think the operation is being run by the same con artists who are selling the counterfeit oil securities."

Ivy thought of the printouts she had in her room and of the names of people in Denver that she had checked in red. "Chris," she said impulsively, "would it be possible for you to bring a list of the names of the people who have been swindled in Denver?"

"Sure, but why?"

Ivy's brain worked frantically. She didn't want to tell Chris about the printouts, but she had to know if the names of the swindled people were on either of the lists she had upstairs.

"Ivy?"

"Yes, I'm still here."

"Why do you want the list of names?"

"If I get a chance, I could run them through our files at work to see if we have information on them. If we don't, wouldn't that put Continental in the clear?" she asked hopefully.

"It would go a long way toward indicating that. I'll bring the list with me when I fly back on Wednesday."

And what if the names are the same as the ones Scott deleted from the files? Ivy thought. Chris would expect her to tell him if she found any reference to the names on the list. *Should I? Could I?* she wondered. *I'd be helping him send my own brother to jail!*

Immediately she regretted having opened her mouth about the list. Now she didn't want to know if the names were the same or not. "Chris, forget what I said about bringing the list. It was a pretty farfetched idea."

"No, it wasn't. At this stage we can use all the help we can get. We've got to put a stop to these people being ripped off. Listen, I've got to go. Do you think you could meet me at the airport Wednesday evening? My flight gets in at seven. We could have dinner together."

"Uh...yes, I'll meet you. Let me have your flight number."

After she jotted it down, he said, "I'll be so damn glad to see you again. You won't believe how much I've missed you." When Ivy didn't respond, Chris prompted, "Isn't this where the lady tells the man she's missed him, too, even if she missed him just a little?"

"There's been so much going on here, that I—" she gritted her teeth "—that I haven't had a chance to think of anything."

"Is it something I can help you with when I get back?"

"No, no. I had to meet with Kim's guidance counselor at school, and some other family matters came up. I know you have to run, so I'll see you Wednesday evening."

"Great. Ivy, I really missed you. See you soon."

"Yes, Chris...soon."

After hanging up, Ivy slumped back against the sofa. She could feel a headache coming on, and she berated herself for asking him to bring the list. But, then, if the names weren't on the printouts upstairs, there would be no problem. It would prove that her brother had nothing to do with criminals.

"God," she murmured as she got up and headed to the kitchen, "you're creating problems where none may even exist."

She reached in the fridge, took out the decanter of orange juice she had squeezed earlier and poured herself a glass. Sitting down, she propped her elbows on the kitchen table, rested her chin on her interlaced fingers and tried to think things through.

Every time she saw Chris, and even when she just spoke with him on the phone, she had this wonderful feeling of being drawn to him. But at the same time, some counterforce seemed to be pulling her from him. And now, being wrenched in two different directions, between him and her brother, was tearing her apart. The mental and emotional tug of war had to cease, she realized—and soon!

It seemed to her that two roads lay ahead. If Scott was completely innocent, then she was free to pursue her relationship with Chris. But if Scott was somehow mixed up with the swindlers, as Chris thought possible, then she must end her involvement with the man who might send her brother to prison.

Once she got her hands on the list Chris was bringing, she would know which road she would have to take.

CHAPTER NINE

AT THE END of the staff meeting Wednesday afternoon, Ivy stayed behind in the conference room, wanting to speak with Bob McDonough in private.

"Good news about Scott," Bob said, pouring himself another cup of coffee from the urn on the credenza. "He'll make a sharp branch manager."

"He will," Ivy agreed, then brought up the matter that Bob had talked about during the meeting. "Just how cooperative do you want us to be with the postal inspectors?"

"As I said, we give them any information they want about how we gather our data and who we sell it to."

"But they don't get into our files."

Bob looked her square in the eye. "Not without a court order, and they don't get that unless they can convince a judge we've got something to hide. We don't, do we?"

"Not that I know of, but did the postal inspector say why they were checking out Continental?"

Lowering himself onto the chair at the head of the conference table, her boss said, "We're just one of the marketing research firms they're investigating. Supposedly, somewhere, someone is conning people out of a lot of money. The Postal Inspection Service is guessing that the kind of information we gather is helping these jokers get to the right people."

"So why not let them check our files?"

Bob leaned forward, his tone became serious. "The consumer information we collect is worth its weight in gold, and we've got a responsibility to the company to keep that information confidential, particularly from the government. Would you want Washington to have a file on you that listed what organizations you sent money to, what magazines you read and what political action groups you belonged to? Never mind the information the IRS would love to get hold of. Why do you think we spend the kind of money we do on security?"

"Surely the postal inspectors aren't going to breach our confidentiality rule."

"Wake up, Ivy. There are good and bad guys in every line of work. Even the inspectors have to spend time checking out internal crime in the post office."

"But what if we do have problems in our company? Maybe we should run a check on our security."

"I appreciate your concern, but let me worry about security. You just keep on with the great job you're doing, and don't let the postal inspectors' nosing around get to you."

Standing, Ivy nodded. "Okay. If you say we don't have a problem, I guess we don't." More than ever, though, she was anxious to see the list that Chris was bringing with him from Chicago.

AGITATED by conflicting emotions, Ivy paced in front of the glass window in the waiting area at Miami International, watching as Chris's plane taxied toward the terminal. In minutes she would see him again. How should she act? she wondered. Casual or joyous? Their few days' separation had made her realize how important he had become to her, and she honestly believed she was important to him.

Every fiber within her wanted their reunion to be happy, but she had a dark, nagging fear of what she might find out once she had the list Chris was bringing with him. What would she do if it indicated that Scott was somehow involved? Would it be proof enough of his involvement with the swindlers? How would she handle the moral ramifications? Would she feel obligated to tell Chris? What of her obligations to her brother, to her family, to Continental?

The arrival notice of Chris's flight echoed throughout the waiting room, and soon passengers began to deplane. Ivy's eyes searched the stream of people arriving, then she saw Chris, his head turning this way, then that, as he anxiously scanned the waiting crowd.

Her heart lurched and her pulse quickened when he sent her a wide smile across the room. For an instant she forgot her anguished concerns, smiled back at him and waved enthusiastically. As he maneuvered through the mob to get to her, she saw that he looked tired.

"Hello again," he said, a world of affection in his quiet greeting. Then he took her in his arms and kissed her.

Ivy barely felt his briefcase bump against her lower back; she was too taken with the lovely feeling of his warm lips and the comforting pressure of his body against hers. Oblivious to the people in the waiting area, she slipped her arms around his waist, settled into his embrace and kissed him passionately.

Drawing his head back, Chris grinned. "If this is the kind of welcome you're going to give me, I've got to take trips more often." He placed an arm around her shoulder, and they headed for the incoming luggage area.

When they reached the carousel, Ivy asked, "How was your trip?"

"Exhausting. I've been working day and night. The bogus health care scam has already spread throughout the Midwest."

"So quickly?"

"That's the way the swindlers operate. By the time people realize they've been had, the con men have packed up and disappeared. It's only a matter of time until we begin to get new complaints from the east and west coasts. Oh, I brought the list you wanted." He reached inside his suit jacket and withdrew two folded pieces of paper. "This is confidential information, Ivy. You won't let it get out of your hands, will you?"

"Of course not." She took the papers and placed them in her purse. "I don't know when or if I'll have a chance to check the names against our files."

"As I said, we need all the help we can get. A lot of innocent people are being hurt."

He spotted his suitcase on the moving carousel and lifted it off. "Where would you like to have dinner?"

Her purse seemed five pounds heavier, now that it contained the list he had given her; she was anxious to get home with it. "Chris," she suggested, "since you're tired, why don't we have dinner another time? You'd probably rather rest."

"You're dead wrong. I'd rather be with you. How about we compromise and have dinner at my place? You can tell me about Kim's problem at school."

Take the list and run, Ivy, she ordered silently, but when she looked at Chris's smiling face, her willpower turned sluggish, and she agreed.

CHRIS'S APARTMENT WAS in a complex south of the airport. En route, they stopped at a Chinese restaurant and ordered a carryout. While they waited, Ivy told him of the meeting she had with Kim's guidance counselor, and also about her concern that the girl was seeing so much of Randy. Their pepper steak, fried rice and egg rolls bagged, they again took off in Ivy's car.

After Chris directed her to pull into a visitor's spot in the parking area next to his apartment building, they went inside.

"This is nice," Ivy said, glancing around the small but cozy living room.

"It's okay as far as furnished apartments go," Chris said from the kitchen as he took the white cartons out of the paper bag, "but it's a little claustrophobic. I don't spend a lot of time here."

Ivy guessed that he didn't. She didn't see many signs to indicate that the room was lived in and enjoyed, and that seemed sad.

From the kitchen doorway, he asked, "Would you like a drink before dinner?"

She turned. "A bourbon and water would be nice."

"Two coming up."

"Would you like me to fix them while you unpack?"

"That's something else I like about you," he replied. "You're thoughtful." He reached down into a cabinet and put a bourbon bottle on the counter. He liked the idea of Ivy's puttering around in the kitchen. It seemed to make his apartment a homier place. "The glasses and coasters are in the cabinet over the microwave."

After he carried his suitcase to the bedroom, Ivy fixed the drinks and placed one on the coffee table in front of the sofa, the other on the little table next to a chair across from it. Sitting on the chair, she took a sip from her glass and wondered what it would be like to live alone in a furnished apartment. She didn't much like the idea.

Ivy had always lived in a house surrounded by family, either with her parents and brother or in her own home with her husband and then with Kim. There had always been noise and laughter as well as mild disagreements. But here in Chris's apartment, everything was so quiet, and the place lacked any real warmth. Yet she felt that Chris had a great deal of warmth in his nature.

Glancing around, she spotted a newspaper and some weekly magazines. On the end table, at the far side of the sofa, she noticed two books, one with a folded piece of paper in it to serve as a bookmark. Curious, she got up and checked the titles. One was a collection of poems by Walt Whitman; the other, Thoreau's *Walden*.

She put them back down and returned to the chair, thinking that there were still many facets of Chris's character she wasn't aware of. But the more she learned about him, the more she realized how complex he was and how deeply she was beginning to care for him.

"Thanks," Chris said when he came back into the living room and saw the drink on the coffee table.

Ivy noted that he had removed his jacket and tie and had rolled back the sleeves of his white dress shirt.

He turned on the stereo and lowered the volume of the soft music, then collapsed onto the sofa and leaned back. "It feels great just to sit and relax with good company nearby."

After gazing at her for a while in silence, he reached for his glass and smiled. "Thanks for coming to the airport. It was a nice feeling, knowing that someone was waiting for me."

"We all need that feeling, I guess," she said, realizing how much she wanted someone like Chris waiting for her.

He took a long swallow of the drink, wondering what it was he saw in Ivy's expression that disturbed him. She seemed content enough, but in her eyes he thought he detected sadness. Concern for Kim, he guessed.

Ivy sipped her drink, aware that Chris's eyes were on her. She could feel the tension between them. It was as if they were each resisting some potent force that was drawing them together. The small talk they were making only seemed to heighten the tension.

Patting his hand on the sofa, Chris said, "Come sit with me."

If she did, Ivy knew what would happen. She wanted to rush to him, but at the same time she wanted to run from him. Never in her life had she felt so vulnerable as she did at this moment. Chris had only to touch her, to talk softly to her and make her aware of his warmth, and she would melt in his arms willingly. But she couldn't permit that. How could she when she was using him and his list to learn the truth about her brother?

"Ivy...please," he whispered.

Unable to fight the plea she heard in his voice, she rose, crossed to the sofa and sat down at the end nearest the window.

He looked over at her and smiled. "Mind if I rest my weary head in your lap?" Before she could answer, he stretched out and did just that. After a deep sigh, he drew her left hand over his head, placed it on his chest and began to stroke her smooth, slender fingers. "I thought about you a lot while I was away," he said, his voice low and melodious.

Ivy's alert senses registered the weight and warmth of his head resting on her thighs, and also the body heat from his chest that radiated through her hand. Each slow stroke of his fingers on hers fueled the fire that she felt building deep within her.

"Did you think about me?" he asked, tilting his head a little so he could look up at her.

Struggling to answer, she said softly, "Yes, I did."

The admission itself turned the tables on her resolve to put some distance between them. As she guided the fingers of her right hand through his thick, wavy hair, her other hand moved with the slow rise of his chest as he inhaled a deep, satisfying breath. When he drew her hand upward to kiss her fingertips, she could feel the soft hairs in the V of his open shirt brush against the underside of her arm.

Without thought, she guided the fingers of her free hand around the curve of his ear before moving them down over his warm neck.

Chris shuddered, then circled Ivy's nape with his hand and drew her face down. He closed his eyes and brought her lips to his in a long, lingering kiss. Whispering, he said, "You won't believe how often I thought of you while I was gone. It was bad enough when I was in Chicago, but when I got to Denver and realized how far away you were, I thought I'd lose my mind for wanting you. I do want you, Ivy. God, how I want you."

In the next moment, he kissed her with an urgency that sent her senses spinning. Aching with her need for him, she loosened another button on his shirt and eased her hand over his warm skin, thrilling at the feel of silky hair and masculine muscles. His deep moan crossed their lips, then she felt her hand being eased down over his belt and onto the hard, protruding flesh that strained his pants.

Ivy felt as though her palm had been scorched, but when she tried to pull her hand back, he pressed it there as he deepened his kiss. Her mind reeled; her heart beat wildly. She thought she was going to suffocate.

In one fluid motion, Chris raised himself, turned his body toward Ivy, pinning her against the back of the sofa. His lips sought hers again, but the momentary respite brought her to her senses, and she tilted her head aside.

"Please, Chris...don't."

He raised his head to examine her face. His breathing was ragged, his voice raspy when he asked, "What's wrong?"

With effort she eased away from him and rose from the sofa. "Everything is wrong," she said, her voice as distraught as his.

Leaning back on the sofa, Chris stared at her for several tense moments. Bewildered, he asked, "Did I miss something? I thought we were both enjoying that."

"I'm sorry, Chris, but I wasn't thinking," Ivy said distractedly.

"Ivy, what is there to think about? We care for each other. When I'm not with you, I'm miserable. Is it so wrong that I want to make love with you?" When she said nothing, he swung his feet onto the carpet. "I guess I was taking too much for granted again in thinking you did care for me."

"Chris, I care too much," she admitted. "All you have to do is touch me, and I go crazy."

"So what's wrong?" he asked again.

She looked at him and saw that his face and neck were flushed. "Chris," she said with forced calm, "I have a lot more at stake than you do. You have only yourself to think about. I have a family to consider. Anything I do affects them somehow."

Reaching for his drink, he asked, "How is our making love going to affect your family?"

"I'm not sure I'd be the same person afterward."

After a hardy swallow, he took time to examine her expression, then he asked, "Are you saying that you'd think less of yourself for going to bed with me?"

"No, I'm not saying that."

Resentment blazed in his eyes. "I don't know what the hell you're trying to tell me, Ivy, but I sure don't want you having sleepless nights because of horny ol' me." He got up and made a point of buttoning his shirt. "Suddenly I've lost my appetite. Would you like to take the pepper steak home with you?"

Heartsick, Ivy reached for her purse. "No, but you should eat something, Chris."

"Is that concern I hear?" he asked wryly.

"A friend's concern."

"Well, friend," he said, starting toward the door, "let's call it a night. Apparently I need some time to work on my manners."

As she drove home in the darkness, Ivy wiped at the moisture stinging her eyes. She didn't like herself very much at the moment. She wished she hadn't spouted off about family and responsibility to Chris. In her heart she now knew she had used them as excuses to mask the real problem: her need to protect her brother. But what a price she was having to pay to protect Scott.

For a while back in Chris's apartment, Ivy had felt the full impact of her longing for him and her deep desire to know him intimately. She had wanted to make love with him more than anything else in the world. She had wanted to feel lost in his arms, surrounded by his masculinity, to have him be a part of her. But a barrier had loomed up in front of her like an impenetrable wall.

Chris had offered himself to her, and she had pushed him away, hurt him without meaning to. Ivy knew she would never forgive herself for that. Her one hope was that the list he had given her would prove that her brother was in the clear. If it did, she would run to Chris and beg his forgiveness.

When Ivy reached the house, neither Kim nor her father was home yet, so she rushed upstairs to her bedroom and closed the door.

Her despair was like a heavy weight as she went over the papers spread on her bed. Each name she had checked in red appeared on the list of swindled people in Denver that Chris had given her.

"Oh, Scott, why?" she whispered, her words sounding like a long, desperate moan.

Ivy stared down at the papers again, trying to find some excuse for her brother. She tried telling herself it was merely a coincidence, but she couldn't really believe it was. For deleting those names, she realized that at the very least Scott could be accused of being involved in a cover-up of some kind. But for whom? Whom was he protecting, and why?

Biting down on her lip until it throbbed, she decided she had to find out, and now! Quickly she circled the bed, went to the phone on her night table and placed a call to the Palmer House in Chicago.

"I'm sorry," a pleasant voice said. "We don't have a Scott Chandler registered."

"But you must have," Ivy insisted. "He was to arrive there last Wednesday. Would you check again, please?"

Moments later the desk clerk said, "He did arrive Wednesday night, but he checked out Thursday morning."

"Thursday? I see. Thank you." Ivy replaced the receiver slowly and sank onto the bed.

She hadn't been surprised that Scott hadn't sent them a postcard from Chicago; he wasn't one to write home at all. But if he wasn't at the Palmer House, where was he? And why had he changed his plans?

"Emily, of course!" she concluded.

But how could she contact her? All Ivy remembered was the woman's last name: Domsha. She thought hard and recalled that Emily had lived with her parents in the north section of the city. "Well, how many Domshas can there be in Chicago?" she asked herself and reached for the phone again.

After three wrong numbers, a woman said that she did have a daughter named Emily.

Ivy breathed a sigh of relief and explained, "I'm phoning from Florida, Mrs. Domsha. My brother, Scott Chandler, is a friend of Emily's."

"Oh, yes, I remember Scott."

"He's on vacation in Chicago, and it's urgent that I speak with him. Since Scott went there to see Emily, I thought she would know where he's staying."

"To see Emily?" the woman repeated oddly. "That's impossible. Emily married and moved to California more than a year ago."

Her words hit Ivy like a ton of bricks. Collecting her wits, she murmured, "I see. Thank you, Mrs. Domsha. I'm sorry I bothered you."

After hanging up, Ivy walked slowly to the bottom of her bed and stared down at the papers strewn over the spread. She realized that her brother had lied to her about going to Chicago to patch things up with Emily. Why did he lie? And why did he buy a one-way ticket to Chicago, as Chris had told her he did?

As she gathered up the papers from the bed, Ivy's confusion turned to concern for her brother. Where was he? Was he safe? she wondered. Her worry mounted to fear, and she thought of phoning Chris.

No, she couldn't! she realized immediately. If she told Chris she couldn't locate Scott, there would be too many questions, and that was the last thing she wanted right now.

Her eyes fell to the papers she was clutching; the red check marks she had made glared brightly. She tossed the printouts back into the bottom drawer of her dresser and slammed it shut.

Leaning against the brass rail at the foot of her bed, she grasped it firmly, wondering what to do about the incriminating information she had uncovered. What about her loyalty to Continental? Could she ignore her moral obligation to report what she had found? Ivy covered her mouth with her fingers, knowing she had to do something. But Scott was her brother!

No, she wouldn't do anything just now. She would wait until he returned to Miami, then she would have it out with him.

In her office the next morning, Ivy told Dolores, her secretary, not to disturb her for a while, then she phoned Leon Torell in Chicago.

"It's good to hear from you," he said, his voice sounding chipper.

"Leon, have you heard from Scott in the past week?"

"No, should I have?"

"He's in Chicago on vacation, but I haven't been able to contact him. I thought he might have stopped by to see you."

"Sorry, Ivy. I didn't even know he was coming here. Is there some kind of a problem I can help you with?"

She hesitated. Leon had been a close friend once, and she desperately needed to talk to someone. She was at her wits' end worrying about her brother, and she was still nervous from having to answer questions put to her by Ellen Roth, a postal inspector, earlier in the morning. But Ivy realized she couldn't tell Leon what was bothering her.

"No," she said quietly, "there's no real problem. I'm just concerned about Scott. We haven't heard from him since he left."

"If he does get in touch with me, I'll tell him to give you a call. Don't worry about him. He's probably off somewhere having a ball."

"Yes, I suppose he is," she mumbled. "Well, I'll let you go, Leon. I'm sure you're as busy as I am."

"Ivy," he said quickly, "have you people in Florida had any visitors from the Postal Inspection Service?"

"I'm afraid so. I just got through with one of them."

"What's up? They've been nosing around here, too."

Lowering her voice, she said, "It seems that some group has been using the mails to swindle a lot of people across the country. The inspectors think that criminal elements might be using the information we collect."

"I see. Are they just grabbing at straws, or do they have something concrete to go on?"

"As far as I know, they don't. We're just one of several companies they're checking on."

"Well, if you hear anything definite, or if they come across anything at any of our branches, you'll be sure and give me a call, won't you? What affects one branch affects the whole company, right?"

"Right, and I will let you know. Bye for now, Leon."

"Ivy, I'm thinking about flying down to Miami after the Christmas holidays. Could we get together, have dinner, maybe? It could be like old times."

No, it couldn't, Ivy thought, but to Leon she said, "Sure, Leon, that would be nice. Call me when you get in."

"Will do. Take care."

AFTER WORK ON FRIDAY, Ivy made it home just in time to see Kim take off with Randy for a birthday party at a teammate's house. Ivy was relieved that Kim was finally making friends, but she was still leery of the girl's growing attachment to Randy. She could see it in Kim's face every time she spoke about him. There was a light in her eyes that Ivy had never seen before. And Randy really worried Ivy. The young man was barely able to keep his eyes or his hands off Kim.

"She's growing up, isn't she?" Walt said to his daughter in the living room.

Laying her purse on the table, Ivy went to the front window and watched Kim get into Randy's Camaro. "Too fast as far as I'm concerned."

"You can't hold on to her forever, you know."

"I hardly think at least until she's eighteen is forever." She turned from the window. "Would you like some iced tea?"

"No, I've got to rush. I'm taking Trudy to dinner."

"Again?"

Smiling, he asked, "You got something against your ol' man being a swinger?"

"Walter Chandler, a swinger," Ivy said with a lilt in her voice.

"Darn right, and it wouldn't hurt you to do a little swinging. I'd like to see some grandchildren before I die.

You should start thinking about getting married again. What about Chris? He's eligible, he's got a good job and Ivy Laval has a ring to it. No pun intended."

Ivy recalled how Chris had just about thrown her out of his apartment Wednesday evening. "There's little chance of my name becoming Ivy Laval."

"Why not? The two of you make a good-looking couple."

"It takes more than that to make a successful marriage."

She headed for the kitchen, and her father followed. Leaning against the doorjamb, he watched her pour herself a glass of iced tea. "What would you think about my remarrying?" he asked tentatively.

Ivy stared at him, nonplussed for a moment. "Trudy?" she asked, and he nodded. "I'd think you might be rushing the relationship. You haven't known each other very long."

"Just how much longer do you think I have, darlin'?"

"Unless you and your doctor are keeping something from me, I'd say long enough to regret jumping into something that serious."

"Statistics show that being unmarried slashes about a decade off a guy's life."

"One of Trudy's bits of information, I take, it," Ivy remarked with a smile.

"She's a very with-it lady."

"I'm beginning to understand just how with-it she is."

"So what do you think?"

"About your running off to Niagara Falls?"

"Or to Las Vegas. Trudy's never been there."

Ivy realized how serious her father was. She knew that he was basically a down-to-earth man who knew what he wanted from life. She did want him to be happy, and if he found that happiness with Trudy, so be it. Trudy certainly had a lot of stamina, and though Ivy had to admit that the woman got on her nerves, she realized she wouldn't be the one to have to live with her.

Going to her father, she kissed him on the cheek. "I hope you'll at least wait until Scott gets back so he can be your best man."

"Can you see yourself as a matron of honor?"

"I suppose you have Kim lined up for a bridesmaid."

"What's wrong with making it a family affair? Chris and Randy could be ushers."

"Oh, really? Are you planning to fly all of us to Las Vegas?"

"That's for the honeymoon."

"Tell me, Dad. Does Trudy have an inkling about this trip you're planning?"

"She will, when the time is right." He checked the clock on the kitchen wall. "Speaking of time, I'd better get moving. Trudy's a stickler for punctuality."

Ivy watched him hustle away, thinking how busy the love bug had been in their household. First Kim became smitten with Randy, and now her father wanted to provide his daughter with a stepmother. Well, she thought, he'd have to plan on an usher other than Chris. That much was for certain.

The ringing of the telephone on the kitchen wall interrupted her musings, and she answered it. To her surprise it was Chris.

"I think I owe you an apology," he said.

"For what?" she asked, attempting to sound nonchalant.

"For that scene in my apartment. I must have come on too strong. I'm sorry."

Leaning back against the kitchen wall, Ivy said, "It wasn't that, Chris. The timing was just bad."

"How's the timing tonight? I'd like to be with you for a while. I need to be, Ivy. If you don't have plans, I could pick up two pizzas, and maybe Kim could invite Randy over."

"They've gone to a party tonight."

"Does your father like pizza?"

"He's having dinner with Trudy." There was a pause at the other end of the line.

"Do you like pizza?" he asked.

"Yes," she said softly, feeling like putty in his hands again.

"Good. I'll bring a bottle of red wine. In about an hour, okay?"

"Okay, Chris."

She heard the click and replaced the receiver, thinking just how easy it was for him to make her forget everything else. What was happening to her? she wondered. Had the love bug gotten to her, too?

CHAPTER TEN

"THAT LOOKS AND SMELLS delicious," Ivy said, watching Chris put a huge wedge of the pizza on each of the two plates she'd placed on the kitchen counter.

"Would you pour the wine while I zap these in the microwave?"

As she did, Ivy had difficulty keeping her eyes off him. He looked so masculinely attractive in the tan pullover and khaki slacks he wore. The tuft of brown hair that was exposed by the deep V in the pullover reminded her of the evening in his apartment. It was ridiculous, she thought, but just the sight of the curly brown hair made her fingers tingle.

"Ready?" he asked. Chris saw her avert her eyes, then sit down at the kitchen table. After serving the pizza, he joined her and raised his wineglass. "To friendship," he toasted.

"Yes, friendship," she said quietly and sipped the red wine. As she cut into the pizza with a fork, she remarked, "You're pretty handy with a microwave."

Chris had his slice in hand. "When you live like I do, a microwave is a necessity."

"It was sweet of you to bring Kim the Billy Joel tape."

"I didn't know what kind of music she liked, but I thought it might help her drum up conversation with the kids at school."

"Every little bit helps. So many of the things that kids talk about are foreign to Kim. One day she came home and asked who Elvis Presley was."

"How did she learn English so quickly?"

"Her aunt taught her some. She worked in Saigon while the Americans were there. When Kim was in the Philippines, she went through a six-month intensive program in English. Now she takes special classes at school. She's a bright young lady."

"Takes after her mother."

Ivy looked over at Chris and saw the sparkle in his eyes. Smiling, she said, "It's only been two years, but I feel like she's been with me much longer."

"How about another piece of pizza?"

"Uh-uh. This is fine."

Getting up to put another slice in the microwave, Chris remarked, "You're not eating very much. I thought you liked pizza."

"I do. It's just that—" *What, Ivy? Is it just that you're wondering if he's going to ask if you've checked the list he gave against the files at work? Are you wondering if you should tell him that Scott has disappeared from the face of the earth?* "It's just that I'm not very hungry tonight."

Chris leaned back against the kitchen counter as he waited for the beeper on the microwave to sound. Crossing his arms, he grinned. "They say that physical exercise builds up an appetite. Do you jog or anything?"

Wondering what other kinds of physical exercise he might be thinking of, she said lightly, "I get all the exercise I need at the office."

Taking his plate from the microwave and sitting down, Chris remarked, "Ellen told me she met you at Continental yesterday. She said you were more help than the manager was. Ellen's top-notch, one of our best inter-viewers. She's got a sixth sense about people.''

"And what did her sixth sense tell her about me?"

"You impressed her. She said you knew more about what's going on at Continental than some of the depart-ment heads, especially Lew Frazer in the communica-tions division.''

Where Scott works, Ivy added to herself, wondering if Chris was visiting for business or pleasure. "I started in the communications department. I should know some-thing about it."

"Bob McDonough wasn't too helpful. He's not going to let us near the files unless we get a court order. How well do you know him?''

"I've known Bob for nine years now. He hired me."

"He's a pretty okay boss, I take it."

"I think so. I've been a guest in his home many times, and before Bill died, Bob and his wife were guests in ours.'' Not appreciating Chris's questions about fellow employees, Ivy asked, "Do you always take your job home with you?''

Chris saw her expression cloud over. "Let's not talk business anymore tonight. Let's talk about us."

"What about us, Chris?" she asked as she poured more wine in their glasses.

"I need to make sure there still is an *us.*''

"A little while ago we toasted friendship. Doesn't that cover it all?''

"Not for me, it doesn't. Is that enough for you... friendship?''

No, Ivy admitted to herself, *but it has to be that way.* To Chris she said, "Don't underestimate a good friend. Trudy says a friend is someone who's here today and here tomorrow.''

"Smart lady, that Trudy," Chris allowed, then bit into his slice of pizza.

Ivy asked, "Do you keep in touch with friends you've made traveling around the country?"

"Not religiously, but since you're now a friend, a buddy—" he tacked on the latter with a grin "—let me tell you about this gorgeous lady I met recently. She has beautiful blue eyes, lovely auburn hair and a slight overbite."

Smiling, Ivy said, "She sounds familiar."

"Only one problem. She has this thing about her family...thinks about them at the strangest times...even when I try to make love to her."

Becoming more edgy by the second, Ivy said, "My family will always come first, Chris."

"Look, I'm not trying to tear you away from your family. I just want to be part of your life."

Ivy's eyes darkened. "For as long as you decide to stay in Miami, right?"

"I've been completely honest with you about that. I could have kept my plans to myself and let you think I was putting roots down here, but I'm not." Beginning to feel exasperated, he said, "Ivy, if you were just any woman, I wouldn't be sitting here, trying to make a case for myself. Soon after I met you, I knew I wanted to make love to you, but I didn't expect I'd be falling in love with you."

A lump welled up in Ivy's throat, and she fought hard to control it. She honestly hadn't expected to ever hear Chris say that he was falling in love with her. His admission, though, forced her to acknowledge that she was falling in love with him. God help her, but she was.

Getting up from the table, she moved her plate with the half-eaten slice of pizza on it to the kitchen counter. Determined not to betray her true feelings, she said coolly, "People seem to fall in and out of love frequently nowadays."

"Does that make love less of a wonder?"

"For someone like me it does. I guess I was a late bloomer, but Bill was the first serious love in my life. Unlike you, I don't know what it's like to fall in and out of love each time you move to a different city."

"That's a low blow, Ivy, and you're far from being accurate. I've known a few women intimately, but I've only told two that I loved them . . . Kendal and you."

Ivy looked away, ashamed of her outburst. Trying to steady her voice, she said slowly, "Are you telling me that you love me, Chris?"

"Yes, Ivy," he replied softly. After a brief pause he added, "I guess I would feel safer if I didn't."

Turning to face him, Ivy asked earnestly, "Why? Are you so afraid of being vulnerable, of losing that control over your life that's so important to you?"

"Yes," he answered quickly. "It's as important to me as your family is to you. As far back as I can remember, people have been trying to tell me what I could or couldn't do with my life. When my stepfather took charge of the family and the restaurant, he dictated that one day I'd run the place. Well, I proved him wrong. In college, the coach told me I'd never be a class A runner. I proved him wrong, too."

Chris stood, leaned back against the kitchen counter and braced his hands on it. With his eyes moving nervously, he continued. "Then in Vietnam I came up against an inexperienced second lieutenant who wanted his platoon to walk into a sure ambush. I wouldn't do it. I lost my sergeant's stripes after knocking the idiot on his ass, but the platoon survived.

"Along came Kendal, and she decided she'd reorganize my life. She wasn't satisfied with a husband and a lover. She wanted to turn me into a puppet she could manipulate. She didn't succeed, either." He looked sideways at Ivy. "No, I wouldn't be the man I am today if I hadn't maintained control over my own life."

Ivy had been watching Chris as he spoke. Now she stared down at the countertop and said quietly, "Obviously your life has been quite different than mine. What you've just said, though, helps me to understand why you're not going to let anyone influence the decisions you make for yourself."

Softening his tone, Chris said, "Maybe you think my loving you can't amount to very much because I won't settle down here, but—"

Ivy looked up and said quickly, "I'm not trying to put a ball and chain on you, and I'm not trying to bargain with you, either. I'm not saying, if you do this or that, I'll go to bed with you."

"I didn't say you were," Chris replied. "I'm just trying to explain that I can't make anyone my top priority. I already have one, achieving the goal I've set for myself. I work hard, very hard, to be successful in my job."

Her heart hammering, Ivy asked, "Is being a postal inspector a job or an obsession with you?"

"Perhaps being a success at it is an obsession, but if I give up on being a success, I'm giving up on myself. Please try to understand that."

Slowly Ivy sat down, placed her hands on the table and interlaced her fingers. In a steady voice she said, "I can understand that, Chris, but you've got to understand that for me an intimate relationship, even a temporary one, needs to be worked on with the same patience, energy and plans that you give to your work. I won't accept second place now and wait to feel important to you if and when it's convenient for you."

Chris sat down again, his expression a mixture of surprise and admiration. "Well, I guess no one can say we don't thrash things out honestly. I don't know about you, but I feel kind of limp."

Shaking inside, Ivy took several deep breaths, then suggested, "Maybe some fresh air would help. Why don't you go out on the deck. I'll be out in just be a minute."

"Can I take the wine bottle and the glasses with me?"

"Just take your glass," she said, trying to calm down. "I won't be long."

"Ivy," he asked slowly, "is everything still . . . all right with us?"

"As right as it's ever been, Chris," she answered, then began to straighten up the kitchen.

CHRIS RESTED BACK in one of the lounge chairs on the deck that overlooked the garden. Although it was only a week before Thanksgiving, the evening temperature hovered above the eighty-degree mark, but the humidity was low and a breeze made the night air comfortable.

Sipping the wine, he thought about what Ivy had just said. He wondered if Kendal had felt the same way. Maybe, he considered halfheartedly, if she'd had the same honesty that Ivy did, their marriage would have had a chance.

He smiled to himself, realizing he was happy it hadn't. Ivy was twice the woman Kendal was. But even though Ivy had said that she understood him, he didn't think she actually realized the pressure he felt to succeed in his work. Society expected that of him. A woman was applauded if she happened to succeed, but a man would be considered less than a man if he didn't.

Yes, he told himself—as he had so often in the past—
he would get to the top, and then he would have time to
think about settling down. If only Ivy would accompany
him, though, be at his side while he worked to reach the
goal he'd set for himself. That would be the best of both
worlds.

If he understood one thing clearly now, however, it was
that she wasn't a woman to be pressured into anything.
But two years was a long time. People could change, and
maybe Ivy would.

But why should he think she would change? he wondered. Maybe because women were supposed to be
changeable; men weren't.

"It's beautiful out tonight, isn't it?" Ivy commented,
her expression drawn as she came out onto the deck.

Chris looked up at her and smiled. "It is now. Sure you
won't have some more wine?"

"No, thanks." Sitting sideways on the lounge chair
near his, Ivy moistened her lips, then looked down at her
hands. "Chris, I was thinking about what you said inside, that you were being honest with me."

"I was:"

She looked up and hesitated before saying, "This is
extremely difficult for me, but I feel that I have to be just
as honest with you."

"Ivy, I'm all for this openness between men and
women, but don't you think we've said enough about
that for one night?"

"I'm not talking about us again. I have to tell you
about—" the words came hard "—the list you gave me."

"Yes?" he said, sitting up and giving her his full attention.

"When I was at the home office, when we first met, I
switched a disk for Scott." She could barely get the words

out. "It contained a mailing list. He told me that after he sent the disk to Georgetown, he discovered that he had made an error in merging certain information. When you and I arrived back here, I made a printout of the mailing list before I gave the disk to Scott."

Her heart was beating so hard that Ivy had to stop. She stood, clasped her hands together and moved toward the steps to the garden.

"And?" Chris prompted.

Turning, she said, "My brother had substituted another disk for the files here in Miami, a duplicate of the one I left at the home office. I also made a printout of that mailing list. Then I compared the two of them. Scott had deleted some fifty names from the company's records. After you gave me the list of the people swindled in Denver, I discovered that their names were . . . the same as the ones that Scott had deleted from the files."

Chris leaned forward, rubbing his palms together as he assessed the implications of what Ivy had just told him. Finally he looked up at her and asked urgently, "Who other than Scott knew you were switching the disks?"

"No one. Why would he have told anyone else?"

"I'm thinking about the man who tried to steal your purse. Maybe he thought you had the disk in it."

"I did, but why would a complete stranger know anything about it or want it?"

"Your brother might be able to tell us. Where is he in Chicago?"

Ivy slipped back down on to the lounge chair opposite Chris and grasped the sides of it. "That's something else that has me terrified. I don't know where Scott is. He told me he'd be at the Palmer House, but when I tried to reach him there, they said he arrived Wednesday and checked out the next morning. Chris, I'm worried sick about him.''

"So am I. The people he's dealing with can play rough.''

"I won't believe he's knowingly involved with criminals!"

Chris wasn't going to argue the point with Ivy right now. He saw that she was upset enough. But if he was going to help her brother at all, he knew what he had to do. "Ivy," he said evenly, "I have to report what you told me to headquarters. There's no way that it's merely a coincidence that the names matched.''

"I know it looks bad, but there has to be some reasonable explanation."

"There is. Your brother or someone is feeding your company's information to the swindlers.''

"But maybe Scott didn't realize what he was doing. For the past two years he's been working his tail off at Continental, and now he's been accepted into their managerial training program. He wouldn't jeopardize a solid future with the company to knowingly help criminals.''

"I'd be jeopardizing my future if I withheld this kind of information.''

"He's due back at work next Monday. Couldn't you wait until he gets here and see what his side of the story is?''

"What you're asking me to do is to turn my back and look the other way. That could be as bad for your brother as it would be for me.''

Slowly Ivy rose and went down the two steps leading into the garden. Stopping, she crossed her arms and grasped them tightly with her trembling fingers. Chris followed and stood behind her, taking hold of her shoulders.

"All right," he agreed, hating himself for doing so, "I'll wait until he returns to Miami. It's going to play hell with my conscience, but I'll do it."

Ivy swung around, clasped his neck and kissed him. "Thank you, Chris, thank you," she whispered.

Taking hold of her waist, he offered her a less than convincing smile. "I thought you weren't going to bargain with me."

Her chin rose slightly. "I'm not bargaining. I was only following an impulse."

"I like your impulses. Don't stifle them."

A movement caused Ivy to look back toward the house. Seeing Kim and Randy standing on the deck, she drew her arms from Chris's shoulders. "I didn't expect you home this early." As Ivy started toward the youngsters, she saw that Randy had a bruise on his cheek. "What happened to you?"

"He had a fight," Kim said, "but he won't tell me why."

Chris joined them and tilted the boy's face toward the light on the deck. "It doesn't look too bad."

"You should see the other boy," Kim said quietly.

"Randy," Ivy said, "this is Chris Laval, a friend of mine."

Randy extended a hand. "Good to meet you, sir."

"Same here." After shaking hands, Chris said, "C'mon, let's go take care of that."

"There's a first-aid kit on the wall in the downstairs bathroom," Ivy said, feeling uneasy about the cause of Randy's fight. She hoped it had nothing to do with Kim.

CHRIS TOSSED the damp cotton ball he'd just used to clean Randy's bruise into the plastic basket under the bathroom sink, then checked the young man's face. "I had a few of these when I was your age. What was the fight about?"

"Eddie the nerd made a crack about Kim."

"Like what?" Chris asked, squeezing a dab of anti-biotic ointment onto a finger, then applying it gently to the bruise.

"He wanted to know if Orientals were good lays."

"Did Kim hear that?"

"Uh-uh."

"This Eddie doesn't know what being a real man is all about, does he?"

"Aw, he's all mouth. There's not a girl at school who'd let him touch her."

"There," Chris said, checking the job he'd done, "that should take care of it."

"Thanks, Mr. Laval."

"Make it Chris." He rinsed his fingers and dried them on a towel draped through a brass ring on the side of the sink. "You like Kim, don't you?"

"She's something special...makes me feel good all over. When I'm not with her, all I do is think about her." As Randy checked his face in the mirror over the sink, he asked, "Chris, how do you know if you're in love or not?"

Chris smiled, crossed his arms and braced a shoulder against the wall. "You just about said it all. When a woman gets under your skin, and you can't do much other than think about her, I'd say that's love."

"Then I think I'm in love with Kim, but how can I be sure?"

"Well, if you find yourself taking time to listen to her and to realize that she has feelings just like you do, you can be fairly sure. Not just physical feelings, though."

"Like wanting to have sex, you mean?"

"Right," Chris said emphatically.

"You know what I think?"

"What?"

"I think that if you really love a girl, you gotta be concerned about what happens to her and if she's happy or not. Like, I want Kim to always be happy."

"And healthy," Chris slipped in purposefully. "Kim's a wonderful girl, but she's too young to be having sex."

Randy shook his head. "Not to worry. She set me straight about that. No fooling around while we're going steady, and I'm gonna wait until she's a little older before I ask her to marry me."

Chris's arms dropped to his side, and he stood erect. "To marry you?"

"Oh, not until she finishes high school. Listen, man, this is just between us, right? You won't tell Mrs. Austin I said that, will you?"

"No way." Chris could hear Ivy now. "Your secret's safe with me. Let's get back to the ladies," he suggested.

When they returned to the deck, Kim checked Randy's cheek. "I could have done that for you," she said, casting Chris a glum look.

"Chris and I had some man-to-man talk to do."

"Oh?" Ivy remarked, lifting her eyebrows.

"Say, Chris," Randy said enthusiastically, "Kim and I are going to Crandon Park tomorrow. Why don't you come with us. You, too, Mrs. Austin."

"Randy!" Kim's tone indicated she wasn't as enthused with the idea.

Ivy started to decline. "I don't think we—"

"That's a great idea," Chris interjected. "I haven't been to the beach since—" he grinned at Ivy "—the Cayman Islands."

"Then it's settled," Randy said, ignoring the daggers Kim was sending him with her narrowed green eyes. "What time should we leave?"

"Ivy?" Chris asked.

"Well . . . about nine o'clock?"

"Nine it is," Randy said. "I'd better head on home now."

Her eyes still sparking, Kim said, "I'll go to the door with you."

Once they were outside, she asked, "Why did you invite Mr. Laval?"

"Why not? Don't you like him?" When she didn't answer, he said, "Hey, c'mon, lighten up on him. Chris is a great guy, and he thinks you're wonderful."

"He told you that?" she asked dubiously.

"Yeah, he did, almost made me jealous." Bending down, he kissed her cheek. "See you in the morning."

"And don't forget to bring your books," she called after him as he jogged toward his car.

CHAPTER ELEVEN

A SEA BREEZE from the Atlantic tempered the strong Florida sunshine that spilled down over Key Biscayne and warmed the white sand at Crandon Park beach. Ivy and Randy lay on mats near one of the rental cabanas, while Chris and Kim were busy at a barbecue pit under a clump of coconut palm trees.

Turning the cooking chicken halves, Chris asked, "How do you know when these are done?"

Kim stuck a fork into a chicken thigh. "When you don't see blood near the bone," she answered, her face unsmiling.

"Should I turn these over now?"

"Okay." As he did, Kim brushed some more barbecue sauce over the chicken. Without looking at him, she said, "Thank you for the Billy Joel tape, Mr. Laval. My mother and I listened to it last night."

"I'd like you to call me Chris, Kim. Mr. Laval makes me sound very old."

"That wouldn't be respectful."

"Sure it would, as long as I ask you to."

"I don't think so, Mr. Laval."

Chris could see that gaining the girl's friendship was going to continue to be an uphill battle. Hoping to break the ice, he asked, "Did you like the tape?"

"I couldn't understand all the words. My mother liked the song called . . . baby something."

"'Baby Grand.' That's one of my favorites, too."
Holding the long barbecue fork as though it were a gui-
tar, Chris rocked his head and sang a verse from the song.
He looked down at Kim and smiled.

Straight-faced, she said, "It didn't sound like that
when Billy Joel sang it."

"Ri-i-ight," Chris agreed, but he wasn't ready to toss
in the towel yet. "Did you like 'Goodnight Saigon'?" he
asked hopefully.

"I prefer country music."

"So do I. You know, Florida reminds me a lot of
Vietnam. There are palm trees here and sandy beaches,
and the state is rather flat."

"Vietnam also has mountains and jungles," she
pointed out.

"True. I remember how it used to rain cats and dogs
there and the sun would be shining. That happens here,
too, I'm told. And Florida has hurricanes."

"At home we have monsoons."

"Yeah, monsoons." After a lengthy silence, he asked,
"Do they have orange groves in Vietnam?"

"They have rubber plantations," she told him as she
checked the chicken halves.

"That smells good, doesn't it? I have three younger
sisters. When they were your age, they couldn't cook half
as well as you do."

"How do you know how well I can cook, Mr. Laval?"

"Your mother brags about you a lot. She said that you
make the best lasagna in the world, and I love lasagna."

"It's not difficult. You just have to be careful with the
sauce and not overcook the pasta."

"My parents would love you. They own a French restaurant in Maryland."

"Lasagna is an Italian dish." Kim lifted the cover from a crockery pot and began stirring the baked beans she and Ivy had fixed at home.

"Italian, right. My folks have branched out, though. They serve a few Italian dishes, too. Have you ever fixed lasagna for Randy?"

For the first time since they started working together at the barbecue, Kim gave Chris serious attention. "No, do you think he would like it?"

"I can almost guarantee it. Randy's a nice young man, isn't he?"

Kim smiled and nodded. "He is what you call a hand-some dupe."

"Handsome dude," Chris corrected her gently, then asked, "Should I turn the chicken again?"

"No, not yet." Kim looked up at him. "Mr. Laval, do you think that a girl of fifteen is too young to go steady?"

He feigned pondering that, then said, "It would depend on the girl. Now, if she were someone who was as intelligent and as emotionally mature as you are, I certainly don't think so."

"Randy wants me to go steady with him, and I said I would. I'm not sure my mother would want me to, though."

"You're not going with anyone else now, are you?"

"No."

"Then your mother already knows you're going steady with Randy."

With a questioning expression on her face, Kim thought about that for a while, then she looked up at Chris again. "Doesn't to go steady mean the same as *se fiancer* in French?"

"To become engaged? Uh, no, not quite, Kim. When you go steady, you only date the same person, but to get engaged is a lot more serious. It means you definitely plan to get married." Recalling his private conversation with Randy, he added, "Girls here don't usually get engaged until they're eighteen or older."

"There are girls my age at school who have babies. They aren't married, but they must be engaged, no?"

"Let's hope so," Chris said, realizing how little he knew about talking to teenagers. "Has Randy asked you to be engaged to him?" Chris asked tentatively.

"He gave me his gold chain." She smiled softly as her fingers touched the slender chain around her neck. "Randy said it bound us together. Isn't that like being engaged?"

"What did your mother think about the chain?"

"She said it was too expensive a gift for him to give me, but Randy convinced her to let me keep it."

"I don't suppose you mentioned this *se fiancer* business to your mother," Chris said, glancing over to see Ivy chatting casually with Randy.

"Not yet. Do you think I should?"

That's a tough one, Chris thought, knowing he'd have to be careful how he answered. If he advised Kim to tell Ivy, he was fairly certain she'd freak out—and Kim would probably never speak to him again. But he couldn't advise her not to tell Ivy something that crucial.

"Mr Laval, do you think my mother would permit me to be Randy's fiancée?"

"Uh... I know she likes Randy, and it's my guess that she's happy you're going steady with a guy as nice as he is." Chris took a deep breath. "Tell you what. Let me talk to your mother before you ask her about becoming engaged."

"You would do that for Randy and me?"

Chris drank in the way Kim was looking at him, as though he were suddenly some kind of a hero. "Sure I would," he said, thoroughly enjoying his new status with Ivy's daughter. "And don't worry about it. Your mother will probably be thrilled."

Smiling demurely, Kim said, "Mr. Laval, if you still want me to, I'd like to call you Chris."

His smile broadened and he winked.

"Turn the chicken now," she directed, and as Chris did, Kim said, "My father's name was William, but my mother called him Bill. Is that a nickname like Chris?"

"It's a shortened form, really," he said. Then he asked, "You miss your father a lot, don't you, Kim?"

"I was very sad when he died. When I was little, I used to pray to see him just once, but I...I saw him for a whole year. I thought he would be ashamed of me, and I did not expect him to love me, but—" she glanced up with misty eyes "—I believe he truly did."

Placing a gentle hand against Kim's face, Chris asked softly, "How could a father not love a daughter like you?"

IVY WATCHED CHRIS AND KIM as they talked and laughed together. She had hoped that Kim would warm up to him. It certainly hadn't taken Randy long to like him. But it was ironic, Ivy thought. Two men had recently entered Kim's life, and both of them would be leaving.

Stretched out on the sand with his eyes closed, Randy mumbled, "Boy, this is relaxing."

Sitting up on her beach mat, Ivy applied some more sunscreen to her arms. "It's a shame Carol couldn't come with us."

"Yeah, that night work is the pits. That was one of the gripes Lamar had."

Ivy wasn't about to mention some of the gripes Carol had regarding her ex-husband.

Rolling over onto his stomach, Randy propped himself up on his arms. "I hated to see them get divorced."

"A divorce is never pleasant," Ivy agreed.

"When I get married, it's going to be for good."

"I'm happy to hear that," she said, but she wasn't particularly happy that marriage was on his mind as well as Kim's. "You know, Randy, I'm sure most people feel that way when they get married, but statistically half of them lose that feeling somewhere down the line."

"I won't, and the girl I marry is gonna know beforehand that we're marrying for the rest of our lives."

Ivy was touched by the sincerity in Randy's voice. "For a young man, you certainly have your head on straight," she said, smiling.

Randy laughed. "If I didn't, my dad would kill me while my mom cheered him on."

"How are you parents? I haven't seen them for quite a while."

"They're both fine. Dad still travels a lot."

Ivy knew Randy's father had something to do with the aerospace industry, but if Carol had told her exactly what, Ivy had forgotten. She did know that Randy hadn't introduced Kim to his parents yet.

Wondering if there was a reason for it, Ivy said, "The next time your mother and father visit Carol, I'm sure Kim would like to meet them."

Randy hesitated before responding. "Mrs. Austin, they don't exactly know that Kim's the only girl I'm seeing now."

"Why not? Don't you think they'd like her?"

"Sure they would, but they've talked to me about...well, you know...about not getting serious about any one girl until I'm older. They think it might interfere with my plans to become an officer in the air force."

"They're wise people. I'm sure you know of teenagers who've found themselves in situations they hadn't planned on."

"Yeah, but that won't happen to me. I'm gonna get my second lieutenant bars before I get married." After a lengthy pause, he said, "I think it's great that you want Kim to go to college. She'll make a good doctor."

"A doctor?" That came as a shock to Ivy. "Did Kim tell you she wanted to be a doctor?"

"Uh-huh. She's always asking Carol about the doctors at the hospital and what they do. Kim isn't sure what kind of doctor she wants to be, but I think she's leaning toward gynecology. With her aptitude for math and science, she's a good candidate for med school."

Ivy felt as though she were caught in some kind of time warp. Kim was barely fifteen, and suddenly Ivy was worrying about her breezing through medical school. She was on the verge of pressing Randy for more information regarding Kim's interest in medicine when Chris yelled to them, saying that the chicken was ready.

After they ate, Randy and Kim decided on a walk down the beach. As Ivy packed the picnic basket, she glanced over at Chris, who was lying in the shade of the cabana. "You and Kim seem to be hitting it off nicely."

"She's a sweetheart, easy to grow fond of very quickly. You're doing a fine job with her." He decided to wait before giving Ivy the good news that she was bordering on becoming a mother-in-law.

"Kim's growing up so fast," Ivy remarked pensively, remembering how frightened and confused the girl had been when she first came into her life. "I just learned from Randy that she wants to be a doctor."

"That would be wonderful," Chris said, closing his eyes.

Ivy looked down the beach to where Kim and Randy were talking to some other teenagers. "She's intelligent enough to succeed at whatever she wants to do. I'm so proud of her."

"I enjoy the time I spend with your family," Chris said. "Thanks for letting me be a part of it."

From her kneeling position, Ivy glanced briefly at Chris, then she closed the lid on the basket. "If you're starting to enjoy family life, you should think about having one of your own."

Chris shook his head. "The time's not right."

"Because of your work?"

"Uh-huh." He opened his eyes to see Ivy pulling her beach mat next to his in the shade. "Ever think about leaving Continental?" he asked casually.

"I've been doing a lot of thinking about Continental lately. My job there has become fairly routine. I'm ready for more challenging work."

"Doing what?"

"Liz, a friend of mine, works for the government in urban planning. That would be a job where I could use my skills in researching people and places. Miami's growth has been phenomenal in the past decade, and there's a big need for redevelopment of the older communities. Some of the neighborhoods are really run-down. It would mean returning to the University of Miami for an advanced degree, but Liz told me the M.A. program includes an internship that would give me practical work experience in the field."

"You'd probably find urban planning a lot more satisfying than marketing research. You'd be helping people more directly."

"As you do in your work?" Ivy asked.

"You could say that, I suppose."

Wanting and needing to know more about what made Chris tick, Ivy asked, "Is that why you became a postal inspector, to help people?"

Her question caught him off guard, but he was pleased that she was interested. He welcomed the opportunity to discuss his innermost feelings with Ivy. It made him feel closer to her.

Sitting up, he raised his knees and crossed his arms over them. "It's not just a matter of helping people in general. I like helping people who aren't able to help themselves. Helpless victims, I guess you'd call them."

Chris had intended to end his admission there, but when he glanced over at Ivy and saw the intense interest in her expression, he decided to open up to her even more.

"I know what it feels like to be helpless," he said quietly. "When my father was killed by a thug robbing the restaurant, there wasn't a thing I could do about it. I felt as though I had lost the only friend I had in the world. Then, when my stepfather took over, I felt so damn helpless again. I guess that's when I decided I had to become powerful myself."

"To get some control over your life," Ivy said softly, beginning to understand why Chris felt so driven to reach the top of his profession.

That realization, Ivy saw immediately, highlighted a big difference between her and Chris. He had reacted to tragedy by arming himself as best he could, as if by doing so he would be able to ward off future disasters. Whereas

Ivy, when she lost her mother and then her husband, had turned to her family for support. But Chris hadn't been able to, she thought sadly.

About to comment on that to him, she saw Kim and Randy running toward them.

"Mother," Kim asked, half out of breath, "one of Randy's friends invited us to a pool party this evening. Can I go?"

"Who is this friend?" Ivy asked Randy.

"A guy on the basketball team."

"Will there be any drinking?"

"Only punch and colas, Mrs. Austin."

Ivy turned to Kim. "All right, but get me the boy's telephone number and be home by eleven."

"Okay," Kim said, beaming. Then she and Randy headed back to the group they'd left down the beach.

Chris chuckled. "At their age, life is one big round of parties, isn't it?"

"Kim's long overdue for some fun. I just wish she weren't spending all her time with Randy."

"Why? He's a good kid."

"I know that, but did you notice the gold chain Kim's wearing? Randy gave it to her."

"Yeah. Kim showed it to me." *This is definitely not the time to split hairs about the difference between going steady and becoming engaged,* Chris told himself, guessing that Kim would never make it to the pool party if he did.

"I want her to be happy," Ivy said, "but I don't know how she'll take it when Randy leaves." She tilted her head toward Chris. "Don't misunderstand what I'm going to say. I'm thrilled that Kim's warming up to you, but I don't want her getting too attached to you while you're here in Miami."

Confused, he said, "Run that by me again."

"Look, Chris. Kim's at a vulnerable age, and she's a girl who grew up never having a father to relate to. Suddenly she had one with Bill, and I saw her take to him with all the love and warmth she had stored up inside. I also saw how deeply crushed she was when Bill died. I hadn't thought about it before, but while I was watching you and Kim earlier, it dawned on me that you could become a father figure for her. I don't want her to experience another loss like that."

"It seems to me you're trying to organize her life down to who she can and who she can't see."

Slightly miffed, Ivy said defensively, "It's not a role I choose to play. It's a responsibility I have."

"You handle that responsibility exceedingly well. I've got to give you that. I honestly respect your dedication to Kim, but I feel like you're using her as an excuse to hand me my walking papers. Are you?"

The way he asked gave Ivy a sinking feeling in the pit of her stomach. Each time she tried to keep Chris at a safe distance, she wound up hurting him—and herself. Why did things have to be so complicated between them? she wondered.

"Frankly," Chris said, "I don't know what to make of you at times. You seem to have a bagful of excuses to keep us from really getting to know each other. First, you're afraid I'm going to send your brother to jail, and now you make it sound like I'm going to abandon your stepdaughter."

Ivy's voice became little more than a whisper. "Isn't that true on both accounts?"

"Maybe it is," Chris allowed. "But what I can't get a hold on is where you fit into the picture. What is it you think I'm going to do to you?"

You've already done it, Ivy thought. *You made me fall in love with you.* To him, though, she said, "I don't know."

"That's not the honest answer I expected from you."

Facing him, Ivy looked deeply into his brown eyes, which reflected the sunlight. She wanted to place her hand on the side of his face and move her fingertips over his lips, lips that she longed to feel on hers once more. "All right," she said softly, "I'll tell you what I'm afraid of. I'm afraid that I'll miss you even more than Kim might when you leave."

"A lot can happen in two years," he said, then slipped his arm around her shoulder. "We could both be hurt a lot more if we miss a chance at the happiness we could share together during that time. I want to be a part of your life, Ivy. Don't keep trying to push me away."

His words were as warm as the arm he had around her, and the bare thigh she felt against her own. She placed a hand on one of his knees and admitted, "I don't think I can push you away. As much as I probably should, I'm afraid I can't."

Leaning his head down, Chris kissed her soft hair, then said quietly, "Spend the evening with me, Ivy. I want us to make love. I want it desperately."

His words caused a chill to ripple across Ivy's skin. Her momentary excitement abated, however, when she thought of how dedicated Chris was to his work. After their talk last evening, she knew he was determined to eventually report what her brother had done. Only her plea had persuaded him to wait until Scott returned from vacation. And then what? she wondered now. No clear answer came; her mind was too muddled by conflicting emotions.

Her feelings for Chris, though, were too strong to be dismissed. Chris had awakened emotions in her that she had buried with Bill, feelings that needed expression as surely as she needed air to breathe. Each time she was with Chris, those emotions and feelings were nourished by his kindness and his warmth. He had made her blossom again, made her aware of all of her feminine needs and capabilities. But how could she permit herself to give in to her feelings?

Yes, she wanted to make love with Chris. She needed to desperately. She had thought about it day and night, had fantasized being enveloped in his arms, exchanging intimate touches, learning and savoring each and every part of him.

And now, huddled so close to him, his arm around her, his warm body snugly aligned with hers, Ivy felt her private war rage with a new intensity.

"Will you come to my apartment this evening?" he asked in a whisper, his breath feathering her ear.

"Chris, I . . . I . . ." she stammered and felt his fingers press into her shoulder more firmly.

"Please, love," he said huskily and brushed his lips over her sensitized ear. "I need to hold you close, lose myself in you, feel you lose yourself in me. I need that so much. Say that you want it, too."

Tightening the grasp she had on his knee, Ivy sighed deeply. In a wisp of a voice, she said, "Yes, Chris, it is what I want."

CHAPTER TWELVE

CHRIS PACED ANXIOUSLY as he waited for Ivy to arrive. If she were half as nervous as he was right now, he was afraid she might have an accident driving to his apartment. He checked his watch again: it was a quarter after eight. Had she decided not to come? he wondered. No, she would have phoned.

He picked up his glass of bourbon on the rocks and drained it. When he started to fix another drink, he changed his mind and took the glass to the kitchen, where he accidentally dropped it in the sink. It shattered and he muttered a curse, wondering what was wrong with him. Deep down, though, he knew: he was losing control of his emotions, and that scared the hell out of him.

"You've kept a pretty tight rein on them up to now, so what's your problem?" he murmured as he dumped the broken glass into the trash.

The problem, he answered himself grimly, was Ivy. Where she was concerned, he could see his control slipping—no—shooting away. He could hardly keep his mind on his job anymore, and already he'd done the unthinkable. He had held back information on a criminal investigation, just because she had asked him to. And it was eating away at him. He couldn't break free of the guilty feeling that more people might be taken in by the swindlers while he procrastinated.

He'd spent last night tossing and turning, trying to rationalize the promise he'd made to Ivy to wait until Scott returned before alerting headquarters. If only he could convince himself that she was merely using him to protect her brother...but he couldn't believe that. She was just terrified for Scott. Chris couldn't blame her for that. After all, Scott was family.

"Family," he mumbled, checking his watch for the tenth time. That was all Ivy thought about. He wondered why he was so ambivalent about getting too used to feeling like a part of her family. It was a little late to worry about that, he realized, knowing that he was already more than slightly interested in what was going on in Kim's life. He liked Randy, too, and Walt. But he loved Ivy. That was what really unnerved him. What would she demand of him if she returned his love? And why was it so damn important to him that she did?

After tonight, though, he'd calm down and stop being so tormented by thoughts of her. All he was going through, he told himself, was the peak of emotional strain. They'd make love, and he'd feel more in charge of his emotions again. There was nothing wrong in looking at the situation that coolly. It wasn't as though he was taking advantage of her. She was the one who had insisted there be no commitment between them.

"Come on, man!" Chris ordered. "Get your act together. No one's been able to take control of your life from you, and neither will Ivy."

More confident now that he'd given himself a locker-room pep talk, Chris threw back his shoulders and stood tall, sensing a new strength hardening his leg muscles. But the minute he heard the sound of the buzzer, his knees buckled. Dashing to the door, he opened it wide.

Ivy stood there, looking gorgeous in a silky beige dress, her auburn hair shimmering in the hallway light, her eyes glistening like stars.

"I thought you'd never get here," he said, his breath ragged. He stepped aside and followed her with intense eyes as she entered.

"I'm sorry I'm late," Ivy said. "Kim changed outfits a half dozen times before Randy finally said he was leaving without her if she didn't hurry."

Chris closed the door, leaned back against it and extended his arms.

Ivy went to him happily. For anxious minutes she had remained downstairs, wondering if she was doing the right thing. Now that she felt his arms move around her and draw her close, she knew she was.

The moment his lips covered hers, her arms circled his shoulders, and she held to him as though to life itself. Everything that was hers to give, she wanted to offer him; she would take everything he would offer her. When Chris rested his head alongside hers, she heard his deep sigh and felt his chest rise and fall.

"I can't believe you're actually here," he admitted in a strained voice.

"I am," she assured him.

Releasing her reluctantly, he took hold of her hand and led her into the living room. "Would you like a drink?"

"No, thanks." After an uneasy silence, she said, "I have to be back before Kim gets home."

Chris couldn't understand why he felt so awkward. He didn't want this time with Ivy to be rushed. He wanted their lovemaking to come slow and easy, whatever it cost him to wait. He wanted her to be relaxed, to enjoy every minute of it—to want more lovemaking from him. But, he realized, she was rushing him.

Silently he led her into the bedroom. The drapes were drawn. Moonlight rayed over the trees in the park across the street and spilled into the small room. Ivy saw that he had pulled down the spread and had carefully angled back the white sheet on one side of the bed.

Then Chris was behind her, lowering the zipper on her dress, leaving gentle kisses on her skin as the material parted. The garment slipped down to the carpet below, and he unhooked her lacy bra. It fell beside her dress. Ivy shuddered when she felt his lips at the side of her neck and his hands slip under the swell of her breasts. Slowly and gently he lifted the soft mounds, running his thumbs over her puckered nipples, all the while leaving a trail of warm kisses across her shoulder.

It had been too long since Ivy had felt the intimate touches of a man. She had tried to minimize her natural need for love and affection by giving all the love she had to caring for her family. But now as Chris caressed her, her repressed longings and desires broke free.

Turning in his arms, she loosened the buttons on his shirt, parted it and pressed herself against him. The warmth of his body seared her own, and she flung her arms around his neck, kissing him with a passion that took him by surprise.

"Oh, Ivy," he murmured against her lips, then swooped her up in his arms and gently laid her on the bed. His excitement mounted as he slipped off the remainder of her clothes, and he had to conquer his urgent need to immediately satisfy the hunger he felt for her. Moments later his clothes lay on the carpet, and he sat on the bed, gazing down at her, filling his eyes with the lovely curves and valleys of her slender feminine form.

Ivy closed her eyes, savoring the tantalizing tingling of her skin as his hand moved slowly upward over her thigh and onto her hip. Her body was alive, anticipating each gentle stroke of his searching, warm hand. Every part of her trembled at his touches, his caresses, his kisses. She could feel the soft hairs on his thigh brushing hers. When his lips began to follow the trail of his hand's slow explorations, she shuddered and murmured his name.

"You're so beautiful, love," he whispered as he ran his fingers through her silky hair, which waved over the pillow. Leaning to her, he nuzzled the side of her neck, then brushed his lips across her cheek before kissing her softly once, twice, then again.

She felt the weight of Chris's leg as it moved over hers; her thighs burned from the heat of his throbbing erection. Giving herself totally to the wonder of his deepening kiss, she slid one hand over his shoulder and eased the other downward between them.

Chris moaned when she grasped him and began to stroke him slowly. "Love, take it easy," he pleaded, then raised himself onto his arm and gazed down at her, marveling at how beautiful she appeared in the moonlight. "I've imagined being with you like this so many times, but I never dreamed it would be as wonderful as this."

His eyes lowered to her small, firm breasts, and he brushed his fingers over one peak, then the other before lowering his head to suckle with his lips and tongue.

Writhing beneath him, savoring his sweet caresses, she clasped her hands behind his neck when he began to slowly massage the silken hairs between her thighs. Deep within she felt like a tightly coiled spring ready to snap. She wanted to give in to the involuntary tremors that raced through her, but she held back; the mounting tension she felt was too exquisitely exciting.

Slowly she raked her fingertips over the smooth skin of Chris's muscular back, and she arched upward to meet the increasing pressure of his palm. Inside her body, she felt an emptiness, a tingling hollow feeling that craved to be filled. The sensation became a torment, and she whispered, "Now, Chris, please . . . now."

He moved over her and slipped between her legs. "Take me into you, love," he requested, his voice husky and low.

Through half-closed eyes, she saw him poised over her, his face flushed, his eyes burning with need. As she guided him into her warm moistness, she saw his eyes close and his anxious expression transmute to sheer delight. She gasped when he took control and eased deeper within. Closing her eyes, she stretched out her arms and wadded the bed sheet in her clenched fists.

"Ohh!" she moaned, feeling his pulsating flesh penetrate deeper and deeper. She fought to catch her breath as her senses reeled. Finally the lovely pressure ceased, and she felt his arms encircle her. But then, something was brushing the tip of her nose.

"They say the Eskimos like this."

"What?" Ivy asked, somewhat disoriented.

Chris drew his head up. "Rubbing noses," he answered, grinning.

Opening her eyes, she smiled up at him and drew her arms around him. "It's not your nose that I'm thinking of at the moment," she admitted.

"Umm, we do go together nicely," Chris said, twitching inside her and relishing the exquisite feel of being one with her. But when he felt her muscles tighten around his sensitive erection, he advised, "Keep that up and it'll be rockets'-red-glare time."

Threading her fingers through the wavy hair that draped over his forehead, she asked, "What's the matter? Are you getting low on breath?"

"Uh-uh . . . high on hormones."

Ivy felt her own hormone level surge, and she wrapped her legs around his warm thighs and arched up to meet his tantalizing extended thrusts. "Chris," she murmured, "I don't think I can...hold back...much longer."

"Don't hold back. Let it come, love. I'll be right with you." He covered her lips with his own and quickened his thrusts.

Ivy dug her fingers into his back muscles, his frantic kiss stifling her sighs and moans as every nerve end in her body began to quiver. Her sensations reached a feverish pitch, and she clutched him desperately, sighing his name again and again. Sweet release came in wave after wave, fragmenting her sense of time and place. Her only reality was the exquisite joy of being one with the man she held in her arms.

Breathless moments later, still secured in Chris's embrace, Ivy could feel her heart pounding in her chest, the rapid thudding of his meeting the pace of hers. She held him, never wanting to be farther from him than she was at this moment. Nothing mattered to her, other than their intimate union. Never had she felt so utterly feminine, so desired, so loved.

Rolling onto his side, Chris let his head fall back on the pillow and rested a hand over his forehead. "Sweet heaven," he exclaimed, "I thought I was never going to stop." He tilted his face toward hers and smiled. "You are one hell of a woman." Drawing her to him, he placed her head on his heated chest and began stroking her hair. "God, I love holding you like this, and I love your holding me. Don't ever stop."

Ivy closed her eyes and snuggled closer. "I won't," she whispered, her thoughts totally on the comforting warmth she felt in his arms. Seconds later, though, she caught a whiff of something sweet. Opening her eyes, she raised her head slightly and asked, "What kind of cologne are you wearing? It smells like roses."

Chris extended his arm and switched on the lamp by the bed. Ivy followed his movement, and next to the lamp she saw a small vase of yellow roses. Removing one, Chris slipped it between her breasts and drew her down again, encasing her in his arms. "I wanted this evening to be special," he said softly.

Inhaling the flower's sweet perfume, Ivy whispered, "It has been special, Chris, so very special."

After chuckling he said, "I'm tempted to ask you to spend an entire night with me, but I don't know if my heart could stand it."

With her fingers, Ivy traced an imaginary circle through the soft hairs on his chest, then slid her arm around his waist. "There's nothing wrong with your heart...or anything else about you," she said languidly.

"So you approve?"

"Mmm, yes," she admitted.

"Can you?" he asked quietly.

"Can I what?"

"Work it out so you can stay over some night."

Ivy thought long and hard before responding. "I can't, Chris."

"Why not?"

Slowly she raised herself and rested her arms on his chest. The rose slipped from between her breasts. She retrieved it and waved it under his nostrils. "I can't very well lecture Kim on being careful with Randy if I don't set some kind of example myself. Actions do speak louder than words."

"Kim is only fifteen. You're an adult."

"Ever try using that kind of reasoning with a teenager? She's my daughter, and my responsibility." Sitting, Ivy drew up her knees and covered them with the sheet, then she looked down at Chris. "I have to be realistic about my responsibility to Kim and to my father. I don't want either of them believing that I'm sleeping around."

Propping himself up on his arms, Chris placed the rose back in the vase and said, "I hardly think spending one night with me would qualify as sleeping around. Just what do you suppose Walt is doing with Trudy?"

"That's different," she said quietly. "He's thinking about marrying her." The instant Ivy heard her own voice, she regretted having said that. She looked over at the travel alarm clock on the night table. "I've got to leave if I'm going to be home before Kim."

She started to get up, but Chris took hold of her wrist. "Neither Kim nor your father is going to know what we're doing, unless you tell them," he pointed out. "Besides, you just got here."

Becoming anxious, but not knowing why, she insisted, "I have to get home."

Chris leaned back against the headboard, stared at her, then let go of her wrist. "Did I miss something again? A few minutes ago we were acting like lovers, and now you can't wait to get out of here. Why the sudden change, Ivy?"

Running her fingers through her hair, she asked herself the same question. She tried to blame it on his attitude toward Kim and her father, but she had to dismiss that as the reason. The truth was that she felt guilty being with him like this.

While she had been pacing downstairs earlier, she had questioned her sanity. She had told herself she loved Chris, but she had also asked herself if she needed to feel loved so badly that she would accept a temporary affair. She had become more confused when she reminded herself that Chris could be instrumental in putting her brother in prison for a long time. Despite her strong misgivings, though, her strong feelings for Chris had made her enter the building.

"Why the change?" Chris asked again.

Summoning all of her emotional strength, Ivy rested her arms on her knees and replied quietly, "Because I realize I shouldn't have come here tonight."

"Oh? Why did you?"

She faced him. "It's difficult for me to say no to you, Chris."

"Then why make things difficult for yourself? I told you I was in love with you, and you said you cared for me. We agreed to see where our relationship took us."

Ivy's gaze drifted over the bed. "This is where it did."

"And now you're sorry?" he asked quietly.

"No, I'm not sorry," she confessed.

Chris extended his arm and slowly ran his fingers over her back. "Let's promise we'll never be sorry, no matter what happens."

No matter what happens, Ivy repeated silently, assuming that Chris was thinking of Scott, just as she was. Could she promise never to regret this evening with Chris? she wondered. Her heart told her she could, but her reason tormented her with thoughts of being disloyal to her brother and betraying him.

Yet the wonderful feel of Chris's hand stroking her and the solace she had experienced in being so intimately close to him gave her the strength to once again block out thoughts of everyone but him. She would dwell only in the moment, she determined, and would think only of him.

Lowering herself next to Chris, Ivy moved an arm over him and began stroking his side. "I don't know what's wrong with me," she said softly. "So much has been happening lately, I guess I'm losing my perspective on what's important and what's not."

"You worry too much about Kim," he said, believing Ivy was relaxed once more. Thinking of Kim, Chris decided not to postpone the talk he'd promised her he would have with Ivy. After a deep breath, he said, "When Kim and I were barbecuing at the beach today, I was able to clarify a little confusion she had about her going steady with Randy."

"What confusion?" Ivy asked, her eyes closed, her concentration on the slow rise and fall of Chris's warm chest under her cheek.

"You know the gold chain that he gave her?"

"Uh-huh."

"Kim thought it was—" He modified his words. "Kim and Randy think of the chain as an . . . engagement present."

Chris felt Ivy lurch and he tightened his arm around her.

"Engagement present?" she repeated and pulled loose from his hold.

Smiling, Chris said, "Sweet, isn't it?"

"Sweet? Are you crazy?" She stared down at him. "Why did Kim confide in you and not in me?"

"She was afraid you might not like the idea."

"Well, she's right about that! Just wait until she gets home tonight."

"Wait a minute, now," he said quickly. "Don't get so upset. I told Kim that you'd probably be thrilled to hear it."

"You told her what?"

"Randy's a great guy. What more could you want for Kim?"

"Some time to grow up, for one thing. Just what possessed you to do my thinking for me?"

"Whoa, now. I care about Kim. Is it so bad that I take an interest in her problems?"

"I resent your behaving as though you were her father. Kim is my daughter, not yours."

Chris realized that Ivy was pushing him away again. He didn't like it one bit. Rather abruptly, he informed her, "She's not your daughter. She was your husband's."

His words stung, deep and painfully. Glaring at him, she said, "I wouldn't expect you to understand a loving family relationship. How could you? You don't even like your own family."

"How the hell did my family get involved in this discussion? We were talking about Kim and Randy. For your information, I care about those kids."

"Only because it's convenient for you at the moment, just as I am."

A ponderous silence filled the air as Chris's eyes narrowed and his expression turned grim. "You're right," he said darkly. "I should mind my own business." Tossing back the sheet, he jumped up from the bed.

As he strode to the closet and jerked a short robe from a hanger, Ivy realized that she had done it again; she had turned on Chris and had hurt him because of her own confused feelings. With effort she slipped out of the bed and began dressing.

"I'll fix us some coffee," Chris said in a monotone and headed for the kitchen.

Ivy went to the living room to locate her purse, then to the bathroom to straighten her hair. As she ran her small brush through it, she could feel tears stinging her eyelids. Looking into the mirror, she asked silently, *What the hell is wrong with you? Chris was just trying to be helpful, and you cut him down.*

In her heart Ivy knew the reason for her reaction. She had fallen hopelessly in love with Chris, but, knowing that things could never work out for them, she was using every possible circumstance that came along to build barriers between them. Each time she was with him, the previous barrier she had erected would collapse. So now she had just built another in the last one's place. And she hated herself for doing it.

You knew what you were getting into with Chris, she told herself as she jerked the brush through her hair. *Now you're behaving like a wounded doe. Face it, you agreed to settle for an affair, and that's all that it is. You take it or you leave it.*

She tossed the brush back into her purse, wiped her eyes and returned to the living room, where she saw Chris sitting on the easy chair. He had placed her coffee cup on the table in front of the sofa.

"It's instant. I hope that's all right," he said, his tone distant, colorless.

"Fine." She sat down and took a sip, noting that Chris didn't touch his coffee. After putting down her cup, she began, "I'm sorry if I was a bit edgy before, but—"

"You don't have to apologize for speaking your mind," he interrupted. "I'm not going to apologize for speaking mine. Tomorrow I'm going to file a report on what you told me about Scott's manipulating the files at Continental."

Ivy felt an icy chill tear down her spine. "But you said you'd wait until he got back from vacation."

"I know, and I was wrong telling you I would."

Glancing at her lap, she saw that she was digging one thumbnail into the palm of her other hand. Not looking up, she asked, "Are you doing it because this evening hasn't turned out the way you expected?"

"No, but I want to point out that you're making me crazy. One minute you have me feeling like I'm on top of the world, and in the next you make me feel like I should crawl under a rock." Exasperated, he asked, "What is it you want from me!"

Your love, Ivy said to herself, not able to admit it to him, knowing she shouldn't even admit it to herself.

When she seemed to ignore his question, Chris said tightly, "The way this evening has turned out has nothing to do with my reporting what you told me. I'm doing it because I have to. I spent a miserable night mulling it over. I just can't withhold the information any longer."

"I see," she said quietly, not at all certain that she actually did. "It's a matter of honor with you, I suppose."

"It's a matter of what's right and what's wrong, not to mention what's legal and what's not. Our keeping quiet about this could make both of us an accessory after the fact."

Her eyes shot up. "What fact? We don't even know if Scott has committed a crime."

"If you honestly believe he hasn't done anything wrong, why shouldn't I file my report?"

Ivy grabbed her purse and jumped up. "File your report, Chris. Maybe there'll be some kind of an award in it for you, and you'll make it to Washington ahead of schedule.''

Chris sat immobile, staring straight ahead as he heard the door slam behind her. "Time to get back under the damn rock," he muttered.

SUNDAY AFTERNOON, Ivy tried to keep herself busy by working in the garden. Before Randy had picked up Kim to go roller skating, Ivy had had a long talk with her, insisting that she return Randy's gold chain to him. She hated herself when Kim began to cry, but Ivy laid down the law as firmly as she could, explaining why becoming engaged was out of the question for the fifteen-year-old.

Again, Walt was of no help. When she tried to discuss Kim's situation with him, her father had left the house quickly, explaining that he was taking Trudy on the luncheon cruise that left from Haulover Marina.

Alone in the garden now, planting a new bed of purple salvia, Ivy felt miserable as her thoughts returned to the previous evening.

She had been a wreck when she left Chris's apartment, and now in the bright light of day she berated herself for having acted so erratically. "You've got no one to blame but yourself," she mumbled, pulling a plant from its pot with her gloved hands and centering it in the hole she had dug with a trowel.

Adding a mixture of dirt and humus around the plant, she began firming it down, wondering what would happen to Scott after Chris filed his report. She was pondering that problem when she heard Carol call her name.

Ivy turned toward her neighbor's yard. Carol and her mother were on the other side of the viburnum hedge that separated their property. Smiling, she waved, thinking how much Louise Wilson reminded her of Lena Horne.

"Hi, Mrs. Wilson," Ivy called cheerfully, then she stood, removed her work gloves and went to the hedge.

"Your garden looks beautiful, Mrs. Austin," Louise remarked in her smooth, rich voice.

Before her mother could point out the contrast between Ivy's multiflowered garden and her own sparsely landscaped lawn, Carol said, "Ivy, if you've got a minute, my mother would like to speak with you."

"Certainly." Ivy guessed that it had something to do with the woman's being on the board of the Miami Opera Guild. She had talked Ivy and Carol into buying season tickets to last year's performances. "Bring your mother over. I just made some limeade."

"She'd like to talk with you alone," Carol said, her tone more controlled than usual.

Ivy deduced it wouldn't be about opera tickets. "Fine," she said.

Standing behind her mother, Carol mouthed the words *Randy and Kim*.

Smiling uncertainly, Ivy said, "I'll take a minute to wash my hands and meet you on the deck, Mrs. Wilson. It's so beautiful out, we can talk there."

Minutes later, Ivy came onto the deck from the house, carrying a tray with a carafe and two glasses. After placing it on the round redwood table where Louise Wilson was sitting, she poured the limeade. "It seems more like April than November, doesn't it?"

"It certainly does. My husband has spring fever."

Your son does, too, Ivy thought, wondering if she should broach the subject first. She didn't have to.

"Mrs. Austin," Louise said, accepting the white linen napkin and glass that Ivy handed her, "I think we need to talk about my son and your stepdaughter. They've been seeing quite a bit of each other, and frankly it has me concerned.''

Ivy sat down on the other side of the table and crossed her legs. ''It's had me concerned, also, Mrs. Wilson.''

''May I call you Ivy?''

''Of course. Randy is a fine boy, and he's helping Kim make some difficult adjustments.''

''I know. Carol told me about your stepdaughter's problems at school.''

''Louise, I think of Kim as my daughter.''

''Oh, yes . . . of course. Well, as Randy's mother, his future is my first concern.''

''That's understandable. Kim's future is foremost in my mind.''

''My son has his heart set on becoming an officer in the air force, just as his father was. Jonathan was a helicopter pilot in Vietnam, you know.''

''No, I didn't,'' Ivy said, feeling a tenseness in her facial muscles. She had a premonition that the woman was going to say that her son and Kim were no longer to see each other. After the talk Ivy had had with Kim this morning, the idea seemed attractive at first thought, but she knew how devastating it would be for Kim. Ivy certainly didn't want her falling back into her old pattern of keeping to herself.

Ivy drew a deep breath and said, ''Surely you don't believe that Randy's dating Kim is going to change his plans.''

''They are both very young, especially Kim. Randy told us she was only fifteen.''

''Yes, she is.'' Recalling her talk with Carol, Ivy wanted to get one thing out in the open immediately. ''Louise,'' she asked evenly, ''are you at all bothered that Kim is an Amerasian?''

For tense moments, the woman was silent, her blue-gray eyes fixed on the glass she held. Then she looked up at Ivy, her expression suggesting both worry and pain. "Ivy, a black man has problems enough finding approval in our society. It's something my son is going to have to deal with daily in one way or another. Jonathan and I don't want his life to be any more difficult than it has to be."

"Louise, the kids are just dating each other. In a few months Randy will leave, and that will be the end of it."

"I know my son. He has more on his mind than seeing Kim just until June. He's quite taken with her, and I hope to God he doesn't find himself in a position where he has to marry her."

Ivy felt her pulse throbbing at her temples. She had recently read that on the average, by the time American boys were eighteen, they'd had sex with five girls, and that more than a million teenage girls became pregnant each year. These facts had precipitated the talk she'd had with Kim about the dangers of early sexual involvement. Having done so, Ivy had put the matter to rest, but now Randy's mother brought her fear to life once more. Certainly, she realized, she couldn't blame Randy's mother for being as concerned as she was at the moment.

Composing herself, Ivy said, "I've talked to Kim about abstinence, Louise, and she's fully aware of the consequences of having a sexual relationship at her age. If it helps any, I truly can't see her becoming involved in one. Have you and your husband spoken to Randy about his responsibilities?"

"We've discussed the matter with him several times during the past few years . . . and recently, when he told us about dating your stepdaughter."

Ivy watched Randy's mother sip from the glass of limeade. Seeing that the woman's fingers were shaking confirmed that the conversation they were having was difficult for both of them. When Louise set the glass down, Ivy asked, "Do you think they should stop seeing each other?"

"Randy is too old to accept that from his father or me. However, since your stepdaughter is so young, we thought perhaps you would have control over whom she dated. I should think you'd feel better if she went out with boys closer to her own age."

"I would," Ivy said honestly, "but Kim is shy, and she's had difficulties in making friends at school. Randy is making a big difference in her life. Because of him she's beginning to be accepted by the other kids."

"I see." Louise Wilson thought seriously about that, then asked, "Aren't there any Oriental boys in her classes?"

Ivy tensed. "Why do you ask?"

"I would think your stepdaughter would be happier with someone of her own kind, an Asian boy, perhaps."

Sitting erect, Ivy said as calmly as she could, "Louise, Kim's mother was an Asian, but if you remember, her father was a white American."

"If your husband were still alive, do you think he'd be pleased to know his half-white daughter was involved with a young black man?"

"With a young man as fine as Randy, Bill would have been delighted." Ivy felt her scalp tighten. "I'd like to think you felt the same way about Kim."

Tensing, Louise said, "I repeat, my son is my only concern. I don't want to see him throwing away what could be a bright future. Randy is my flesh and blood, and if you think of Kim as being your *daughter*, you might want to give some consideration to her future, as well."

"Louise," Ivy suggested with all the control she could muster, "let's both calm down. You're upset and I'm upset. Our being so won't help Kim or Randy. I wish she were dating boys her own age, and you wish your son were seeing someone else. But that's not the case, and I don't believe that forbidding them to see each other is realistic. For one thing, they both attend the same school, and I'm sure that neither one of us is going to follow them around after school. Whether we like it or not, they have become friends, and we're going to have to live with that."

"I guess there's nothing more I can say." Louise stood and looked down at Ivy. In a conciliatory tone, she said, "I hope you understand why I felt it was necessary to discuss this with you. It's not easy being a parent nowadays, is it?"

"No, Louise, it's more difficult than I ever thought it would be."

After the woman returned to Carol's house, Ivy sat on the deck, again wishing that she didn't have to cope with situations like this alone. As she ran her fingers over the limeade glass, she wished that she could call Chris and ask him to advise her.

But she couldn't, and that made her even more depressed.

CHAPTER THIRTEEN

IVY ASKED DOLORES to hold her calls, then she phoned Leon, asking if he had yet heard from Scott.

"Not a word. What's wrong? You sound upset."

"I'm worried about him."

"Why? He's old enough to take care of himself."

"That's what I keep thinking, but I'm afraid he might be in trouble."

"What kind of trouble? Does it have anything to do with our being hassled by the Postal Inspection Service?"

Ivy didn't respond. Friend or not, she was afraid that if she told him that Scott had doctored the files, Leon would most likely feel he had to report it.

"Does it have anything to do with the company's being investigated?" he asked again.

"I'm not sure, but Scott lied to me about why he went to Chicago. He said he was going to see Emily, but I found out that she moved to California a year ago."

"Maybe he never came here," Leon suggested.

"I know he did. He checked into the Palmer House a week ago last Wednesday, but he left the next day."

"Did you tell the postal inspectors that?"

"I didn't have to. They know Scott took a plane to Chicago."

"They're following him?"

"Leon, they're following all of us down here in Miami."

"What the hell do they expect to find out?"

"I don't know. It's got something to do with the swindling racket they're trying to track down."

Leon chuckled. "What could Scott possibly have to do with that?"

Ivy decided she had said too much already. "Nothing as far as I know. Please, if he contacts you, tell him to phone me immediately."

"I will, and you keep me advised on what the postal inspectors are up to."

Minutes after she had concluded her conversation with Leon, Bob came into her office.

"How's it going?" he asked, smiling.

"Fine. I'm going over the results of our alumni survey. I'll have everything ready for the communications division this afternoon. They should get the disk to the home office this week."

"Good. I just had a visit from a postal inspector, a Chris Laval."

Chris! Ivy started at hearing his name. "What did he want?"

"He asked again if our files would be open to him. I told him no, not without a court order. I think he may try to get it, but I doubt that he'll find a judge who'll give him one."

"What if he does get a court order?"

"Then we comply. Our files are in good shape. I just don't want to make it too easy for anyone to come in off the street and pore over our confidential information. How did your session with that lady inspector go?"

"Ellen Roth," Ivy reminded him. "She asked a lot of questions, but I followed the guidelines you gave me."

"Did she say anything about why they were so interested in our files?"

"No," Ivy answered honestly. The woman hadn't.

"She didn't, huh? Well, if the postal inspectors are involved, it must have something to do with mail or wire fraud. Chris Laval was real closemouthed, too, but I guess they have to be careful about making any charges until they've got evidence to back them up."

"What kind of evidence?" Ivy asked, feeling her pulse quicken.

"Like I said, they must be working on some kind of mail fraud case. What they don't seem to realize, though, is that we just compile and sell the mailing lists. If one of our buyers is using them to swindle people, it's not our problem. That would be like blaming General Motors for every holdup in which a car was involved."

Mentally, Ivy leaped at the idea that it was a buyer, and not someone in the company, who was involved in the swindles that Chris had told her about. That would mean that Scott was innocent. But immediately she thought of the names Scott had deleted from the files, and her moment of hope vanished. If only she could talk with Scott and find out what was going on, she thought. And what had happened to him in Chicago? Not knowing was driving her crazy. She had to do something!

"Well," Bob said, "if any of the inspectors should phone you and want any more information, just transfer the call to me."

"I will," she said, her mind working rapidly. "Bob," she called as he turned to leave, "I need a few days off. Could I have the rest of the week? It's important. A family matter has come up."

"Okay. With Thursday being Thanksgiving, this will be a short week, anyway."

"Everything's in good shape in my department," Ivy assured him. "If you need anything, Dolores can handle it."

"Is anything wrong with Kim or your father?"

"No, it's just something that's going to take a few days for me to work out."

"Fine. I'll see you next Monday, then. Have a good turkey day."

As Bob walked through Ivy's secretary's office, he heard Dolores speaking to her boss on the phone.

"Chris Laval on line three."

Bob paused, glanced back at Ivy's closed door, then returned to his office.

HURRYING ACROSS Biscayne Boulevard, Ivy saw Chris waiting for her in the park.

"Thanks for meeting me," he said when she approached him. He took her arm and started walking toward the yacht basin. Thinking of the way she had stormed out of his apartment on Saturday, he asked, "How was your Sunday?"

"Busy, as usual," she said briskly. "I have a household to run, remember? How was yours?"

"I spent it at headquarters."

Feeling a twinge in the pit of her stomach, she asked, "Did you file your report?"

"No, but I told Matt about what Scott did." He felt her arm stiffen.

"Did he order you to arrest me, or what?" she asked curtly.

"He was very appreciative that you volunteered the information. What we do need are the two printouts you have."

Ivy jerked her arm free. "I suppose you also told him that I switched the disks in Georgetown."

"I didn't, and I won't unless I have to."

Looking out over the bay toward Dodge Island, where the cruise ships docked, Ivy wished for the millionth time that she had never heard about the damn disks.

Quietly she asked Chris, "What will happen to Scott if I do give you the printouts?"

"That depends on his involvement. If he was manipulating a cover-up, we have to find out if he knew what he was doing, or if he was only following orders. It's who gave him the orders that we're interested in. That would lead us to the people on top, the ones we're after."

"Will Scott be arrested?"

"Unless he turns himself in, he will be, but if he cooperates and is wiling to testify, he may not have to serve time."

Ivy faced Chris. "Do you mean that?" she asked hopefully.

"I can't guarantee it without knowing what else he might have done, but this would be his first offense. If he only leaked company information, it's possible that with a good lawyer handling a plea-bargain session, he could get off with probation."

Ivy chewed her lower lip, then asked, "What if I don't give you the printouts?"

"You'll be faced with a search warrant." He saw her eyes narrow and guessed what she was thinking. "Ivy, if you destroy the printouts, you'll be guilty of impeding a criminal investigation."

"Please, Chris, can't you just wait a few more days? I'll find Scott in Chicago and—"

"What do you mean you'll find him in Chicago?"

"I'm going there tomorrow."

"That's crazy."

"Is it any crazier than my sitting down to Thanksgiving dinner, wondering if my brother is dead or alive?" In a calmer voice, she said, "If I can talk to Scott, I'm sure he'll turn himself in and answer any questions that you have. Just give me a few days to try and find him."

"Suppose you do find him and he won't cooperate?"

Ivy's expression was grim. "Then I'll give you the printouts."

Again, Chris felt his control slipping away. Ivy was the only person he'd come up against in his entire life who could make him do just about whatever she wanted him to do—and that was scary. "All right," he conceded uneasily. "I'll wait a few days, but what do we tell Carol about our not showing up for Thanksgiving dinner at her house?"

"We?"

"You don't think I'm letting you go to Chicago alone, do you? If you should find your brother, you can't be sure what kind of trouble you'll find along with him."

"But I—"

"Ivy," Chris said firmly, "whether you want me to or not, I care about you and what happens to you. I'm going with you to Chicago."

TUESDAY EVENING, as the taxi pulled away from the terminal at O'Hare Airport, Ivy drew the collar of her blue wool coat closer around her throat. She hadn't worn it in ages, but the change from the eighty-degree Florida weather to Chicago's twenty-nine made her happy that she had kept the warm garment.

She looked over at Chris, who was sitting beside her. "Now that we're here, I'm not sure where to start looking for Scott."

"When we get to the Palmer House, I'll talk to the manager, and in the morning I'll take his picture to headquarters. They'll make routine checks of the hospitals and—" he almost said the morgues "—and hotels. Do you know the names of any of the people Scott knew when he lived here?"

"Just Emily Domsha, but she's in California now. And there's Leon Torell, the branch manager for Continental. I talked to him on the phone yesterday, but he still hadn't heard from Scott."

"Still?"

"I called him last week when I couldn't reach Scott at the Palmer House."

"Are Leon and your brother good friends?"

"He did me a favor by keeping an eye on Scott when he followed Emily back here."

Chris thought about that and made a mental note to see what the local inspectors had turned up in their check on Leon Torell.

As the taxi neared the city, Chris asked, "When you visited your in-laws here, did you get to see much of Chicago?"

"Not really. They lived in Winnetka. I do remember a lovely fountain all lit up in a park across from the Auditorium Theater. Bill's parents took us there one night for a concert."

"That's Buckingham Fountain in Grant Park. The gardens are beautiful in the spring. I'm sorry we're not here under more pleasant circumstances. I'd like to show you around the city."

"How long did you work here, Chris?"

"A little more than two years. Chicago's a great little town. You can go to a different restaurant every night of the year, and it's got just as many clubs."

It started snowing just as the taxi pulled up in front of the Palmer House on East Monroe. After they checked in, Chris got Ivy settled at a table in Trader Vic's lounge and went to talk to the manager.

Sipping the rum and fruit juice Chris had recommended, Ivy rethought her feelings about him. He was certainly going out of his way to help her and her brother, but she doubted that Scott would appreciate that.

"Chris," she said softly, wondering just where their relationship stood now. When he'd checked them both into the same room, she had started to say something, but her silence had said enough, Ivy supposed. She didn't believe he had forgotten the upsetting words they'd had in his apartment; she certainly hadn't. Apparently, Chris wasn't a man to carry a grudge.

If only she could get her thinking straight, Ivy pondered. There was just too much going on, though. Kim was growing up before her very eyes, her father was about to make a new life for himself, and this business with Scott was driving her to despair.

She tried to remember even one of the jobs that her brother had said he had while in Chicago, but he'd been quite vague about them at the time. Maybe Leon would know, she thought, and decided to go to his office in the morning while Chris was at headquarters.

Something else was percolating in Ivy's brain, however. The more she thought about the downside of marketing research—the way the personal information they gathered could be misused—the more she determined it was time for her to change careers. Chances were she would lose her job, anyway, if the company learned that she had switched the disks at the home office.

Going back to school would be expensive, she knew, particularly with no salary coming in. Fortunately she and Bill had saved during the years, and his insurance money and the funds from the sale of their home would make returning to the university possible. Still, it was a big step to take.

By the time Kim finished high school and went on to college, though, Ivy was sure she'd be employed again. If her father and Trudy were to marry, she and Kim would move to an apartment nearer the University of Miami. That would simplify things for both of them.

Yes, there were so many things to think about and to plan for, and in an odd way she was thankful for that. It gave her less time to think about Chris.

But even as Ivy came to that conclusion, she knew it wasn't true. Chris was constantly on her mind. She had tried to put distance between them because she was torn between her feelings for him and her loyalty to her brother, but she hadn't been able to. What should she do now? she wondered.

Be thoroughly modern, she ordered silently. *For better or for worse, admit that you love Chris and enjoy whatever time you have together. You got over Bill's death, and you'll survive Chris's leaving, too.*

"Sure I will," she mumbled and reached for her glass.

"You will what?" Chris asked as he sat down across from her at the little table.

Ivy smiled weakly. "I'm talking to myself...again. I've been doing a lot of that lately."

"I do that sometimes. It helps."

"Did you learn anything from the manager?"

"Uh-uh. He showed me the card Scott filled out when he arrived. It indicated he left the next morning. The only forwarding address he left was his apartment in Miami."

"Do you think the postal inspectors here will be able to find him?"

"We've tracked down a lot of people in our day. It just takes patience and time."

Ivy sipped her drink again, then said, "When Scott returns to work Monday, I hope to God he has some reasonable explanation for what he did."

Chris wisely decided not to comment. Instead, he remarked, "You didn't eat much on the plane. Are you sure you aren't hungry?"

"I'm not. This is what I need right now." She lifted her almost empty glass. "I'm hoping it will help me sleep."

Chris signaled the waitress and ordered another drink for Ivy and the same for himself. He couldn't understand Ivy's blind loyalty to Scott. Couldn't she see that her brother had used her?

For Chris, family was an accident of nature, a group of individuals temporarily forced together by circumstance. He tried to imagine how he would react if he found out his brother had done what he was pretty sure Scott had. The only thing he could picture was telling his brother that he had made his bed and he would have to lie in it.

Yet as Chris examined Ivy's worried expression, he again perceived that he was missing something in life: the emotions and the caring that bound a close family together. Thinking about that, he felt an emptiness inside that he had never experienced before. It was as if he were suddenly totally alone in life, with little future, except for his work, of course.

Continuing to study Ivy, he knew that she was the cause of his disturbing thoughts. But then, there were a lot of things he hadn't thought about until he met her.

For one, he knew that he would feel incomplete without her. He thought about having children with her, to protect and raise to be every bit as wonderful and caring as she was. Yes, he had to admit, for the first time in his life he wanted to be part of a family, to experience whatever it was that made Ivy so committed to hers.

Family. The word brought his own family to mind again.

"You seem a million miles away, Chris," Ivy said softly.

He grinned. "I was just thinking about Claude, my brother. He became a father about two years ago, and I've never seen my niece."

The waitress placed their drinks on the table, and Chris lifted his glass. "Here's to little Debra."

"You'll probably see a lot of her after you transfer to Washington," Ivy suggested. "Is Bladensburg far from there?"

"Only a short drive."

Chris thought that maybe his timing was lousy, but he had to know where he stood with Ivy. When he had checked them into a single room, she hadn't objected, but it was possible that she was too preoccupied thinking about her brother to have taken note.

"Ivy," he asked, focusing his eyes on the fingers curved around his glass, "when this business with Scott is settled, where does that leave us?"

She hesitated, then said, "To be honest, I don't know. I guess I won't until I see what happens to him."

Looking over at her, he asked, "What about me?"

"What about you?"

He forced a wry chuckle. "You make me sound so incidental."

"I didn't mean to, Chris."

He glanced at the people at the next table. "Could we go to our room? This isn't the greatest place for a private conversation."

She nodded, and he led her from the lounge.

Once in their room, he asked, "Should I have something sent up?"

"Not for me," she answered, then sat down in one of the chairs by the wide window.

After hanging up his jacket and removing his tie, Chris sat in the chair opposite her and rolled back the sleeves of his shirt. Leaning forward, he said, "When I hand over Scott's picture to headquarters, they'll send it by fax to all our offices. Sooner or later he'll be picked up for questioning."

"And he'll have a reason for deleting those names from the files," she insisted.

"I hope so...for his sake, for yours *and* for mine. Also, I'm going to see Leon Torell when I finish at headquarters. You said that—"

"Please, Chris, let me talk to him first. He may remember some of the people my brother knew when he lived here in Chicago. I might be able to find Scott and talk to him before your people arrest him. Scott will cooperate. I know he will!"

"If he doesn't, is it over between us?"

Rising from the chair, Ivy began to pace nervously. As she neared Chris, he reached out and took hold of her hand. Looking up at her, he said quietly, "I love you. Doesn't that count for anything?"

Ivy felt a stinging sensation at her eyelids, and a heaviness filled her chest as she gazed down at him. For silent moments his pleading eyes held hers, then he gently drew her down onto his lap. Closing his arms around her, he rested her head on his shoulder and asked in hushed tones, "What am I going to do, love? You've turned my life upside down."

"Oh, Chris," she said softly, slipping her arms around his neck, "my life is topsy-turvy right now, too. I can't even think straight."

"Let me do the thinking for both of us now," he suggested, wanting to ease the worry that he knew was tormenting her.

Lifting her head from his shoulder, Ivy tried to smile. "Thank you, but I can't let you do that. I used to run to my father whenever I had a problem, then I went to Bill. But I've learned to meet difficulties head-on now. It's not always easy, but I like myself better for doing so. I wish I could tell you that no matter what happens, things won't change between us, but in all honesty... I can't."

Again she smiled; this time the smile was almost real. "Carol once gave me some good advice. She said that sometimes it's necessary to take things one day at a time. That's what I have to do now."

Chris slid an arm under Ivy's legs, and he raised himself to a standing position. "One day at a time it is," he repeated. "And one night at a time."

He carried her to the bed and laid her down gently. Soon their clothes were discarded, and Chris was lying beside her, holding her close.

"Ivy," he whispered, "this feels so wonderful, it has to be right for us."

Nestling against him, she placed her hand on the side of his face and turned it toward her. "Kiss me," she said softly.

Their lovemaking was slow and tender, their climax sweet and soulful. As Chris held the sleeping Ivy in his arms, he hoped that they would find her brother soon. But experience had taught him not to hope for too much.

AFTER THEY ATE breakfast together in their room, Chris left for headquarters, and Ivy headed for Leon's office in the Hancock Center on North Michigan Avenue.

As soon as his secretary informed him who was waiting to see him, Leon came charging out of his office. A wiry, dark-complexioned man with piercing eyes, he rushed to her, a smile on his face. "What are you doing in Chicago?"

"Am I interrupting anything?" Ivy asked.

"No, no. C'mon in." He turned to his svelte secretary. "Hold my calls, Rhona."

Inside Leon's plush office, Ivy glanced out the window of the high rise, seeing the morning sun sparkle on Lake Michigan. "You have a breathtaking view here," she remarked. "I envy you."

"Did you make the trip to check out the view from my office?" he asked with humor in his tone.

"I wish it were as simple as that," she said uneasily.

"How about some coffee?"

"No, thanks. Have you heard from Scott?"

Leon went to the credenza by the paneled wall, his steps over the plush carpet inaudible. While pouring himself a cup of coffee, he said, "Not a word."

Ivy sighed, then sank onto the brown leather chair next to his desk. Crossing her legs, she began to pump her foot. "I'm really worried about him this time, Leon."

"I don't understand what you're so uptight about. Scott's a fun-loving guy enjoying a vacation somewhere. So he came to Chicago. So what? Maybe he met another girl like Emily and followed her to Paducah or to Boise. What difference does it make? He'll show up for work when he's supposed to. I guarantee it."

He sat down behind his curved desk and leaned back in his executive swivel chair, focusing his eyes on Ivy, then narrowing them when she remained silent. "We go back a long way," he said smoothly. "If Scott's in some kind of trouble, I want to know. Maybe I can help."

Torn between her desperate need to locate her brother and a feeling that she shouldn't divulge anything to a Continental employee, Ivy thought for long, difficult moments before saying, "Scott may be in big trouble."

Leon leaned forward. "What kind of trouble?"

"With the company."

"Be more specific."

"I need you to promise you won't say a word about this conversation."

"You've got it. Now what's going on?"

Ivy's words tumbled out, leaving her with a mixed feeling of relief and heightened worry as she told Leon about switching the disks for Scott and her discovery that the names he had deleted from the company files were the same as the names of some people recently swindled in Denver.

Seeing Leon's face pale, she realized that he was as shocked as she had been.

"Damn!" he muttered, then got up and took slow steps to the window.

"It could just be a coincidence," she said, trying to alleviate his concern. "If I could find Scott, I'm sure he'd have an explanation."

Leon turned from the window. "You've got to get rid of the printouts the second you get home. And for God's sake, don't breathe a word about them to anyone."

"It's too late. The postal inspectors know."

"What! How the hell did they find out?"

Ivy looked down at her fingers, which were tugging at the straps of her purse. "I . . . I told one of them."

Groaning, Leon covered his eyes with a hand. After a few seconds he removed it and stared at Ivy. "You know that you've destroyed Scott's future with the company, and he'll probably be put away for a long time."

"Not if he gives himself up and agrees to cooperate. That's why I've got to find him. I thought maybe you could tell me the names of some of his friends here in Chicago. One of them might know where he is. Leon, I'm half out of my—"

"Wait, wait," he interrupted, raising a hand. "Give me a minute to think." After thumping a fist against his palm, he asked, "What did the postal inspectors say?"

"Chris said—"

"Chris?"

"Chris Laval. He's an inspector who works out of the Miami office."

"Has he seen the printouts?"

"No, I only told him about them."

"Has anybody else seen them?"

"No, why?"

Leon crossed the room, rested back on the edge of his desk and softened his voice. "Ivy, if the inspectors never see the printouts, they can't prove a thing against Scott in court. And if you deny anything this Chris Laval might say about the disks and the printouts, they've got no case. In fact, they wouldn't have anything to even take to court."

"But that would be lying, and if Scott was coerced or talked into helping someone get access to our files, that's got to be stopped. You know how easily he can be influenced. If somebody put him up to misusing our mailing lists, I'm going to find out *who*. I've got a moral obligation to do so."

"What about your obligation to your brother? Do you want to see his career *and* yours go down the drain? Do you want to be able to see him only during visiting hours? Think about it. And what about the company? What would the publicity do to the integrity we've all worked so hard to maintain? Continental's been too good to you, and to Scott, to hand it a deal like this."

Rising slowly, Ivy began to pace in silence, then she faced Leon. "I've thought about that until it's making me ill. Scott and I are just two people who are going to be hurt by whatever mess he's gotten himself into, but Chris said that hundreds of innocent people are being swindled out of their life savings. He said that if Scott cooperates with the authorities, he may not have to go to jail."

"This Chris has you pretty brainwashed, doesn't he?"

"I trust him, Leon. Look, all I want to find out now is if you remember anyone that Scott knew here in Chicago."

"You're not going to destroy the printouts, are you?"

Ivy shook her head slowly. "I can't, I just *can't*. If I'm unable to find Scott, I'm going to give the printouts to the postal inspectors."

For tense moments Leon stared at her with dark eyes, then he nodded and returned to the seat behind his desk. He picked up a pen and began to tap it against the phone. "Scott did have a good friend in Winnetka. What was his name? Dirk something...Boman, Broman...Bower. Dirk Bower."

He pulled a phone book from a wide drawer in his desk and began leafing through the pages. "Here it is." Using the tip of the pen, he punched the numerals and waited. "This is Leon Torell. I'd like to speak to Dirk Bower."

Ivy sat down again and listened attentively.

"Oh, he's not. When do you expect him? The O'Hare Airport? Do you know who he was meeting? Well, thank you, Mrs. Bower. I'll try to reach Dirk later."

Hanging up, Leon said, "That was Dirk's mother. He went to the airport to pick up a friend. She didn't know who, but it could be Scott. She expects both of them to be at the house in about an hour." Seeing the excitement in Ivy's eyes, he said, "I'd drive you up to Winnetka, but I've got important meetings all afternoon."

"I know where it is. My in-laws lived in Winnetka. It's just north of the city. I'll get a cab. Let me have Dirk Bower's address."

After Leon jotted it down and gave her directions, Ivy said, "Thanks a million," and turned to leave.

"Don't be in such a hurry. A taxi there and back would cost you a fortune. You can take my car. It's parked on the tenth floor."

"In this building?"

"We have parking from floors six through twelve." He reached into his trouser pocket. "Here's the key. It's a blue Porsche. I'll call down to the attendant, and he'll show you where it's parked."

Taking the key, Ivy kissed Leon on the cheek. "You don't know how much I appreciate what you're doing. It's just got to be Scott who Dirk Bower is meeting."

"Let's hope so, and be careful driving. The streets are icy."

"I will," she promised, flashing him a wide smile before she hurried from the room.

THE MOMENT IVY CLOSED the door, Leon punched the same phone number. "Dirk, it's me again. Yes, never mind what I said before. I'll explain later. Scott's sister is on her way there. She's driving my car. I didn't want a cab company having a record of leaving her at the house. Keep her there until I find out what we should do with her.''

After hanging up, he made two quick phone calls to Florida.

CHAPTER FOURTEEN

IVY HELD the steering wheel so tightly that her knuckles were white. Having to maneuver the car on the slippery roads didn't help her frazzled nerves any, but she would have driven through fire if it meant finally locating Scott.

As she passed through Evanston, it began to snow, and she groaned. "Wouldn't you know," she muttered and searched for the switch to turn on the windshield wipers. Leon had told her to follow Green Bay Road past Wilmette, that Winnetka would be only a few miles north.

She had mixed emotions about how to approach her brother when she saw him. Her first impulse would be to take hold of him and shake him until his teeth fell out, but she knew she would be too relieved to see him safe to do that. Most likely she would just hug the breath out of him.

Suddenly she felt elated, thinking that Chris would be proud of her having found Scott. She'd been right in talking to Leon before he did. Leon wouldn't have told Chris a thing.

Chris? She glanced at the clock on the dashboard. It was a little before noon. Most likely she and Scott would be back at the Palmer House before Chris even got there. He had said not to expect him to return until later in the afternoon.

But what if Dirk Bower wasn't meeting Scott at the airport? she thought, and her mood plummeted. *It has to be,* she insisted. *It just has to be!*

When she reached Winnetka, she pulled into a service station and asked for directions to the address Leon had given her.

"Be careful of the roads," the attendant warned. "That's in a pretty desolate area over by the lake."

Ivy didn't care if the house was in the boondocks; she'd locate it.

Following the attendant's instructions, she drove along an isolated road that paralleled Lake Michigan. The falling snow made it difficult to read the addresses on the few houses she passed, but she could tell from the numbers that she was headed in the right direction.

The road curved slightly, and she drove for several minutes without seeing another house. Then, just ahead on the right, she spotted what looked like an old mansion. Pulling up alongside the mailbox, she pushed the lever to roll down the window and checked the number.

"This is it," she said and examined the Victorian-style edifice. The snow had slackened, and she could see that the house was in need of repair and a good coat of paint.

Well, she thought as she hopped out of the car, *Scott didn't tell me about any millionaire friends he made in Chicago.*

She slipped the car keys into her coat pocket, put on her gloves and trudged through the calf-high snow and up the steps to the front door. Not seeing a buzzer, she took hold of the brass knocker on one of the double doors and tapped it several times. She waited impatiently and was about to knock again when the door opened.

"My name is—" Ivy began, but when she looked into the brutish face of the dark-haired man who loomed before her, she thought he looked familiar. But how could he? she wondered. Then her blood ran cold.

He was the mugger who had tried to steal her purse in Georgetown!

CHRIS SAT SLUMPED over a desk at postal inspection headquarters on West Van Buren Street. He was reviewing the latest complaints that had come in from elderly citizens who had been ripped off by con men selling a bogus catastrophic health care plan. When the office door opened, he looked up to see Carlos returning.

He had worked with Carlos Hernandez for two years, and they were good friends. Happily married with three children, Carlos had done his best to convince Chris to hold on to his marriage with Kendal. He always maintained that a man without a wife was like a meal without jalapeño peppers.

Running his fingers through his wavy black hair, Carlos said, "Your Scott Chandler hasn't been checked into a hospital or a morgue. I've had his picture sent by fax to all our offices, so now we wait."

"He's worth waiting for. Chandler's the closest thing we have to getting a lead on where the main base is for the floating swindling operation."

"If he's still alive," Carlos said, his dark eyes narrowing. "When a man just disappears the way Chandler has, it makes me wonder."

Chris had been wondering, too, but for Ivy's sake he hoped her brother was alive. Still, he could think of several other possible explanations for Scott's disappearance.

Leaning back in his chair, Chris said, "There could be a reason he seems to have disappeared. He might be a smurf for the operation."

"A money runner?"

"Yeah. Miami's working on a money laundering case now. One man funneled fifteen million dollars in deposits into more than 150 accounts at thirty Miami banks."

Carlos cocked his head. "How did cash deposits that large get by the IRS?"

"They weren't all cash. The larger deposits were cashier's checks issued by banks in the Cayman Islands. Chandler could be busy smuggling cash out of the country to an offshore bank. The money could be transferred to banks back here electronically, or he could be bringing back a mess of cashier's checks."

"And the IRS would be none the wiser," Carlos added. Seating himself in a chair, he grinned at Chris. "Why are you taking such an interest in this Chandler guy? We could have put a trace on him without your being here. And don't tell me you miss the ice and snow of the Windy City."

"His sister's here looking for him."

"Ah, so it's not all dedication. If I'm right she's a looker with million-dollar legs."

Smiling, Chris said, "You're right."

"Wait a minute. If she's his sister, she's the one who works at Continental, the lady that tipped you off about Chandler... Ivy Austin, isn't it?"

Chris's smile evaporated. "Right again."

"Hmm. That must put you between a rock and a hard place, unless she's got a beef with her brother."

"Uh-uh, she doesn't, and the squeeze gets tighter all the time. She's really close to him and would do just about anything to protect him."

"You serious about her?"

"I'd just as soon give up breathing as give her up."

"So if you show Chandler that crime doesn't pay, she shows you the door, huh?"

"I can hear the knob turning now." He glanced at his watch. "Gotta run, friend. I don't want Ivy worrying any more than she is already."

IVY WASN'T WORRIED; she was terrified. Locked in a room on the second floor of the old house, she had checked every nook and cranny for something to pry open the window that had been nailed shut.

She held her hand under a table lamp, the solitary light in the room, and checked her watch. It was almost six o'clock. Again she went to the window and peered out at the snow flurries falling in the darkness. Pressing her face against the cold glass she trained her eyes on the narrow ledge below the window. If there was some way she could get onto it, she thought she might be able to reach the sloping roof over the first floor, a few yards away.

"Then what?" she murmured. She hadn't passed another house within a good mile. The snow blocked her vision now. Earlier she had seen a small boat lying upside down on a pier. But, she thought, there was no way she was going to row out into Lake Michigan in the snow.

Looking down at the ledge again, Ivy didn't know what she was going to do *if* she could escape. She had to warn Chris, though. Leon had sent her into a trap, and he'd do the same to him. She was sure that Chris would go to Leon's office when she didn't turn up at the hotel. Again she attempted to force the window open, but it was no use. Her fingers ached from trying.

Ivy rested her forehead against the cold glass as she thought desperately. Suddenly she had an idea and placed her hand against the windowpane. It was thick, but maybe she could break it!

And the crash would bring the brute downstairs charging up, she told herself.

Ivy wondered what he was doing now. When he had pulled her inside the house, he'd had to drag her kicking through the living room and up the stairs. No one had helped him, so Ivy guessed he was alone in the house.

Going to the locked door, she strained her ears and listened. The sound she detected seemed to be that of sports fans going wild. She'd heard that yelling often enough at home, and she imagined the man downstairs was watching a game on TV.

As quietly as she could, she struggled and dragged an empty dresser in front of the door and piled a chair on top of it. Then she scanned the room and pulled the blanket from the bed. Putting her scarf back on, she closed the top button on her coat, then unplugged the lamp.

She'd have to be quick, she told herself. Her chances of escaping were almost nil, but she had to try, not just for her own sake, but for Chris's.

A silent prayer on her lips, she tilted her head back, closed her eyes and raised the lamp. Using all her strength, she swung the metal base against the window.

With an earsplitting crash, the glass shattered. Her heart pounding, Ivy used the lamp to punch away the sharp edges. Sliver after sliver of sharp glass spewed onto the snow two floors below.

She heard a wild thumping behind her. She glanced back at the door and gasped when she saw it was vibrating as her captor attempted to break in. Terrified, she tossed the blanket over the windowsill, the man's pounding and cursing rioting in her ears.

"Please, God," she cried and lifted herself onto the sill. In one swift movement, she swung her legs up and jerked her body around, holding tightly to the sill as she sought desperately for solid footing on the snow-covered ledge.

Bringing herself to a standing position, she hugged the side of the house. The icy wind stung her face; the snow almost blinded her. She moved one foot, then the other, inching her way along the narrow ledge. Her hands and cheeks were freezing, but she forced herself on. Shivering from the cold and raw fear, she quickened her precarious steps toward the sloping roof, now only a few feet away.

A sickening crash came from inside the room. The man had broken in! Ivy glanced down at the snow on the ground two floors below, then forced her feet to move faster. She was almost at the slanting roof.

"You bitch!"

Ivy jerked her head back toward the window. He had one leg over the sill, and was coming after her.

"I'll break your damn head when I get hold of you!" he yelled.

Her heart pounding so that her chest ached, Ivy looked down. She was above the sloping roof. She crouched on the ledge, planning to lower herself to the roof below. A powerful gust of wind whipped along the side of the house.

She felt herself falling backward!

Ivy screamed and tried to grasp the ledge, but her fingers slipped.

Down she plummeted.

She groaned as her back hit the roof. Like a bobsledder, she slid down and down. She hit the snowdrift at the side of the house with a muffled thud, her breath momentarily knocked from her lungs.

Her legs were wet and numb, but she struggled to her feet, gaining strength from her terrible fear of the wild man cursing at her from above.

Instinctively she scurried through the deep snow as fast as she could toward the only building in sight, a wide, dilapidated garage at the end of the driveway.

Halfway there, she heard another thud and glanced back. Her captor was sliding down the roof.

At last she reached the side door to the garage. It was stuck. Throwing all her weight against the door, she forced it open, lunged inside and slammed it shut behind her.

With a swift swat of her hand, she slapped the dead bolt in place. Her breathing deep and painful, she peered into the darkness around her. There was one automobile parked in the three-car garage. She ran around the car. At the far end she could make out a long, high pile of firewood near a workshop area.

Her head snapped toward the door when she heard the man throwing himself against it.

Ivy gasped and shuddered, then rushed behind the pile of firewood. The only light coming into the garage was from a small window near the door, but behind the firewood it was pitch-black.

Crouching in the darkness, she began to tremble. Her legs were shaking, and her hands were sweating despite the freezing cold. Her breaths came in ragged, painful gasps, and she closed her eyes, attempting to control her terror.

The pounding against the door built to a terrifying roar. She covered her ears with her trembling hands. Then she heard a deafening crash and the angry man screaming at her.

Ivy's eyes shot open, and she groped frantically in the darkness, trying to find something, anything, to use in self-defense. Her fingers touched a fallen piece of firewood. She grasped it tightly and waited.

"C'mon lady. The more difficult you make this for me, the madder I'm gonna be. Get your ass out here."

Shivering from the cold and fear that gripped her, Ivy covered her mouth with a hand. The horrifying sound of his footsteps came closer and closer. Suddenly the footsteps receded, and she realized he was moving toward the other end of the woodpile.

Ivy glanced behind her and saw a tall metal cabinet against the wall about two feet away. Cautiously, she crawled backward and silently raised herself to a standing position at the side of the cabinet, the foot-long log clenched tightly in her trembling fist.

"I know you're in here," he growled, "so you may as well make it a little easier on yourself."

Ivy pressed her back against the concrete block wall, tears running down her face as she heard the shuffling sound of his feet coming closer and closer.

"And if you tell Leon you got away from me—" he was so near that Ivy could smell the acrid odor of beer and sweat "—I'll break every bone in your body."

Her movements a blur, Ivy raised the log and brought it down on his head.

The man yelled in pain and fell against her. She screamed!

When he dropped to the floor, she stood immobile against the stone wall, petrified. Then she fixed her eyes on the pale light streaming through the sole window near the door of the garage and started to move around his body.

She shrieked when a rough hand grabbed her ankle!

Again she raised the piece of firewood and struck him. His hand dropped from her ankle; his head slumped onto his other arm.

Gasping for breath, she staggered toward the door. If she could only make it to her car!

The man had forced the door off its hinges, and she had to step around it to get outside. It had stopped snowing; a full moon brightened the silent night. Ivy's fear slowly subsided, and she trudged through the snow as fast as she could.

Just as she neared the back of the house, she saw the headlights of a car pulling in off the street. Quickly she tore from the driveway and darted behind a thick, leafless hedge.

She peered through the branches and saw two men get out of the car. One opened the side door of the house as the other pulled an unconscious man from the back seat—Chris.

Through her despair, Ivy thought desperately. Should she get to her car and try to find help? But that could take more time than Chris might have. No, she had to find out what they were going to do to him right now!

As soon as the men dragged Chris into the house, she started toward the side door. Then she thought better of it and went around to the back of the house. There she found a cellar door, unlocked, and entered.

The cellar was pitch-black. Disoriented in the darkness, she felt her fear returning in force. Her breathing became ragged again; she began to feel dizzy; her teeth started to chatter.

No! she ordered, balling her hands into fists. *You can't give in to fear. You've got to think of Chris and the danger he's in!*

Taking several deep breaths, she inhaled dank odors of mildew and acrid stale air. She peered around the darkness, then groped her way through the damp cellar, bumping against tables with covered objects on them.

Her eyes began adjusting to the darkness, and she lifted one of the covers. It seemed to be some kind of small printing press. She removed another cover and found another press and then a computer. Cautiously she moved toward the wall and ran her fingers over a row of filing cabinets.

Chris had told her about floating boiler room operations, out of which swindlers worked for a time and then moved on before authorities could track them down. The equipment here could certainly belong to such an operation, she thought.

She heard scuffling sounds above, and she turned toward the nearby stairs leading up to the first floor. "Chris," she murmured and silently moved toward the staircase.

As quietly as she could, she mounted the steps and stopped at the closed door at the top. She listened and heard one man call, "Dirk!" Hearing the sound of footsteps going up to the second floor, she eased the cellar door open a crack, peeked out and saw it led to a kitchen. The door from the kitchen to the next room was closed.

"Dirk and the woman are gone!" she heard one man yell as he retraced his steps down to the first floor. "We'd better tie this guy up and look for them. Help me get him off the floor and onto that chair."

Ivy moaned, wondering how badly they had hurt Chris, then she entered the kitchen and tiptoed to the closed door.

"Use this drapery cord and tie his hands to the chair," one of the men said.

Anxiously Ivy waited, hoping both men would leave to search for her and Dirk. She'd untie Chris, and they could make a run for it.

"That oughta do it," a gruff voice said.

Her heart beating wildly, alert for any sounds from the next room, Ivy let agonizing moments pass before placing her trembling fingers on the doorknob. Slowly she turned it.

She screamed when rough hands dug into her shoulders and spun her around.

It was Dirk!

Ivy felt a crushing blow on the side of her head, then darkness swept over her.

"IVY...IVY!"

Coming to, she heard someone whispering her name. She forced her eyes open and saw Chris tied to a chair a few feet away. Disoriented, she glanced around. They were alone in a dining room. When she tried to move, she found that she was tied to a chair, also.

"Chris," she murmured, "are you all right?"

"Never mind me. How are you?"

Ivy had an awful headache, but she disregarded it and nodded. "I'm okay. I saw them bring you in. I was so worried about you."

"You should have gotten the hell out of here when you had the chance. I heard Dirk tell the other two how you got away."

"I couldn't just leave you here." She tried to jerk her hands free, but they were securely bound behind her. "What do you think they'll do with us?" she asked in a hushed voice.

"I don't know," he said, but he had a pretty good idea.

Her thoughts clearer, Ivy asked, "How did they get you here?"

"When you didn't show up at the hotel, I visited your friend Leon. He said if I ever wanted to see you alive again, I had to go quietly with those two bruisers who brought me here."

"Oh, Chris, I'm so sorry I got you into this. I still can hardly believe that Leon would do this to me or that he's mixed up with the swindlers."

"Believe it," Chris said, tugging at his ropes.

Remembering what she had seen, Ivy whispered, "Downstairs in the cellar, they've got printing presses and filing cabinets."

"Here?" Chris thought quickly. "We've got to find a way to notify headquarters before those guys take off with the files." He wrestled with the ropes again. "If I could only—"

Dirk loomed up at the dining room archway and glared at them. "You two shut up," he growled, "or I'll shut you up." He laughed gruffly, then strutted back into the living room.

After several moments, Ivy whispered, "Chris... I guess it's times like this that make us realize how we really feel about someone. I love you."

"And I—" He cut himself off. "One of them is dialing a phone."

They listened intently.

"Yeah," Dirk said, "everything's under control here. What do you want us to do with 'em? The lake? No problem. I'll give 'em enough weights to hold them down into the next century."

Ivy's frightened eyes darted to Chris's.

"Let's not go quietly, love," he said in a hushed voice.

A cold shiver coursed down Ivy's spine, and she nodded.

"I'll go to the pier and get the boat ready," they heard Dirk say from the living room. "Bring 'em down in a few minutes."

Ivy jumped when a door slammed, and she looked over at Chris, who was trying to shuffle his chair nearer to hers.

"Gettin' restless?"

Her head jerked toward the archway. She saw the two men who had brought Chris in coming toward them. The shorter man began untying her hands as the other laid his gun on the dining room table and started to loosen Chris's hands.

As soon as Ivy's hands were free, the man pulled her up from the chair. She rubbed her sore wrists, watching closely until she saw that Chris's hands were free, too. Then, with all her strength, she jerked her knee upward and aimed it at the man's groin. He groaned, and she pushed him backward as hard as she could.

Chris's movements were just as swift. His fist flew full force onto the taller man's face, knocking him against the wall.

"Get to the car and take off!" Chris yelled as the man came back at him.

"You bitch!" the shorter man growled, his beady eyes burning.

Ivy grabbed a heavy glass bowl from the dining room table and swung it, striking him in the shoulder. The man staggered, and she darted to the front door and headed for the car.

Under the snow, the walkway was icy. She slipped, but gained her balance, leaped into the car and turned the key in the ignition. She heard a grating noise, but the motor didn't turn over. "Please, God," she pleaded and turned the ignition key again. This time the motor whirred sharply.

Chris had told her to take off, but she wasn't going to leave him now!

Ivy winced as she listened to the ruckus coming from inside the house, but in the next moment she saw Chris charging down the walkway toward the car. She threw the door open on the passenger side, and he jumped in.

"Hit it, love! The guy's got a gun."

Her foot crashed onto the gas pedal. A shot rang out. A second hit the rear of the car as she tore down the road, a death grip on the steering wheel as the car swerved and skidded on the ice.

Minutes later, they were back on the road to Winnetka. Spotting a roadside bar, Chris directed her to park in the rear. Inside he phoned the Winnetka police, identified himself and told them to move in on the mansion. He also phoned postal inspection headquarters in Chicago and told them to arrest Leon Torell.

CARLOS HANDED Ivy another cup of coffee, then faced Chris. "The three men were gone, but the Winnetka police have sealed off the house. Our inspectors are there now, going through the evidence."

He showed Ivy a list of numbers he had jotted down when he'd talked to one of his men who had phoned from the house. "Do these codes mean anything to you? They're part of a listing that was found in one of the filing cabinets."

Emotionally and physically exhausted, Ivy studied them for a moment. "No, they aren't codes we use at Continental."

Chris took the paper from her and examined the numbers. "They could be bank account codes. Have you asked Torell?"

"He's not saying anything until he sees his lawyer." Carlos looked back at Ivy, then sat down in a chair next to her. "Mrs. Austin," he said quietly, "several bank account executives have already identified your brother from the picture you gave us. I'm afraid he's in this operation up to his neck."

Ivy's eyes darted over to Chris, who avoided her gaze. "Are they certain?" she asked Carlos. "Couldn't it just be someone who looks like Scott?"

"I'm afraid not," Carlos said sympathetically. "Some banks are being extra cautious and are filming individuals opening new accounts with large sums of money. Our people have checked thoroughly. We're sure the man is your brother."

Slowly Ivy rose and put her coffee mug down on the desk, then she turned away, heartsick. From the beginning she had tried to make herself believe Scott was innocent, but now she had to face the truth.

Chris got up from his chair and stood behind her. "I'm sorry that it's turned out this way, but Scott obviously knows what he's doing."

Turning, she said, "But we don't know why he's doing these things. Maybe he's being forced to."

"Maybe," Chris agreed, trying to ease her hurt.

Ivy looked over at Carlos. "What will happen to him?"

"When we pick him up, he'll be charged with conspiracy to defraud by mail, participation in a racketeering activity and interstate transportation of money obtained by fraud... for starters."

"Chris," Ivy said as she looked into his eyes, her one word a cry of despair.

"Why don't you two go back to the hotel," Carlos suggested gently. "There isn't anything else you can do here tonight."

Chris nodded. "You'll give us a call when you…if you hear anything?" He almost said, "When you pick Chandler up."

"Sure. Listen, if you and Mrs. Austin don't have plans for Thanksgiving tomorrow, you're both invited to share dinner with me and my family."

"Thanksgiving," Ivy repeated morosely and reached for her purse.

"I'll let you know," Chris said, then he and Ivy left for the hotel.

CHAPTER FIFTEEN

DEPRESSED AND STILL STUNNED by the day's events, Ivy sat dejectedly in one of the chairs by the window in their room at the Palmer House. Chris was seated on the foot of the bed across from her, wishing to hell that he were running the French restaurant at home, rather than running down her brother. He realized her heart was breaking, but he didn't know how to help.

On the verge of tears, Ivy smiled painfully, and she shook her head. "Scott was such a good baby. I mean he hardly ever cried, and he loved attention."

"Who knows why some people turn out the way they do?" Chris asked rhetorically. "People can have four kids. Three can either become priests or nuns, and the fourth can get into all kinds of trouble."

"I don't know," Ivy said quietly. "Scott was thin in grammar school, and it used to torment him that he was always the last player picked when the kids chose sides before a baseball game. Then in high school, he wasn't as popular with the girls as some of his friends were."

"Those things can get to a young boy, especially in our competitive society."

Ivy was so caught up in her thoughts that she barely heard Chris's comment. "Scott and my father never really got along. Dad was gone most of the time, either covering games or interviewing sports figures all around the country. Maybe if he had been at home more, Scott would have turned out differently."

"My stepfather was always on top of me, giving me a hard time," Chris recalled. "He had a nasty way of trying to turn my mother against me. Any little thing I did wrong, he'd blow all out of proportion." Chris chuckled dryly. "When I told him he could take the restaurant and shove it, he said that I was being disloyal to the family and that I'd never amount to anything. That bothered me for a long time, but it made me decide to work even harder, just to show him how wrong he was."

"Were you close to your mother?" Ivy asked listlessly.

"I was before she remarried. Then after I announced that I didn't want anything to do with the restaurant, the whole family considered me a traitor."

"Scott and my mother were very close. When she became ill, and died a few years later, he took it hard. We all did, but I think it changed him, made him become colder inside."

Ivy dragged herself up from the chair, went to the window and gazed down at the moving car lights on Monroe Street. "I guess it's partly my fault," she said dejectedly.

Moving behind her, Chris folded his arms around her. "What kind of thinking is that? How could you be responsible for what your brother's done?"

"Maybe I should have been closer to him. When I was in high school, I was busy with girlfriends and boyfriends. Then I went on to college, and that took a lot of time and work. After that my job became important, and then Bill and Kim did."

"You were doing the normal things people do, and you've handled your share of tragedy. Thinking that you're somehow responsible for the choices your brother made is ridiculous."

Ivy turned in Chris's arms. "I need to believe that, I really do," she whispered. "Hold me, Chris," she pleaded. "Hold me tightly."

He did, and during his intermittent sleep that night, Chris agonized over how unhappy and restless Ivy was. In his heart, he knew he would never love another woman the way he loved her. Once this business was over with, he was going to ask her to marry him.

THANKSGIVING MORNING, Ivy and Chris had breakfast at the hotel. When he reminded her of Carlos's invitation to dinner, she declined the offer. Chris phoned him and learned there was no word yet regarding Scott's whereabouts.

Midmorning Ivy said she needed to get out of the hotel, and they walked toward the lake, turning right on Michigan Avenue. The temperature had risen, and the sun was bright. Most of the snow on the street had melted, but drifts were piled along the sidewalk.

Traffic was light on the usually busy thoroughfare, and Ivy remarked matter-of-factly, "I guess everyone's home stuffing a turkey. That's where I should be, I suppose."

"Your family's having dinner at Carol's," he reminded her and put his arm around her shoulder.

"Yes, that's right. What am I thinking?"

"You're thinking too hard. Try and relax a little."

As they walked, he saw that she was still deep in thought, so after they crossed Van Buren Street, he said, "Buckingham Fountain is just over there in the park."

"Oh," Ivy said with little enthusiasm.

Chris led her across Michigan Avenue and over one of the short bridges leading into Grant Park. Ivy glanced down at the railroad tracks below, then they crossed another street, and she saw the mammoth circular fountain directly ahead.

Silently she viewed the sculpted green sea creatures spouting water from their mouths as pipes from the three-tiered fountain shot water high into the air.

"It was all lit the night I saw it," Ivy remarked languidly and turned to watch some children playing in the snow-covered park.

As they started to walk around the fountain, Chris took hold of her gloved hand. "Are you cold?"

"Uh-uh. The sun feels good." She glanced absently at the row of high buildings that paralleled Michigan Avenue, then stopped and set her worried eyes on Chris. "What if Scott agrees to make restitution for any money he's got from the scam? Would that make a difference? If he can't pay it back, I will, somehow."

"That will be up to the courts," Chris said honestly. "Scott's best bet would be to cooperate and tell us everything he knows. If he helps us get to the people at the top, it can only work in his favor."

"I see," Ivy said, and they began to walk again. "How long do you think it will be before they . . . arrest him?"

"That's hard to tell. He was seen in Iowa, Missouri and Tennessee. He might be working his way back down to Florida."

After a moment, Ivy said, "Chris, let's go back home. Is there any reason we can't?"

"No, but I thought you might want to stay here a day or two in case Scott was . . . located." He knew what she was thinking. "I'm just guessing that he might be heading for Florida. He could circle back and cover other northern states."

"I want to go home now and be with my family. I've got to prepare them. It's going to be a shock when they find out the kind of trouble Scott's in. I don't want my father and Kim hearing about it on TV."

"All right, love. When we get back to the hotel I'll phone Carlos and let him know we're leaving."

THE WARM AFTERNOON SUN shone down over Miami as Ivy and Chris exited the airport. She carried their coats while Chris carted their suitcases to his parked car.

Driving toward Coral Gables, he glanced over at her. "Carol will be pleased that you'll be having dinner with her."

"You are, too, aren't you?"

"After I drop you off, I'm going right to headquarters to see what's going on, but I'll try to make it."

"Can you take a minute to say hello to Kim and talk to my father? He's going to have questions that I won't know how to answer."

"Sure," Chris said, offering her a tender smile.

When they reached the house, Walt told them Kim and Trudy had gone next door to help Carol prepare dinner. Before she went to Chicago Ivy had told her father briefly why she was going so suddenly, but he was shocked now to learn the extent of his son's involvement and that several federal agencies were hunting him down.

As Chris was about to leave for headquarters, he asked Ivy, "Could I have the printouts now?"

She knew she had to turn them over to him, but she hated to do it, because the papers represented her role in exposing her brother's wrongdoing. "Yes," she said in a strained voice. "I'll get them."

Slowly she went upstairs to her bedroom, but moments later she rushed back down, her face pale.

"Chris, they're gone! I can tell that someone's been going through my room."

Her eyes swept to Walt, as did Chris's.

Confused, her father said, "Don't look at me. I haven't been in that room for years, and certainly Kim wouldn't have taken whatever you can't find."

Chris asked him, "Have you been here all the time since we left?"

"Tuesday night Kim and I were here, but last night she and Randy went out, and I was at Trudy's."

Ivy said, "Someone got in here and stole the print-outs."

"You're sure they're not upstairs?" Chris asked.

Hurt by the implication of his words she said, "It would be rather foolish of me to get rid of them now. Half the world knows I have them."

"Who knows besides postal inspectors and now Walt?"

"I told Leon when I was in his office."

"He could have passed that information on to some-one else, someone right here in Miami," Chris said.

Perplexed, Ivy asked, "but who would know exactly where to look?"

"Your brother would."

"You think my son was here?" Walt asked.

"I don't know, but if the printouts have conveniently disappeared, someone was here. I'd better get to head-quarters." He kissed Ivy on the cheek and picked up his suitcase. At the door, he turned. "Tell Carol I'm sorry I can't make dinner."

As soon as Chris shut the door behind him, Ivy, seek-ing reassurance, went to her father and took hold of his arm. She knew that Scott was thought to be somewhere in the middle of the country, and the idea of a stranger prowling around the house and going through her room made her flesh crawl.

DUE TO THE HOLIDAY, postal inspection headquarters was deserted when Chris arrived. He was really worried now. Leon Torell had to have been the one who alerted whoever broke into Ivy's house and made off with the printouts. If it wasn't Scott, Leon had to be working with someone else at Continental. But who?

In his office, Chris began to pore over the surveillance reports he had made on the personnel at the company, checking for anything that he might have overlooked. He picked up his report on Lew Frazer, Scott's boss in the communications division, thinking the two men would make a good pair if they wanted to cash in on the firm's wealth of information. What if Frazer and Chandler were working together? he hypothesized. Frazer could have searched Ivy's room for the printouts.

Tossing the paper down on his desk, Chris leaned back and locked his fingers behind his head. Maybe Ivy's brother *was* in Miami. He was the one person who'd most want to get rid of any evidence that pointed directly to him. Maybe he knew the files in Winnetka wouldn't incriminate him. Maybe he figured his sister wouldn't testify against him. A lot of maybes, Chris thought, then muttered, "Damn, if only the banks were open today."

He knew that postal inspectors, the IRS and the FBI in all fifty states could swarm through the banks and see how far south Scott had gone. They might even be able to pinpoint where most of the swindled money was winding up. Chris had a feeling it would end up in one of the numerous banks in Miami.

It was no secret that laundering money in certain states, Florida included, was a profitable business. He'd been involved in investigations where officers at some banks had accepted millions in cash deposits in boxes and paper bags.

Certain that Carlos would have his men working around the clock, going over the stuff they found at the house in Winnetka, Chris decided to give him a call. Just as he reached for the phone, it rang.

"Laval," he said evenly.

"I thought you might be there when I couldn't get you at your apartment," Carlos said.

Chris grinned. "I was just about to call you to see if you solved the case yet."

"Not quite. We're still sorting through the piles of records we found in the file cabinets. I do have a flash for you, though."

"Yeah?"

"Torell was released on bail just after you left Chicago this morning. This afternoon he was lying on the sidewalk in front of his apartment building. It's possible he could have fallen from his tenth-floor window."

"You don't believe that any more than I do. Did he leave a suicide note?"

"Uh-uh."

"I don't imagine you got anything from him before he was released."

"Not even a goodbye."

"Well, we can rule out *his* taking the red-eye down here and stealing the printouts from Ivy's bedroom."

"They're gone, huh? Why doesn't that surprise me?"

"Anything in the records to implicate Chandler?" Chris asked.

"Nope. So far it's been one big collection of names and addresses that cover just about every state in the country. I think you're right about the codes being bank account numbers, but we'll have to wait until tomorrow to check that out."

"Okay. Keep me posted, ol' buddy, and I'll do the same."

After hanging up, he went back to recheck the report he'd turned in on Lew Frazer.

WITH DIFFICULTY, Ivy got through dinner at Carol's without breaking down, but behind her pleasant facade, she felt long overdue for a good cry. The past few days had been a nightmare. But she didn't want to ruin everyone's Thanksgiving.

During dinner she had been only half listening when the others at the table rattled off their plans for the long weekend. Walt was taking Trudy for an airboat ride in the Everglades and then down to Key West. Kim and Randy were going with Carol and Lamar to Disney World.

"You're sure you won't come with us?" Carol asked again when her guests were seated in her living room.

"Please, Mother," Kim coaxed.

"No, I'm really not up to it." Mickey Mouse was the last thing Ivy wanted to face right now. She turned toward Carol. "In fact, as soon as we get the dishes done, I'm heading home for a shower and bed. I'm exhausted."

Trudy jumped up. "No one goes near the kitchen. Kim and I decided we'd volunteer to straighten up."

Carol beamed as they headed for the adjacent room. "Be my guests, you two."

"I'll help," Randy offered, then followed them.

With a grin, Walt remarked, "She's a winner, isn't she?"

"Who? Kim?" Carol asked, winking at Ivy.

"Her and the Kelly Girl," he said, smiling broadly.

"Kim was a big help today," Carol told Ivy. "She sure has come a long way. I can remember when an all-electric kitchen was a mystery to her. Now, she's a better cook than I am, and you know how I like to eat."

"You should taste the sauerbraten Kim makes," Walt said. "The girl must have some German blood in her somewhere."

Ivy looked over at Carol. "Have your parents gone away for Thanksgiving?"

"They went to my sister's in Tampa."

"Did your mother tell you about the conversation we had?" Ivy asked, her voice hesitant.

Carol frowned and nodded slowly. "She did, or at least I got her version of what went on. I assumed that was the reason you made Kim give Randy back his chain."

"I think I'll go see if I can give the guys in the kitchen a helping hand," Walt said, getting up from his chair. "It'll give you two a chance to chitchat."

"You just miss Trudy," Carol said, smiling as Walt left the living room. Then she turned to Ivy. "Did you tell Walt about my mother's visit?"

"Yes. He didn't understand what all the fuss was about."

"I don't know how much good it will do, but I told my mother she was making a mountain out of a molehill. Actually, I told her more than that. I let her know I thought she had behaved like an idiot."

"Carol, how could you have said that to your own mother?"

"Just because I love her doesn't make everything she does right."

Ivy had to wonder if she was the only one in the world to offer her family complete loyalty. Looking at Carol, she said, "In some ways your mother made a lot of sense. I certainly want Kim's future to be smoother than her past has been. I always thought I could be objective about interracial couples, but when it hits home, I'm learning that it's another matter."

Carol chuckled. "Randy and Kim aren't exactly a couple yet." Then her expression became serious. "Don't think too badly of my mother. She lived through some difficult times while she was growing up. What Mom tries to do now is put all that behind her, to pretend it never existed. Of course, she can't, and she's mighty sensitive about what people say."

"I'd think her experiences would make her more tolerant of Kim's situation."

"She doesn't have a thing against Kim's being Amerasian. It's Randy she's worried about. Not everyone is as broad-minded as you and Walt. My mother just doesn't want her baby boy to have to listen to the snickers and raw jokes that she had to take because she's so light skinned. From what she told me, she got it from whites and blacks."

"What does your father have to say about all this?" Ivy asked.

"Honey, he wouldn't care if Kim was a black Miss America. He doesn't want Randy getting serious with *any* of the fairer sex at this time in his life. He warned Randy that if he wanted to be an air force officer, he needed to put all his energy and concentration toward that goal."

"Sounds like good advice." Ivy chuckled. "It also sounds like something Chris would tell Randy. Chris has his sights set on becoming chief postal inspector in Washington, and nothing or no one is going to get in his way.''

"You told me, but your Chris has a big start on a boy who isn't eighteen yet."

"He's not exactly *my* Chris, Carol."

"Walt told me you two went to Chicago together. I thought you'd come back with big news."

"It wasn't that kind of trip," Ivy said sadly.

"You do know how to keep a girl in suspense. Just what kind of a trip was it?"

"It has to do with Scott. He's in trouble. Bear with me, though. I don't have the heart to talk about it right now." Rising, she kissed Carol on the cheek. "Dinner was lovely, and the turkey was delicious."

Arm in arm, Carol and Ivy walked to the door. "I'll give Trudy a plateful to bring over. I'm sure Randy is eating you out of house and home."

"He's a teenager, isn't he? Remember how we were?"

"Were?" Carol patted her stomach, then opened the door. "I'm sorry Chris couldn't make it. I know how it is to have to work on holidays." When Ivy was outside, Carol lowered her voice. "With everyone gone this weekend, the two of you should make up for his having to work overtime."

"We'll see," Ivy said and waved at her friend.

ALONE IN THE HOUSE, Ivy slumped onto a chair in the living room and rested her head back. Her depression deepened as she thought about Scott. Where was he now? she wondered. Was he still carting money to banks all over the country? And Leon—he had actually ordered her and Chris killed! What was happening to the people she thought she knew? But then she had to ask herself if she had ever really known her own brother.

"Ivy?"

She heard Trudy's voice in the hall. "In here," she called.

"Carol asked me to bring this platter of turkey to you. I'll put it in the refrigerator."

"Thanks," Ivy said.

Following Trudy to the kitchen, Ivy leaned against the doorframe and watched as the woman rearranged some items in the refrigerator, then slipped the platter onto one of the shelves.

"That will make some lovely turkey and cheese sandwiches," Trudy said as she closed the refrigerator door. "Carol is a sweetheart, isn't she? It was so thoughtful of her to invite me to share Thanksgiving with you wonderful people. I'm going to miss all of you."

"Miss us?" Ivy asked.

"I finished typing your father's manuscript yesterday."

"But we'll still see you."

"I'm afraid not. I've never seen the West Coast, so I've decided to work my way from California up to Washington."

"As a Kelly Girl?"

"Yes. You can meet the most fascinating people that way—people like your father. He's such a dear."

"But I thought you two were going to Key West this weekend."

"We are. I'm not leaving for California until Monday."

"Does Dad know?"

"I haven't told him yet, but I will."

"Oh," Ivy said quietly and sank onto a chair at the kitchen table. "He's going to be disappointed." She looked up at Trudy. "My father thinks a great deal of you."

"And I think he's a fabulous man. All he needed was for a brassy woman like me to jolt him out of his doldrums."

"You did more than that, Trudy. Did you know he was thinking of asking you to marry him?"

"He had that look in his eyes a few times, but I'm not ready to settle down again. Bertie and I had a marvelous life together, but he wouldn't budge out of London. Unlike him, I've always wanted to travel. After I've seen the West Coast I plan to go on to the Far East. I hear that Hong Kong is fascinating."

"I envy your being able to pick up and go whenever you choose." Ivy thought of the ties to Miami that would keep her from following Chris.

"I earned it. Bertie and I raised three children successfully. They're happy with their families. So now it's time to please myself. Your father should do the same."

"I've always thought so, too, Trudy, but you've obviously had more influence on him than I did."

"So like a man, isn't it?" she remarked, then sat down across from Ivy. "They become quite comfortable with members of their own family and tend to take them for granted. Sometimes it requires an outsider to get their attention." Changing the subject, Trudy said, "I'm really going to miss Kim. She's such a dear girl. She has a rare combination of beauty, sensitivity and intelligence."

Ivy's lips eased into a smile. "She is a joy."

"Randy certainly thinks so." Trudy laughed softly. "Those two make me think of Juliet and Romeo. But theirs will be a happier ending," she added quickly.

"I don't know," Ivy confessed. "His parents aren't exactly thrilled that he's seeing Kim."

"I've a hunch that won't change the way they feel about each other. Oh, it might make things a bit more difficult right now, but that could be good, considering Kim's age. Adversity can strengthen us all at times. My children were all girls, so I have an idea of what you're going through. At Kim's age, you want them to be popular, but at the same time you're frightened out of your wits that they will be."

"Trudy," Ivy confessed, "I feel so inadequate as a mother. Kids are so different than they were when I was fifteen. I talked to Kim about the emotional and psychological damage early sexual involvement could cause her, but she and Randy seem so serious about each other. Yet I can't bring myself to advise a fifteen-year-old to use the pill, a diaphragm or an IUD. If anything did happen, though—" Ivy couldn't finish.

"Nonsense. Nothing is going to happen. From the talks Kim and I have had, I'd say you've been an excellent mother. The child loves you and wouldn't do a thing to hurt you. You're worrying needlessly."

"You really think so?"

"I do," she said, standing. "Now I'd best get back to Carol's."

"I'll see you before you leave for California, won't I?"

"Of course, dear."

After Trudy left, Ivy realized she would really miss her. The talk they had just had reminded her of conversations she'd had with her mother. She wondered how her father was going to take it when he learned his Kelly Girl was leaving.

And Ivy had to admit she also had a less altruistic reason to wish Trudy were staying. She had gotten used to her father's new independence and was afraid he would revert to being a recluse. If he did, she knew, it would be just one more reason why she couldn't even contemplate leaving Miami. Not that she was, of course.

The phone on the kitchen wall rang, and she rushed to it, thinking it could be Chris.

"Hello," she said excitedly.

"Where the hell have you been?"

"Scott!"

"Is anyone there with you?"

"No, Dad and Kim are at Carol's. Where are you?"

"I desperately need your help, Sis."

"My help? What you need is to turn yourself in before you're arrested! Scott, how could you have—"

"There's no time for that now. I'm in big trouble. Leon's dead."

"What? How? When?"

"I'll tell you when I see you."

"Are you all right? Where are you?"

"Will you promise not to tell the police?"

Ivy felt momentary panic as she thought of the consequences of agreeing to his request. Every fiber in her body told her she shouldn't, for Scott's safety, but how could she deny him now? She had to see him. She'd talk to him and make him realize he had to turn himself in.

"Will you promise?" he asked again, his voice taut now.

"Yes, yes. Where are you?"

"I'm at the airport. I want you to go to my apartment. There's an envelope packed in with my scuba diving equipment. Get it and bring it with you. Meet me in the parking lot at the Hofbrau House on Dixie Highway at ten o'clock tonight. Make sure that you're not followed."

"Scott, you're scaring me!"

"Sis, I'm scared enough for both of us. They killed Leon, and they'll kill me if they get a chance. Can I depend on you to do what I said?"

Her nerves rioting, Ivy asked, "Who are they?"

"I'll explain later. Will you get the envelope for me or not?"

"Yes. I'll find it and bring it to you." She heard the click on the line. "Scott!" she called uselessly.

Slowly she put the receiver down, then checked the clock over the mantel and knew she'd have to hurry.

Upstairs in her bedroom, she found the key to her brother's apartment, the one that he had given her just after he moved in. Then she phoned Carol and asked her to tell Walt that she was going out for a while and would be back shortly. When Carol assumed she was meeting Chris, Ivy didn't correct her.

Right now, the only person she could consider was her brother.

CHAPTER SIXTEEN

SHORTLY AFTER Ivy pulled into the parking lot at the Hofbrau House, a taxi stopped in front of the lounge and she saw her brother get out. Jumping from the car, she called to him and waved. He rushed to her, opened the door on the passenger side and climbed in.

Ivy slipped onto the seat next to Scott, hugged him and breathed a long sigh of relief. "I've been so worried about you," she said, her voice unsteady. Then she sat back and saw how drawn his face looked. "Do you know the police are looking for you?"

"I guessed they would be."

"Scott, you have to—"

"Did you bring the envelope?"

"Yes." She reached into her purse and took it out.

He grabbed it, ripped it open and withdrew a small black book. Shoving it into the inside pocket of his jacket, he asked, "Are you sure you weren't followed?"

"I don't think so. Scott, you've got to turn yourself in."

"I can't. I told you they killed Leon, and they're probably looking for me now."

Exasperated but terrified for him, Ivy demanded, "Who are they, and what happened to Leon?"

Scott slumped down and let his head fall back against the car seat. "I'm beat. I need some sleep."

"Who's trying to kill you? Please tell me!"

"I don't know who, but it's the people at the top of the organization. They're trying to cover their tracks so the postal inspectors can't get to them. I flew to Chicago with the printouts last night, and—"

"You took them from my room?"

"Yes. Leon phoned me in Palm Beach yesterday and told me you had been there to see him and that the inspectors were breathing down our necks. When I arrived at his apartment building, I saw Dirk going in, so I waited outside. A few minutes later, Leon was lying on the sidewalk. I trashed the printouts and came back here to get the envelope you brought me, but I didn't know if the inspectors or someone like Dirk would be waiting for me at my apartment."

"So you used me again," she said, aching with an inner pain.

"I had to, Ivy. No one's going to hurt you."

Ivy smiled wryly, thinking of how close she and Chris had come to disaster in Winnetka. But before bringing that up, she wanted more answers from her brother. "How did you get mixed up with Leon and his organization in the first place?" she asked.

"It's not his organization. He's . . . he *was* just one of the people working for them. When I followed Emily to Chicago, I checked in with Leon like you said to. Well, I needed money." He gave his sister a weak sideways grin. "I loved Emily. I would have done anything for her."

Looking straight ahead again, his voice turned sullen. "Leon paid me to make some deposits for him at various banks under different names, using phony identification. I also made trips to the Cayman Islands, where the banks don't ask any questions. It was his idea that I try to get a job with Continental here in Miami."

"And I helped you," Ivy said bitterly. "Did Leon put you up to applying for the managerial training program?"

"Yes. He said it'd be a sure thing."

"How could he have told you that?"

"Maybe someone at Continental who has pull is part of the organization, too."

"Someone in the home office?"

"It could be, I don't know. Leon's the only contact I had. Anyway, for the past two years I've been keeping a record of the banks I visited and the accounts I made deposits to." Scott patted his jacket pocket. "That's what I've got in this little book. It's my bargaining information."

"Scott," Ivy said firmly, "you've got to turn yourself in and give that book to the postal inspectors."

"And you think they'll protect me?" he asked sarcastically.

"Yes, I do, if you're honest with them and tell them what you've just told me."

"I've got to think about that."

Sitting erect, her voice rose as she said desperately, "You don't have time! For once in your life will you listen to me? People may be trying to kill you. Is that what you want? One of the inspectors said that if you cooperate fully, you might not have to go to jail. You might just be placed on probation."

"Sure. They'd tell you anything to get what they want."

"I trust Chris. He wouldn't lie to me and use me the way you have."

"Chris? You're on a first-name basis with the inspectors?"

"He's a friend. If you can get it through that thick skull of yours, he's trying to help you!" Ivy sighed deeply, then tempered her tone. "Please, Scott, turn yourself in. It's the only sane thing to do. Even if you have to spend some time in prison, Dad and I will do everything we can to help you get your life back in order when you're released."

"I wouldn't bet on any help from Dad. He'd tell me I got just what I deserved. No, I'll have to think this through." He glanced around the parking lot. "And I've got to keep on the move right now, but first I need some sleep. There's a motel a few blocks down the highway. Will you drive me there?"

"You haven't been listening to a thing I've said, have you?"

"I've listened, but I've got to get a few hours shut-eye before I do anything."

Knowing it was hopeless to talk to him any further, she turned the key in the ignition and headed for the motel.

AT HOME, IVY FOUND Chris waiting for her. Kim had gone to bed, and when Walt saw the scowl on the postal inspector's face, he excused himself and disappeared upstairs.

Through a thin-lipped smile, Chris said, "Your father thought you were with me. Did we have a good time?"

"Don't be sarcastic," Ivy warned. "I'm in no mood for it."

"If sarcasm is out, how about a little honesty? Where were you?"

Ivy turned away. She was emotionally exhausted from her encounter with her brother. What was she to do? If she told Chris where Scott was, she knew he would arrest him. If she didn't, Scott would keep on running from the law and from the people who he thought were out to silence him as they had Leon. There wasn't really much choice, she realized. For her brother's safety she would have to tell Chris the truth.

"Well," he asked again, "where were you?"

Ivy turned slowly. In a low voice she admitted, "I was with Scott."

"That's what I thought," he said dryly, then went to the fireplace and propped his arm on the mantel. He waited, wondering if she would tell him where her brother was.

"He just checked into a motel on Dixie Highway."

"Which motel?"

"I'm going with you, Chris," she said quickly. "I've got to explain to him why I've betrayed him."

"You haven't betrayed him. You're probably saving his life. But I don't want you coming with me. It will just make you feel worse."

"Worse?" she cried, her voice shrill with despair. "I couldn't feel any more pain than I do right now. Scott won't understand. He'll think I've abandoned him."

"At some point he's got to realize that he's responsible for his actions. He can't go on thinking you'll get him out of every difficult situation he gets himself into. This is one that you sure as hell can't help him with. What your brother knows is a threat to people higher up in the racket that he's been part of. They don't take kindly to having someone like him hanging over their heads."

Chris didn't want to frighten her any more than she already was, but he had to make his point. "Ivy," he said, lowering his voice, "Leon is dead."

She nodded. "I know. Scott was in Chicago. He saw Dirk go into Leon's apartment building just before—" She couldn't finish.

"That Dirk is a busy man," Chris said, hoping the guy was still in Chicago and not in Miami. "Did Scott take the printouts?"

"Yes," she answered, staring down at her tightly clasped hands. "He was going to give them to Leon."

After explaining how her brother had gotten involved in what he had called the organization, Ivy remembered his saying something that had puzzled her. "Chris, Scott told me that Leon assured him that he'd get into the managerial training program at the home office. But he couldn't have guaranteed that. It's possible that someone in the home office with more authority could be part of the organization."

"Or it could be someone right here in Miami." He took hold of Ivy's shoulder and looked into her worried eyes. "I've got to get to Scott before anyone else does. Which motel is he at?"

"You're going to arrest him, aren't you?"

"I have to."

Once more Ivy felt herself being pulled mercilessly in two directions: toward her brother and toward the man holding her. The emotional tug-of-war became unbearable. She visualized Chris breaking into Scott's motel room. She could see her brother's startled expression and imagine what he would think of her for betraying him.

Something snapped in Ivy's overwrought brain, and she jerked free from Chris's hands. After giving him the name of the motel, she said bitingly, "Now go and do what you have to do."

"I'll come back later."

"No," she said firmly, "I don't ever want to see you again."

"Ivy, that doesn't make any sense."

"Does any of this make any sense!" she cried.

"Ivy, I need you," he pleaded, feeling her slipping away from him.

"A lot of people need me, Chris. Kim needs me, my father needs me, and now Scott is going to need me more than ever. There just aren't enough pieces of me to go around. My family has to come first."

Upset himself, Chris said, "I know your family comes first, but look where your misguided loyalty to your brother got you and him."

Ivy's lips curled into a tormented, twisted smile. "I'd expect that from a man who doesn't know the meaning of family loyalty."

Hating this ceaseless arguing about families, Chris inhaled slowly, then forced out an apology. "I'm sorry. I shouldn't have said what I did. It's just that you always have time and love for your family and so little for me. It makes me wonder where I fit in."

"You don't fit in, not anymore. We agreed to see where our relationship took us, and we found out, didn't we? But I discovered something else, Chris. I was about to make a big mistake. I almost settled for an affair with you for as long as it conveniently fit in with the plans you have for your life. Well, your plans are no longer convenient for me."

She turned, moved away and lowered her voice. "When this thing breaks wide open, I doubt if I'll even have a job with Continental."

"Look, I'll make certain they know how much you helped to—"

Spinning around, she snapped, "I don't want you to help me! I want to get on with my life, and there's no longer any place in it for you. Now please, leave and do your damn job." Taking rapid strides to the door, she flung it open.

At the door Chris asked quietly, "Is that how you really want it?"

"Goodbye," she said, choking on the word.

Closing the door after him, Ivy shut her eyes and leaned back against it, hot tears bathing her stinging eyes.

Then for hours she paced aimlessly in the living room, fearful images building in her mind as she imagined what was happening to her brother. Had they hurt him? Was he locked up in jail now? she wondered, wringing her hands, continuing to walk the floor like a caged animal.

When the phone rang, she jumped as though physically struck and rushed to it.

"Yes!" she blurted out.

"Mrs. Austin, this is Matt Shapiro. I'm with the Postal Inspection Service."

"My brother! Is he all right? Where is he?"

"He's fine and he's being very cooperative."

"I've got to see him!"

"I'm afraid that's not possible right now. For his protection, he's in a safehouse here in Miami. Mrs. Austin, we need your cooperation now, also. We're blocking media publicity as long as we can, so we can follow through on the information your brother has given us. When he doesn't show up for work Monday morning, don't offer any explanation. He went on vacation, and that's all you know. It's important. Do you understand that?"

"Yes," Ivy said in a wisp of a voice.

"Good. Please don't contact us here at headquarters. Your brother is well and safe."

"Thank you, Mr. Shapiro. I'll follow your instructions," Ivy said. As though in a trance, she replaced the receiver and collapsed onto the sofa.

Long minutes later, her mind clearer, she pieced out what had happened. She wasn't at all surprised that Matt had phoned instead of Chris, considering how they had parted. It was for the best, she realized. Right now she had to pull herself together and get her own life in order, for her sake, for Kim's, for her father's and for Scott's.

THE WEEKEND WAS MISERABLE, lonely and depressing. Everyone had taken off, and Ivy dragged herself around the house, waiting for the phone to ring. She spent hours wondering if she should resign before she was fired from Continental. She was certain that would happen when they learned she had switched the disks at the home office. But that didn't concern her most; her thoughts kept returning to Scott—and to Chris.

When Kim and Randy returned from Disney World Sunday afternoon, Ivy did her best to listen attentively as they gave her a detailed rundown of all the things they had seen and done. For the first time, Ivy was truly happy that Kim and Randy had made plans for the evening.

Walt's mood was quite different when he returned from Key West. Trudy had informed him she was leaving for California the following afternoon. After Ivy told her father what had happened to Scott, Walt merely nodded, then went straight to his room.

Monday morning, Ivy called in sick. She was ill, but it wasn't so much physical as it was emotional exhaustion. In the late afternoon, she started to fix herself some coffee and toast, but then changed her mind, went into the living room and sat near the phone.

Her head turned toward the archway to the foyer when she heard her father coming down the stairs.

"Any news about Scott?" Walt asked as he shuffled into the living room.

"No," Ivy said, her own mood as dark as his.

"I knew that brother of yours would get in over his head someday."

"Dad, he happens to be your son as well as my brother."

"Your mother spoiled him."

"Why weren't you around more to correct that?"

"I was busy working to provide for the family."

"If you had loved Scott half as much as you love sports, things might have turned out differently for him."

Slumping onto an easy chair, Walt asked, "Are you saying it's my fault he got mixed up with criminals?"

Ivy didn't want to argue with her father. She knew he was upset about Trudy leaving, and she also knew that deep down he did care what happened to his son.

"No," she said with a sigh, going to her father. She sat down on the arm of the chair and placed her arm around him. "I'm not saying it's your fault. I just wish that when Scott was younger, you had hugged him more often and told him that you loved him just the way you always told me."

"If only Miriam was here," Walt said, his voice breaking.

Don't start that again, please! Ivy begged silently. To get his mind on something else, she ran the back of her fingers over his jaw. "Aren't you going to shave today?"

"Why? I'm not going anywhere."

"Kim and I have to look at you," she said lightly. "If Trudy were here, you'd shave."

"Trudy who?"

"Dad, there's no use in your going into mourning over her leaving."

"Who says I'm even thinking about her? She was an employee, that's all."

"We both know better than that. You thought you were in love with her."

"So now you know how I think."

"I know you. You sat around here moping for two years, then that whirlwind of a Kelly Girl perked up your life, and you liked it. Just because she left this afternoon, that doesn't mean you have to stick your head back in the sand."

"What do you expect me to do? Go play shuffleboard with the old fogies in some senior citizens' club?"

"Your book's mailed off. Start researching another one. Do something that will get you interested in life again."

"I don't have the heart for it, or the energy."

"I still think you should have taken Trudy to the airport."

"Why?"

"Because she's a friend."

"Aw, I'm better off without her. With all the running around she had me doing, she would have put me in an early grave."

"Sitting around the house again will do it even faster."

"Look, you keep up about Trudy, and I'm gonna get grumpy."

Her father's depressed mood was the last thing Ivy needed right now. Standing, she said, "I'm going to make some tea. Would you like a cup?"

"Naw. I think I'll go back to my room and watch a game on TV." He headed for the stairs, but at the archway he turned. "You know, Daughter, I don't know why you keep sticking up for that brother of yours. If he was still a kid, maybe I could understand, but he's a grown man now. What's he ever done to earn the kind of blind loyalty you give him?'' Without waiting for a reply, Walt went up the stairs.

Her father's words struck Ivy as heartless and uncaring, but she excused them because she knew how bad he felt about Trudy's leaving.

Returning to the kitchen, she put the kettle on to boil, then sat down, propped an elbow on the table and rested her chin in the palm of her hand.

Since when did family members have to earn loyalty? she mused. That was what families were all about. If you couldn't depend on members of your family, whom could you depend on? It was her father's describing her loyalty to Scott as being *blind* that bothered Ivy, however.

Had her loyalty to her brother been extended that unthinkingly? True, he had used her and lied to her, but it wasn't the first time. She had been used to his doing that over the years.

But that didn't justify his taking advantage of her, she decided. As though thinking clearly about his behavior for the first time, Ivy began to feel hurt by her brother's treatment of her. No, not just hurt, angry.

Brother or not, she had always treated him with respect and had tried to help him whenever possible. Why shouldn't she expect the same treatment from him?

Perhaps her father was right, she decided. Her idea of family loyalty had blinded her, and it had cost her dearly. Each time she had tried to become close to Chris, really close, Scott's problem had loomed up, creating a barrier between her and Chris. A barrier of her own making, she had to admit....

But it was no use blaming anyone but herself for how she had spoken to Chris. She had made it clear that there was no place for him in her life and that she never wanted to see him again. He had accepted her words and walked out of her life forever. For that, she couldn't blame him.

The teakettle started to whistle, and Ivy got up and went to the stove. She was putting a tea bag into a cup when she heard the chimes in the foyer.

Ivy opened the door. It was Carol. "I saw your car parked in the driveway when I got up," she said. "Are you feeling all right?"

"I'm okay. I just needed a day for myself. Come on in. Are you still on the night shift?"

"Two more weeks, then back to days." Carol sat on one of the sofas near the fireplace. "I can't wait, and neither can Lamar. Ivy, he's a changed man. We had a wonderful time at Disney World. Usually he has a sore neck from ogling every woman that passes, but I saw more of his eyes in the past few days than I did all during our marriage."

Sitting on the sofa opposite Carol, Ivy was glad to hear good news from someone. As she folded her legs under her robe, she asked, "Do I hear second-time-around wedding bells?"

"I'm not jumping into anything, but who knows? How are things with you and Chris?"

"Chris is history, I'm afraid."

"Oh? Randy said he thought you two were headed for the altar."

"We're headed nowhere, not together, anyway," she said sadly.

Carol's eyes drifted over her friend's slippers and robe. "Is that why you've taken to your bed?"

Ivy knew she'd eventually tell Carol about the horrors she had been through recently, but she wasn't ready to talk about them now. The memories were too grim.

"No," she said halfheartedly. "I just woke up feeling like a tired, old lady this morning."

"At times men have a way of making a woman feel like that. Why don't you and I go out on the town next weekend? We could check out the male strippers in Hialeah."

Grinning, Ivy said, "Lamar would love that, or wouldn't we take him with us?"

Carol's eyes lit up. "You know, we should. It might remind him of the kind of a waistline he used to have. Lamar's gone from a slim thirty-four to a size forty-plus belt." She chuckled. "He claims that any middle-aged man who has a flat stomach has got to be gay. Speaking of waistlines, have you eaten anything today?"

"I was just fixing some tea. Want some?"

"No, I'm off to the dry cleaners and the supermarket. So much for life in the fast lane." Standing, she said, "Don't get up, and you take care of yourself."

"I will."

Carol started for the door, but then she turned. "Ivy, are you sure you and Chris can't work things out? I know you, and you're a woman in love."

"That's what hurts so much," Ivy admitted.

"Doesn't he feel the same way?"

"He said he did, but he thinks my family keeps getting in the way."

"You do spread yourself rather thin, and remember, men are sensitive animals. Their mothers spoil them, and they expect the women in their lives to do the same. By the time we get them, it's too late. They're already conditioned."

Pushing herself up from the sofa, Ivy walked Carol to the door. "Chris's problem is that he's already married . . . to his work."

"Just don't give up on him too easily," Carol suggested, then left.

Ivy returned to the kitchen, feeling like a wrung-out dishrag. Thinking of what Carol had said about not giving up on Chris too easily, she eyed the phone on the wall and was tempted to call his office. *And say what?* she asked herself. *"I'd like to speak to the man who arrested my brother?"*

"That's stupid," she muttered and flicked on the heat under the kettle.

After fixing another cup of tea, she put a spoonful of honey in it, then took a sip, thinking how screwed up her once orderly life had become.

"Mom!"

"I'm in the kitchen, honey," Ivy called, noting that she had graduated from being called Mother to the more informal Mom. Some of Randy's casualness was catching, Ivy thought.

"Randy's parents bought him a new car. It's a Mustang, totally awesome!"

Ivy smiled slightly, realizing that Kim's vocabulary was broadening also. "Is it outside?"

"No, Randy had to get back to practice. Are you feeling better?"

Giving Kim a cheery smile, Ivy said, "I'm fine. I was just feeling a little lazy today."

"Randy's mother invited me to their house for dinner Wednesday. Is that all right?"

The invitation came as a pleasant surprise to Ivy. Apparently, after Carol's talk with her mother, Louise had tempered her objections to her son's seeing Kim. "Sure it's all right. If you'd like, invite them over here for dinner some Saturday night."

"This Saturday?" she asked.

"If they don't have other plans."

"Invite Chris, too." Kim suggested enthusiastically.

"He's pretty busy at his job right now, honey."

Sensitive to her mother's moods, Kim asked softly, "You and Chris are still friends, aren't you?"

Thinking that honesty was the best policy, Ivy said, "Not really. I don't think we'll be seeing much of him anymore."

"Oh," Kim said dejectedly. "Was it anything I did?"

Ivy took hold of the girl's hands. "Certainly not. It's just that Chris works very hard. He's ambitious and eventually he wants to work in Washington. He won't be in Miami very long."

"I thought you liked him a lot."

"I do, and I'll miss him when he leaves, just as you'll miss Randy."

Saddened by the news, Kim said, "I'll miss him, too. He was like a—"

When Kim stopped midsentence, Ivy filled in the remainder silently: *Like a father.*

"Randy," Kim said, "is going to write to me and visit when he can. Is Chris going to write to you?"

"I don't think so," Ivy admitted, feeling her throat tighten. To change the subject, she asked, "How about helping me get dinner started?"

As they chopped vegetables for cacciatore sauce, Ivy thought about how fond Kim had become of Chris. It was also obvious how far the girl had progressed since knowing him and Randy, how she was beginning to reach out to people and to trust them.

The reports that Ivy had gotten from Mrs. Miller had proved that to be the case. Kim was making new friends at school every day, it seemed. For that Ivy was thankful, and she determined more than ever not to uproot Kim from the stable life she now had.

Ivy's shoulders sagged a little more when she thought of how much her father and brother needed her now, also.

TUESDAY MORNING, Ivy had just settled in her office when Dolores buzzed her, saying that Lew Frazer wanted to speak with her. Ivy expected that Scott's boss would want to know why her brother hadn't shown up for work yesterday.

"Send him in," she said and quickly busied herself with a file on her desk. When her office door opened, she looked up at the tanned, attractive blond man and smiled. "Hi, Lew."

Closing the door behind him, he moved to Ivy's desk and shoved his hands into his pockets. "Where's that brother of yours? He didn't come in yesterday, and he's not here yet this morning."

"I don't know. I was out myself yesterday." She reached for the phone on her desk. "I'll call his apartment."

"I've done that already. He's not there." Sitting in the chair by her desk, Lew stretched out his legs and crossed his ankles. "If Scott wanted an extension of his vacation time, he should have had the decency to let me know. He's not a manager yet."

As casually as she could, Ivy said, "I'm sure he has a good reason for not reporting back to work."

"Do you have any idea where he is right now?"

"No, I don't." Ivy didn't. Matt Shapiro had only said that her brother was in a safehouse somewhere in Miami.

"If he contacts you, you'll let me know, won't you?"

"I'm certain you'll hear from him first."

Lew glanced over Ivy's desk, then cocked his head. "That was a shame about Leon, wasn't it? Who'd have thought he'd commit suicide? I would have guessed the guy hadn't a care in the world. Inconsiderate of him, too. It's not the greatest publicity for Continental."

Ivy searched Lew's face for some sign of compassion, but found none. "I read about that in Sunday's paper. I guess you never know what's going on in a person's private life."

"Anything going on in Scott's?"

"Like what?"

"He and Leon were pretty good friends, weren't they? I heard he gave your brother a great recommendation." As though suddenly remembering, Lew asked, "Wasn't Scott going to Chicago for his vacation?"

Ivy recalled her brother's suspicion that someone else at the company was working with Leon's group, and Lew's questions now took on an added import. Yet she knew that Lew had wanted his sister-in-law to get the slot in the managerial training program instead of Scott. If Lew were involved in the swindling organization, wouldn't he have supported Scott's advancement? Ivy wondered. Not if his sister-in-law was also involved, she countered.

"Didn't Scott go to Chicago?" Lew asked again.

"Oh...uh, yes. He wanted to visit some people he knew there." Remembering the list of numbers Carlos Hernandez had shown her in Chicago, Ivy asked, "Lew, have you added any new codes for our mailing lists?"

"What's the date on the last one you received from my division?"

Reaching into the top drawer of her desk, Ivy flipped through a folder. "I have the one from August," she said, carefully studying his expression.

"That's the most recent list. Why are you asking?"

Ivy thought quickly. "With the postal inspectors checking on everything, I want to make sure my own files are up-to-date. I guess they've been spending as much time in your division as they have in mine."

"They've been nosing around, but they haven't come up with a court order yet to go through the files."

"Would it be so bad if they did?"

"Our files are none of their business," he said curtly and stood. "Scott's not showing up for work isn't going to look good on his record. If you find out where he is, let me know right away, okay? It's important. You can call me at home anytime."

"I will, Lew," Ivy said, wondering if he could possibly be involved with the swindlers. After learning about Leon, nothing would surprise her now, she realized.

The rest of the day at the office was tense and painful for Ivy. She couldn't attend a meeting or talk with her own staff without the conversation turning to Leon Torell's supposed suicide. By day's end, she thought she was going to scream, but she forced herself to remain on the job. She wanted to do some checking on her own after the other employees left for the day.

Ivy didn't know what she would look for, but if she could find something, anything, that would indicate that someone at Continental was working with the swindlers, she knew it could possibly save her brother's life.

CHAPTER SEVENTEEN

AFTER WORK, Ivy took the elevator down to the communications division. In Lew's office, she leafed through
the pages of his desk calendar for the past few weeks and
noted Leon's name scribbled on several of them. But that
didn't prove anything. Lew often had to contact branch
managers across the country.

His desk drawer and filing cabinets were locked, as
they should be. Ivy wasn't about to try to break into
them. She saw his copy of the company directory on one
of the cabinets and flipped through the section that listed
the branch managers. She was interested to see that
Leon's home phone number was circled. Why would Lew
need to call him at home? she wondered. Then she remembered that the two men had been good friends when
Leon worked in Miami.

Deciding she was wasting her time in Lew's office, Ivy
went to the file room, where she had found Scott shredding documents. The codes that Carlos had shown her in
Chicago had been composed of nine digits, and she knew
that Continental's codes were a mixture of letters and
numerals—unless Lew had begun using a new code that
he was keeping to himself.

Ivy fingered the numbers on the electronic panel that
would open the files, but just as the metal cover slid up,
a man's voice started her, and she spun around.

"What are you doing in here, Ivy?" Bob McDonough asked.

She tried desperately to think of some legitimate explanation for her actions, but none came to mind. Stalling she said, "I thought everyone had left."

"Obviously, but that doesn't tell me what you're looking for."

Even though her boss had been a personal friend for years, Ivy didn't think that she should confide in him regarding her suspicions about Lew. But she also guessed that at any moment the postal inspectors were going to descend on the company with a court order, and Bob would learn everything then, anyway.

Hesitantly she said, "Continental is in trouble."

"Does it have anything to do with the reason Scott hasn't shown up at work?"

"Yes," she admitted quietly.

"What kind of trouble? I've got a right to know."

"Scott was...using the information in our files to swindle hundreds of people."

"What?" Bob went to the electronic panel and closed the file cover. "Who told you that?"

"One of the postal inspectors. It's possible that someone else here or at the home office is also involved."

"Since when did you start working for the Postal Inspection Service?" he asked with a crooked grin.

"I'm trying to help Scott. He's in serious danger."

"And you're playing police by going through our files."

"I thought I might find something that would help the inspectors."

"You know our files are confidential."

"But we can't just look the other way. If someone else is abusing our security, we should give the inspectors all the help we can. Bob, I'm terrified for my brother's safety."

"Where is Scott now? Has he talked to the inspectors?"

"I honestly don't know where he is, but I've got to do something to help him. For the company's sake you should be willing to cooperate with the investigation!"

"Calm down, will you? And stop all this nonsense about swindlers and go on home."

"It's not nonsense, Bob!" Feeling more desperate by the second, Ivy blurted out, "Leon's death wasn't an accident. He and Scott were mixed up with some organization that's running a nationwide racket."

"Who told you that?"

"Chris Laval, the postal inspector who talked to you," Ivy confessed, afraid she had said too much already.

"Do they have anything to go on other than the files they confiscated in Winnetka?"

"I don't think so," she said, her thoughts focused entirely on Scott's little black book.

"Well, the inspectors will do their job with or without our help. C'mon, I'll walk you to your car."

As they rode up the elevator in the parking garage, Ivy felt as if she was coming apart at the seams. Instead of helping Scott, she thought she might have told Bob more than she should have. Well, everyone in the company would know shortly, she realized, and Matt Shapiro couldn't hold her brother much longer without people starting to wonder. She also knew that the Postal Inspection Service wasn't going to be able to keep the raid they had made on the house in Winnetka from the press much longer, either.

The house in Winnetka? Ivy thought suddenly. *That information wasn't in the newspapers on Sunday. How does Bob know about the files there?*

When the elevator stopped at the sixth floor of the garage, Ivy's boss stepped out onto the parking level.

"Bob," she asked, still inside the elevator, "who told you about the house in Winnetka?"

The man's chubby face flushed. He looked around the quiet parking level, then reached inside the elevator and pressed the stop button. Grabbing hold of Ivy's arm, he glared at her with cold gray eyes. "Scott was a fool to get you to switch those disks for him. I could have taken care of that myself if he'd had the sense to tell Leon."

"You?" she murmured, her heart pounding painfully against her chest. "You were working for Leon!"

"The other way around, Ivy. Damn Scott for getting you involved in our organization's business. It cost Leon his life." Tightening his hold on Ivy's arm, he jerked her out of the elevator.

"Let go of me!" she shouted.

Smiling grimly, he said, "I can't. You're despondent about learning that your brother is a criminal. Like Leon, you're unable to face the future."

Ivy's fear turned to terror when she realized that Bob intended to kill her and make it appear she had committed suicide, just the way Leon had been killed. In one swift movement, she lunged against Bob, knocking him back into the elevator. Then she ran for her life toward the parked cars.

The lighting was dim, and Ivy ducked down between two cars, hearing the rapid footfall of Bob's shoes as he traced her path.

Stealthily she made her way around one of the cars, then darted to the next row and doubled back toward the elevator. If only she could make it there without his seeing her!

Slipping between two cars, she listened. There was no sound. She wondered where Bob was. From where she was hiding, she could see the elevator, its doors open.

Crouched, she headed between a row of cars toward it. Just a few more yards, she thought desperately and worked her way quietly to the car nearest the elevator.

It's now or never, she told herself and took a deep breath.

Strong hands grabbed her. She screamed!

"I'm sorry, Ivy," Bob apologized coldly. "Let's get this over with."

She struggled, using all her strength, but he had an iron grip on her arm and his other hand over her mouth as he dragged her to the concrete railing at the edge of the building.

Ivy groaned when her hip hit the chest-high stone wall. Overhead, clouds made the early evening darker than usual, and when she looked down at the street six floors below, she could see the lights from moving cars.

Still struggling for survival, she kicked at Bob as he tried to lift her. Her terrified groan was muffled by the palm of his hand when her feet left the concrete.

In the next moment she felt herself falling!

With a grunt, she landed on the garage floor. Stunned, she looked up and saw Bob fall backward against the wall. Standing over him, a look of rage on his face, was Chris.

A second man grabbed Bob's arms, a third said, "We've got him now. Let us handle it."

"Chris!" Ivy cried.

Reaching down, he lifted her to her feet. "Are you all right?" he asked, his voice ragged.

"Yes, I...I think so," she stammered. "He was trying to kill me!"

"I know. We saw the two of you get into the garage elevator. When I realized he had stopped it, we charged up the steps. Sorry it took so long," he apologized and wrapped his arms around her.

"How did you know I was in trouble?" Ivy asked, trembling as the other two men took Bob into custody.

"Let's get you away from here first," Chris suggested.

Since he had arrived with the postal police in one of their mobile response units, Chris drove Ivy's car. As they rode toward Coral Gables, he glanced at her, concerned, "Are you sure you're okay?"

"When I stop shaking, I will be. I can't believe what just happened," she said, still confused. "If you hadn't shown up when you did, I would..." Her voice trailed off.

"You can thank your brother for that," Chris said. "Using the information he gave us, Carlos and his men followed the trail of deposits Scott had made to forty-five bank accounts in six states. All the accounts were opened under phony business names, companies that were controlled by just three people—Robert McDonough and two former state senators."

"And Scott, what will happen to him?" Ivy asked.

"I don't know. Even though he's cooperated now, he was in pretty deep with the organization. He may have to spend a few years in prison." Seeing her gloomy expression, Chris added, "Then again, he may not."

When he parked in the driveway of her home, he reached over and cupped her hand. "It's over with, Ivy. You don't have to be worried anymore."

"I'm afraid it's not all over for me. The story will be front-page news, and the home office will probably take some kind of action against me."

"Even when they learn how you helped to expose McDonough and his organization?"

"They'll take a dim view of my having switched the disks."

"Do they have to know you did?"

"Yes," Ivy said immediately, drawing her hand from his. "I'm through with lies and half-truths. I'm expecting Scott to be responsible for what he did. I have to own up to what I did."

"This might be a good time for you to change careers."

"That's what I'm thinking of doing, but I was hoping to work until next summer. After I spend two years at the university, this whole business and my connection with it will have been forgotten, I hope."

Two years, Ivy thought then, realizing that was how long Chris planned to remain in Miami. She wouldn't blame him for never wanting to see her again, but right now, all she wanted was for him to take her in his arms and hold her. She was sick at heart, emotionally exhausted, and she saw so many uncertainties ahead of her.

At least the torturous mental war, pitting Chris against her brother, had finally ended. All she could do for Scott now would be to help him in any way possible. But the barrier that had stood between her and Chris had crumbled. She loved him more than ever now, and if they had only two years together, she would grab at them and hold them precious.

She had been foolish, she realized, remembering how she had hurt Chris so often with her vacillations. But she would make it up to him—if he still wanted her.

"Chris," she said quietly, looking straight ahead, "I don't know what's going to happen in the months ahead, but if you still want us to...to try and pick up the pieces—" She cut herself off and faced him. "I love you, Chris," she admitted softly, her mind a crazy mixture of hope and fear.

Grasping the steering wheel tightly, Chris stared through the windshield. "Because of this investigation, I've been offered a promotion and a job at headquarters in Washington," he said with little enthusiasm. "I told Matt I'd take it. I'm leaving Miami the day after tomorrow."

"Oh." Ivy felt as though Chris had just taken hold of her heart and twisted it brutally. Mastering the tears that were welling up in her eyelids, she forced a meager smile. "It's what you've been working so hard to accomplish, isn't it?"

Chris nodded.

"That should make you very happy."

"It should, but...Ivy, I—"

"Please, Chris, don't say anything more. Words won't help. You have your goals, and I have mine. We just can't reach them in the same place. That's not your fault, and it's not mine."

"At least think about coming with me...as my wife," he pleaded.

His sudden proposal hit Ivy like a whirlwind. A warm glow shot through her, and her heart sang with joy. But almost immediately her expression froze, and she felt as if her heart had stopped beating. For one blissful moment, she had thought only of Chris, but now she became agonizingly aware of the family ties that forced her to remain in Miami.

In a voice that sounded like little more than an echo, she said somberly, "I can't leave, Chris, any more than you could stay."

"There are good schools in Washington. You and Kim could be happy there."

Ivy didn't have the emotional strength to remind him that there were other reasons she couldn't leave. Opening the door on the passenger side, she looked back at Chris. "Do you want to take the car, or should I call you a cab?"

Handing her the keys, he said quietly, "No, I need to walk a while."

They both got out of the car and shut the doors. Looking at her over the top of the automobile, raw hurt darkened Chris's eyes. "We would have been so good together," he said, managing no more than a hoarse whisper.

Offering him a final bittersweet smile, Ivy said, "We were good together, Chris. I'll always remember you." Turning quickly, she rushed into the house.

SEATED on the outdoor patio at a restaurant near headquarters, Chris poured ketchup on his hamburger, then handed the plastic bottle to Carlos. "Didn't you eat lunch on the plane?" Chris asked.

"Yeah, but they don't give you enough for a bird to survive on." After dousing his double burger with ketchup, Carlos remarked, "I guess it's poetic justice that Chandler won't be able to use any of that money he stashed away for his defense. He's going to need a good lawyer."

"I know, but the courts have to consider that without his help the organization would still be in operation."

"True." Changing the subject, Carlos asked, "Think you're going to like Washington?"

Chris stared at the hamburger he was holding, then put it down on the plate. "One city is a lot like the next."

"You didn't even take time to get sand in your shoes."

"Can't keep a good man down, they say."

Carlos checked his friend's expression. "How come you don't look tickled pink? You got a promotion and a raise."

Shrugging, Chris said, "The money's nice, but I don't eat all that much."

"That's good. Wait until you see what it's gonna cost you for an apartment in Washington. Or are you planning to commute from Bladensburg? You'd get free dinners at your folks' restaurant."

"Only if I waited on tables during the weekend."

"I'm guessing Ivy Austin isn't going with you."

"Is that a hamburger or a crystal ball?" Chris asked, grinning, then his expression turned glum again. "She feels she's stuck here with family obligations."

"Sounds like a pretty decent reason not to go traipsing around the country after the likes of you."

"I didn't say she didn't have a good reason."

"Sounds like a replay of the Kendal situation."

"Exactly," Chris agreed with emphasis.

As he munched on his hamburger, Carlos asked, "What've you got against settling down and starting a family?"

"Not a thing. To each his own, I guess."

"I take it you're going to go through the rest of your life being a loner."

After a swallow of his iced tea, Chris said, "When the right time comes, I'll settle down and have some kids maybe."

"How? In a petri dish? You're not getting any younger. You'll be what ... forty on your next birthday?"

"Thirty-nine," Chris said flatly.

"So you're almost forty. Take my advice, get married and settled down soon. Running around after a two-year-old leaves you more ragged than army basic training."

Chris propped his elbows on the edge of the table and curved one hand over the other. "I don't know, Carlos. I'm not sure I can spread myself that thin. My work takes up most of my time."

"That's a cop-out, amigo. You're just used to a safer and selfish way of life."

"What's selfish about being committed to my job?"

"It's easier than being committed to a woman. With your job, you get a manual. Follow it, and you got no trouble. With a marriage, you don't get a manual. What you get is a verbal, thinking human being with a mind of her own. Every day is a challenge just trying to figure her out."

"I've been there," Chris reminded him.

"Aw, you and Kendal were like roomies. The first big decision came along, and I bet neither one of you lost much sleep over parting."

Chris knew Carlos was right. He hadn't lost any sleep over Kendal, but he hadn't been able to eat or sleep ever since Ivy had turned down his proposal.

"But with the right lady," Carlos went on, "and Ivy Austin seems like a good candidate, there are lots of rewards. You get a companion, a lover and a good friend to advise you, all wrapped up in one package."

Ivy would be like that, Chris thought.

"You just have to learn to look at things from their point of view when conflicts arise. That's the secret."

"After nineteen years of marriage, you should know. How are Elena and the kids?"

"Driving me up the wall, but I wouldn't have it any other way. You going to eat that burger?"

"Be my guest." Chris pushed his plate toward him and told himself he had a lot of serious thinking to do.

ON WEDNESDAY, Ivy phoned Dolores, saying she wouldn't be in until noon. She spent the morning arranging for an attorney for Scott. Her brother had been transferred from the safehouse to the county jail, and she hoped his attorney would be able to get him out on bail.

Last evening's news broadcasts had been filled with details of how the Postal Inspection Service had broken up a nationwide swindling operation. Shortly after, Ivy had had to unplug the phone so that she, Kim and Walt could try to sleep. In this morning's newspapers, the names of all involved were there in black and white for the entire world to see, hers included.

Now, as she exited the elevator at work, she didn't know what kind of a reception she would receive at Continental.

As she walked to her office, she tried to ignore the stares of her staff and other employees. She was in no mood to answer the questions she knew they would have. Dolores's smile was the first one she'd seen so far.

Ivy stopped at her desk. "Please say you have some aspirins. I used up all mine during the drive here."

"Aspirins and coffee are on your desk," Dolores said. "I thought you might need them. Ernie Williams called. You're summoned to the home office. He wants you there tomorrow afternoon. I booked you on a flight."

Ivy moaned. "This is not going to be one of our better days." She went into her office and closed the door.

It wasn't difficult for her to guess what Ernie wanted. The man in charge of project supervisors nationwide was probably going to either fire her or suggest that she resign. He wasn't a man given to understanding anyone's point of view other than his own, and the morning papers had included mention of her having switched the disks for her brother.

Tossing her purse on the desk, she took two more aspirins and swallowed them down with a gulp of black coffee, wondering if nunneries accepted widows.

CHAPTER EIGHTEEN

A LITTLE AFTER NOON on Thursday, Chris checked in his baggage at the airline ticket counter. For a while he ambled from one waiting area to the next, trying to tell himself he was doing the right thing, but as the time neared for him to board the plane for Washington, his thoughts were as confused as ever.

This business of family had been nagging at him ever since he had seen how deeply Ivy felt about hers. He knew there was little hope of his ever being buddies with his stepfather, but lately he had been doing a lot of thinking about the rest of his family. He wondered if he had cut them off the same way he had cut off Kendal when she wouldn't go along with his picking up and moving every few years.

But Kendal was history; Ivy was the present. Damn, but he wanted her to be the future, too.

For most of the night he had walked the floors in his apartment, ruminating about the talk he'd had with Carlos about settling down. The walls had started closing in on him, and he'd had a premonition that going to a different city to work wasn't going to help him forget Ivy. Nothing would. Ever.

He started toward the next waiting area in the terminal, thinking he'd stop in one of the lounges and get a drink. But that didn't appeal to him, either. Nothing appealed to him now. Nothing ever would again, not without Ivy, he realized.

What was it Carlos had said? That it was sometimes necessary to look at things from the woman's point of view? Chris wondered if he had taken the time to do that, to look at Ivy's situation.

He knew how Kim's life was changing for the better. He couldn't fault Ivy for not wanting to uproot her daughter from the friends she had finally made, and he knew it would break the girl's heart to part with Randy before she had to. Ivy had told him her father was acting like a basket case again, now that Trudy had left. And Scott's fate was still uncertain. Chris could see why Ivy couldn't just pack up and leave him.

So, ol' buddy, he asked himself, *what are your reasons for leaving town?*

Chris rattled them off mentally, beginning with the promotion. *There'll be others,* he challenged. The pay raise. *When will you have time to spend it? All you do is work and sleep. What the hell kind of life is that?* Working at headquarters in Washington was a good reason. *You'll have to play tough politics even to be considered for the big man's job, if that time ever comes.*

No, Chris admitted to himself, *you're not leaving town. You're running away, just like Carlos said you were. Because running is safer than totally committing yourself to Ivy.*

He remembered telling her that a man was what he did, and a woman was what she was. Mulling that over, he suddenly didn't like the idea that the sum total of Christian Laval was his job. He wanted to be what he was. And, damn it, he was in love with Ivy!

His eyes shot around for a public phone. Seeing one on the other side of the waiting area, he rushed to it and made a call.

"I'm sorry. Mrs. Austin is out of town on business," Dolores informed him.

"Where. This is important."

"I can see that she gets a message if you like."

"Lady, my plane's about to leave. If you've got an ounce of romance in your heart, tell me where I can reach her."

"Is this Chris?"

"Yes!"

"Ivy's gone to the home office in Georgetown."

He checked his watch. "What airline?"

"Cayman Airways."

"You're a love," he said, hung up and dashed back to the ticket counter and spoke to the man who had just tagged his luggage to Washington.

"What time does the Cayman Airways plane leave for Georgetown?" he asked.

"It just left."

"Damn. How soon can I get a flight there?"

The clerk leafed through a schedule and told him. When Chris tore off, the clerk called after him, "What about your luggage? It's already on the plane to Washington!"

Chris couldn't have cared less about where his luggage was going. He was heading for the Cayman Islands—and to Ivy.

IN GEORGETOWN, Chris's first stop was at Continental, where he was told that Ivy had left earlier, after she resigned. At the Sunset House, he learned that she had checked in, but that she wasn't in her room. After leaving a message for her, he went to the lounge, where the bartender fixed him a piña colada.

"Bring a swimsuit with you this time?" Danny asked, a smirk on his tanned face.

"No, just the clothes on my back."

Danny commiserated with Chris when he learned that his luggage was going north while he had come south in search of Ivy. "This isn't a big island," the bartender said. "You won't have any trouble tracking the lady down."

"You don't know her like I do."

Chris checked with the desk clerk again, then ordered another piña colada, wondering where Ivy could be. He didn't think she'd be in a mood to go shopping, after re-signing, but then he had gotten used to Ivy's surprising him.

While he waited for her to return, he thought back to the peaceful time they had spent together on the island. That seemed ages ago; so much had happened since then. For one thing, he'd fallen head over heels in love with Ivy Austin.

He thought of that first evening they were together, the dinner and the walk on the beach to the cove she loved so much.

"The cove!" he muttered, hopped off the bar stool and headed for the beach.

His steps in the sand quickened as he passed the thatch-roofed cabanas filled with tourists in a holiday mood. Chris scanned the bathers in the glistening aquamarine Caribbean, his heart thumping in his chest. He started to jog toward the mound of coral rock farther down the beach.

Reaching it, he scampered up the rocks and stood at the top, the sea breeze ruffling his wavy hair. He raised a hand to shade his eyes and spotted a woman sitting alone on the sand at the far end of the cove.

"Ivy!" he exclaimed. In seconds he was on the beach, running toward her.

She turned, saw him and jumped up. "Chris?" she called in amazement as he neared her. "I thought you would be in—"

His arms swept around her, his lips silencing hers with a long, passionate kiss.

Hugging Chris tightly, Ivy felt her heart soar. A moment ago, she had sat alone and dejected, feeling as though she had the weight of the world on her shoulders. But now, held in Chris's loving embrace, she felt vibrant and joyful. She clung to him, cupping the back of his neck with her hands and running her fingers through his hair as if to prove to herself that he was indeed holding her in his arms once more.

Pressing his cheek against her forehead, Chris whispered breathlessly, "I had to see you again. I knew I'd go crazy if I didn't."

With her eyes still closed, clutching him tightly, Ivy asked, "How did you know where to find me?"

"Your secretary told me."

Ivy could feel the rapid rise and fall of his chest against her breasts, feel the warmth of his body melding with her own. It was such a glorious feeling; she wanted never to be farther from him than she was at this moment. Never!

She opened her tear-filled eyes, and in a voice quivering with excitement, she said, "I'm happy you found me, Chris, so very happy."

Drawing his head back, he gazed down at her lovely face, glowing in the sunshine. "I'm not going to lose you again, love. Marry me, and make me the happiest man alive."

The light in Ivy's eyes dimmed, and she slowly withdrew her hands from around his neck. Stepping back, she hugged her arms. "I can't, Chris," she said. "You know that."

His voice turned heavy and dark. "I thought you loved me."

"I do," she admitted quietly.

"Then why won't you marry me?"

"It just wouldn't work out, my living in Miami and your living in Washington. Maybe some couples can handle long-distance marriages, but I know I couldn't, and I won't uproot Kim now. I've never seen her so happy. Not only that, but right now my father needs me."

"Ivy—"

"Please, Chris, let me finish. There's more. I just had to resign from Continental. It was either do that or be fired."

"So what? You plan on going back to school, anyway."

"I don't know what it's going to cost to see Scott through his legal problems. They could go on and on. Dad and I have some money saved, but legal fees can drain anyone's finances, and there's Kim's medical training to start saving for. I've got to get another job."

"No, you don't. I've saved quite a bit over the years. Remember, I haven't been your average playboy."

"Chris, I can't borrow money from you."

"Who said anything about borrowing it? Ivy, I'm not going to Washington." He tilted his head and chuckled. "My luggage is, though."

"You're not?" Ivy couldn't believe her ears. "But what about your promotion?"

Taking her in his arms, he said, "The only promotion I care about now is the one that would make me a loving husband to you and a caring father to Kim. As for the job, I can be just as dedicated in Miami, but my work isn't going to be the focal point of my existence anymore. You and Kim, my family, will be."

Ivy held Chris tightly and smiled through the tears of joy that rolled down her cheeks. "Are you positive you won't regret it later?"

"I've never been more positive about anything in my life. Now, love, will you marry me?"

"Oh, yes, Chris, I will."

He kissed her long and deeply, then took off his suit jacket and tossed it onto the sand. With his arms outstretched, he looked up at the clear blue sky and shouted, "Did you hear that, world? She said yes!"

Ivy beamed. "You're crazy."

"Crazy in love with you." He reached for her waist and swung her around, then kissed her again. Still holding her, he said, "Let's get married as soon as possible, and during Kim's Christmas vacation from school, how would the two of you like to take a trip to Bladensburg to meet the rest of the Lavals?"

"We'd love to meet your family, Chris."

"And I want them to meet mine. Oh, Ivy, we're going to be so happy together. I promise you that."

Ivy didn't see how she could possibly be any happier than she was at this moment, but she was sure of one thing: the wish she had made on a star had come true.

Harlequin Superromance®

COMING NEXT MONTH

From America's favorite author
coming in September

JANET DAILEY

For Bitter Or Worse
Out of print since 1979!

Reaching Cord seemed impossible. Bitter, still confined to a wheel-chair a year after the crash, he lashed out at everyone. Especially his wife.

"It would have been better if I hadn't been pulled from the plane wreck," he told her, and nothing Stacey did seemed to help.

Then Paula Hanson, a confident physiotherapist, arrived. She taunted Cord into helping himself, restoring his interest in living. Could she also make him and Stacey rediscover their early love?

Don't miss this collector's edition—last in a special three-book collection from Janet Dailey.

COMING SOON...

For years Harlequin and Silhouette novels have been taking readers places—but only in their imaginations.

This fall look for PASSPORT TO ROMANCE, a promotion that could take you around the corner or around the world!

Watch for it in September!

★